Dogstar

JEZ CAMPBELL

Copyright © 2014 Jez Campbell

All rights reserved.

ISBN-13: 978-1500140267
ISBN-10: 1500140260

Published in Britain by Merrin Quist

For my wife and children who set me free

Do you remember? Straining your eyes, watching for the first sign of dimming as the lights go down. Then the curtains would be winched back, as the projector strummed to life, and the movie was streamed, crackling and jumping at first, onto the screen through whorls of cigarette smoke.

    Do you remember that?

    Well that's how it starts today. This film has been classified as certificate 18 ... The titles roll and the music thumps, Bowie beats: '... as they pull you out of the oxygen tent ...'

    Dogstar – The Movie.

    And people in the audience are actually clapping and cheering.

JEZ CAMPBELL

HEATHEN

One

All of a sudden, I'm like... boom!

This is the money shot.

There's *shattering* pain in my head. Running up and down inside like daggers, man. Slashing and cutting away, digging the filling out of my skull.

I'm bent double now, a hand on each side of my head, desperately trying to hold it together, stop it from exploding.

I lose my balance and fall to my knees.

Then I burst into flames.

This, I'm saying again.

I'm on fucking fire!

My eyes are white light.

I'm completely blinded.

There's heat inside and over my whole body. Real heat, fire-heat, hotter and hotter, fucking unbearable. I've got rushing and boiling in my ears. I can feel my skin blistering and peeling away. The flesh is melting off my bones, as they crack and blacken.

I'm on fire, man.

All I can smell is myself burning.

I'm retching from this and the dry air.

I want to die.

Let me die.

Make it stop.

And then – after what feels like forever – it does stop.

It stops.

Thank fuck.

It's stopped.

I can feel and hear myself breathing. My lonely one-lung scorched like it's been a sixty fag day. I'm coughing up phlegm, and so fucked up, that I'm not even surprised at how different I sound doing this.

Deeper. Gravel.

I'm trying to open my eyes.

There's something on them, stopping me. I try to raise a hand to wipe it away. As I do, I feel that whatever's covering my eyes is covering my whole body. There's a gentle cracking sound, like snapping charcoal. And then I begin to be able to move, shake my head.

Two

At the front of the picture is me (naturally).

It's an action shot. One of the early photos they use for promoting the movie.

I'm stumbling forward, one arm held out towards the camera. The other arm, my right, is clutching my chest. My knees are bent, like I'm going to end up flat on my face the second after the picture is taken. I'm shouting something. Funny, I don't remember what.

Right behind me are two Brunos, heads rag-wrapped... all flared nostrils, wide-mouthed and big eyes. They've just stopped running, the momentum leaking out of them even in this snapshot.

Back a bit from the Brunos, Ziggy and Lukas and the rest of the Crew. A snarling pack of wolves – figuratively speaking you understand – stringy, muscular, white-skinned (and I mean proper, paper white), hair scraped down to a fuzz, T-shirts, jeans in drain pipes and brown and purple Doc Marts.

That one on the right is Lukas' older brother Tony. You'd think from the streak of Greek running through him that Tony would've been barred from the Crew, on account of their distaste for all things Nonglish. But more than being part of it, he is top dog, and anyone wanting to make a bubble out of it is likely to end up with one of Tone's boots half-way through their face.

Just after this picture was taken, Tony, Ziggy and Lukas caught up to the two Brunos and gave them the kicking of a lifetime. The irony is that the brown-boys ended up in the same ward as me, the last detail of the picture being the blood leaking through my fingers where the fuckers had stabbed me with one of their Bruno blades and popped my left lung.

Three

I open my eyes.

There's something fucked up going on. I don't feel right. Something about how I am. My position, I mean. It feels natural but odd somehow. Like I'm on all fours, but standing on the tips of my fingers and toes.

My eyes are open and I'm looking around and up and down.

I'm realising that those hairy paws used to be my hands....

That I can *see* my own fucking nose in front of my face...

That I can run my tongue around my mouth and feel sabre teeth...

For fuck's sake, I can wag my own frigging tail...

So the first thing I do is panic.

I'm on all fours, heaving, gagging.

Where are you, Pete?

How do I get out of this body?

How the shit am I going to get me back?

I'm under water and I've got no air.

My head's spinning, and after all that heat I feel myself go cold.

I try to stand up.

Sounds easy, but just this simple thing drives me crazy. I'm legs and elbows and what used to be arms. I'm scrabbling around on the wood effect lino on my floor.

Ken's spluttering and rattling in his sleep from downstairs, TV still on. *Okay, I tell myself, we've just got to calm down. We've got to chill out and take some fucking control here.*

Think.

Whatever I saw that night in Kensall Road is what I am now.

Someone else was wearing this belt.

This belt with its dogstar buckle that's wrapped around my middle *under my fucking skin.*

It's the dead old boy.

It was his belt. And he was the thing I saw on Kensall.

What a laugh he's got to be having now...

But the dead old boy was an old boy, not an old something else.

He was human. He'd got the belt off, right? It was lying right next to him.

So you can take the belt off. You can get it out from under your skin.

Yeah, but what if taking the belt off is what killed him? What if he had to dig it out of the meat of himself, and that digging out finished him off?

Oh, shit, am I going to die?

And yah-di-hay-di-yah-di-yah lots of chatting away to myself for a long time about all the bad shit I've said and done, and poor me cos I was brought badly into the world and if there is a God and all that did I think I'd be forgiven, yah-di-yah...

Believe me that takes a long time.

After that...

Some practical stuff.

What the fuck am I going to do if I have to live like this? What am I supposed to eat? I mean, anyone sees me and I'm going to get shot, or caught and put in a zoo or worse.

There's no mirror in my room. I try to get a picture of myself by looking at the bits of myself I can see.

I'm thinking of all the bad eighties movies I've watched while pranged.

Am I a werewolf then? I mean, I look like a wolf, bigger, blacker. If I am, aren't werewolves supposed to be able to change back into people? Isn't that the whole point?

And anyway, who ever heard of a werewolf wearing a belt under his skin? And making a ball of fucking fire while he changes? Who ever heard of that?

And all the while, I'm vaguely conscious of dark turning to light and light turning to dark again. Maybe once, maybe more. I'm aware of feeling hungry. I've taken a piss up against my wardrobe. (A nasty, three legged fuckabout which ends up with me falling over and pissing all over myself). The line's been drawn at squatting down and shitting like a dog.

Finally, I get to the point where I realise that this is not going to go away by itself.

I've got to get this belt off.

The first thing I try is to use what were my hands. I'm lying down on my bed and sort of rolling around and getting one of my front paws down to my waist and feeling for the belt underneath my skin. A paw's nothing like a hand, man. I'm working myself up into a panic again and, as I'm trying to grasp at something with these useless fucking mitts with claws, I'm accidentally slashing at myself and making this mess of blood.

Instinct kicks in.

Before I know it I'm chewing at my own belly button. I'm that mutt in the corner of the room curled round giving his crotch a nice tongue and tooth massage. As I'm doing this I can feel the belt just beneath my skin. I've got to get this out. I have to be me again. I sink these dangerous teeth of mine into my own stomach (choking on a scream that might have been a howl) around the buckle deep in my flesh, and rip.

Okay, so more pain. You have the picture by now.

More blinding light.

More heat.

More burning up.

And when I finally open my eyes again, I'm me. Pete, not the wolf.

The belt's laying across me. There's a scar around my middle to go with the scar down my chest.

And believe it or not, your Pete cries.

Me, lying butt naked on my bed, sobbing myself to sleep.

Four

In the dream, we're laughing.

Me and Ken, I mean. The two of us. We really get to looking back – you know, starting from the beginning, and remembering dear old Mum. And I suppose we're having a bit of a joke about it all, and I say my little bit, and then Ken says his. Like what normal people do, right?

Dearest Mum.

With a bit of persuasion, Ken remembers how the old bitch'd soused herself (and me) with cheap vodka, and rolled joints on her fat belly for a full nine months. And I swear I remember – me, little Pete, a blind, web-handed foetus – hearing from her insides all the licking, tearing and folding of paper, and scrunching of dry tobacco and grass.

Happy days.

Then we talk about how it took tongs, a suction pad and a nurse with hair on her arms and Guinness-breath to rip me out of that womb.

About how I wanted to make a point on exit... all elbows, fists and knees as I passed by Mum's swollen liver ... so I did a neat turn of my head the wrong way, intended to give her a scar she would always remember me by. But that there wasn't much remembering left for dear old Mum to do. She split... in both senses of the word (ha! ha!)... and the nurse handed me over (a ball of slime and filth) to the man who thought he was my dad.

You can hear the canned laughter in the background.

'This is where you come back in, Ken, go on,' I'm saying in the dream.

He goes a bit quiet at this point.

'Come on!'

Well... we'll never know, will we? But something tells me that we're not really all that closely related, me and Ken. Me film-star handsome wasted in this shit-hole, and him the fat ball of grease and piss that he was then and still is.

'Hey, hey, watch it! ... Get yourself under control, Ken.'

He's struggling.

Rude, really, I'm trying to talk.

So now I'm telling Ken all I remember. How he distinguished himself when we were growing up with his unquenchable thirst for Special Brew, and the occasional urge to cuddle up to some soft skin when he'd filled his own with beer. How when I was little, he saved that special attention for Debs, my hard-faced sister. How she jumped off the tower block when she was eleven, pumped so full she thought she'd fly right out of the Links. How she wasn't lucky enough to die straight away, was she? So now we're remembering how she spent the next four years in bed making conversation by blowing into a straw, before drifting away, alone, on a wet Thursday in April.

And do you remember, Ken, how after she jumped, you turned to me for comfort? All grunting and fumbling and licking at my neck, as you worked away on me.

Do you remember that, you fuck?

Of course, he can't really answer me now, cos in my dream I've tied him down and stuffed his mouth full of his own socks (real stinkers, never been washed). I've put on the belt, it's disappeared into my flesh and I've burst into flames so I can return the favour and work on him – in my own way, of course (ha! ha!).

Oh, it's coming as a shock, isn't it?

What's that?

He's crying and trying to beg, and then sort of squealing through those socks as he sees me burn and get four-foot shape. His eyes are wide and he's snotting everywhere, and me, I'm getting angrier and *angrier thinking I've got to eat this lump of puss.*

Just as I'm starting to chow down – legs first, I really want to make the pain last – he's managed to spit the socks out.

'Stop! Please... please stop...' he's shouting.

Then a little later...

'You little shit, I'll get you...!'

Really going crazy, you know, right out of control.

I'm going at a reasonable pace, and carefully working around the major arteries, so I manage to eat a good half of him before he dies. Sure, he passes out from time to time... you know, drifting in and out of consciousness and all that, but not enough to spoil the fun.

Five

I wake up.

It's quiet. Fuck knows how long I've been out. I'm trying to work out what's been real and what's been a dream. Maybe I dreamt all of it, right? Then I run my hand around my middle and feel the scar, and I catch sight of the belt laying on the floor.

First:

I'm going to burn the belt, bury the dogstar buckle.

That's right.

I'm going to get rid of the sodding thing.

I'll have myself right back on the ganja and spend six months puffing so hard I'll forget about Kensall Road, forget about what I saw, forget about the old boy and forget about the belt.... forget about who I am. Yeah, six months of no-brain will work all that pain out of my body.

I mean, why me?

I was in the wrong place at the wrong time, trying to cause trouble on Kensall Road bang in the middle of Brown-Town. I saw something I wasn't supposed to see: the old boy belted up wolf-ways. Most likely, I was lucky to get away alive.

After that he was on a hunt after me. Waiting for the right time to take me down.

That's more like it.

And there was me thinking all kinds of shit before. That the old boy was tracking me to find his replacement. That I was *supposed* to find the belt. That I was supposed to be the next in line for dogging it up.

No, man.

He was hunting me to kill me. I was the one who saw him for what he was. And so he wanted me dead.

I'm kidding myself, man. It didn't choose me, the old boy didn't choose me. I'm not supposed to have this fucking belt.

Yeah, this is more like it. I have to get rid of this belt.

Next:

After I've washed in cold water in a cold bathroom (neither Ken nor me is much into wasting money on the gas meter), nicked a couple of quid from Ken's coat pocket hanging on the banisters (one advantage of having a soak for a 'dad' – he'll never learn) and been out of the house to sit on a wall and eat fish and chips.

This is the first proper meal I've had for almost a week.

I realise I'm starving.

Aching all over. Feeling burnt still, everything just a little bit sore like the top layer of my skin has been taken off by a blunt razor.

And I start thinking:

How can I just chuck the belt away?

Maybe I'm not going to put the bastard thing on again, but I can't get rid of it.

I've got to find out something about it. What if it's worth something? Would I talk to Jack about it? Could I trust him? I've never really thought too much about the kinds of people outside the Links that he sells his shit to. Maybe one of them collects belts that turn you into a monster.

Much later:

Two weeks later, in fact.

When I began to wonder *how* I'm going to find out more about it. I can't ask the person I got it from because he's dead. There isn't anyone else I can talk to about it who wouldn't think anything else apart from this was Pete on some kind of trip taking the piss.

What about Lukas? I mean, he was there that night, right? Did he see it? Could he feel it?

Maybe the thing was following him around too. Maybe Lukas is exactly the person to talk to. I mean, look how fucking loop the loop he's gone (joke intended), maybe he's going as crazy as me because the old boy was stalking him too.

Six

'What do you want, man?' I said as I pulled open the door, and Ziggy was there all frantic and worked up like he always was.

'It's Jack's... he's been done over...'

I'm grabbing my jacket and we're out the door.

'Who did it?'

'A bunch of Brunos -'

'What for, man?'

Ziggy was puffing on a joint now, tucking it behind his thumb after each toke.

'Dunno... maybe something he's got came from one of them...'

'Give us some of that.'

We stopped for a minute to pass the zoot back and to. Then it occurred to me to ask something.

'What did they do to Jack? He all right?'

Ziggy nodded.

'OK,' I said.

We carried on across the Links. Twenty-two acres of grey concrete towers and low level maisonette blocks caste on chipped tarmac and brown dirt. Littered with ice cream wrappers, flattened beer cans, fag butts, and petrified black and white dog shit. Low grade graffiti in a scrawl over every wall and on every door. The odd burnt out car, the odd drunk passed out in a doorway, the odd whore hanging out of a *second storey window.*

'Someone said he got in the lock-up room at the back and they couldn't get to him...' Ziggy was puffing, trying to keep up.

'Fuck me,' I said, almost at a jog. 'Things are really going to kick off now.'

This was Jack we were talking about, after all.

Jack bought and sold everything. Anything you wanted – gear aside – Jack was the man for it. He had the biggest place on the Links, two ground floor maisonettes with a door knocked through between them. One he lived in, the other was his office. Story was he could get you anything you wanted. Some of the old folk called him Harrods Jack on account of a shop they'd read about.

But we called him Halloween Jack after the song. A real cool cat with a silicon hump and a ten inch stump. He creaked around his office, pulling up dusty sheets in the half-light, peering under them and rummaging through piles of junk.

'Have you got one, Jack?' we'd yell, hanging in the doorway. Maybe trying to catch a glimpse through the archway that had been hammered through to his home next door.

'Shut the fuck up and wait...' he'd growl until he limped out, blinking in the light with whatever we'd asked for.

When we were kids, we'd have him looking for music or something to play it on, wheels for a bike or something to make a go-kart out of. Later it was things to make trouble with – baseball bats, balaclavas, knives, and, later on, a gun.

As time went on, we started to work for Jack. As much to pass the time as for the cash he gave us. By now we'd got a bit of a reputation – me and Ziggy and Lukas – for doing jobs around the Estate, but the truth was that in this shit-hole everyone nicked from everyone.

That's how our little economy worked – mainly us passing round what we'd nicked from one to the other in an endless circular current with Halloween Jack in the middle making the whirlpool turn.

Davie sold me some gear and used the money to buy music. I robbed his place, nicked the music and sold it to Jack (for money to buy more gear), and Davie bought his records back from Halloween Jack with his gear stash. Round and round she goes, making your head spin.

So it was no great surprise for me and Ziggy when we rounded the corner to Jack's place and found Tony and a bunch of Crew-boys. Tony was bang in the middle of giving Lukas a slapping...

'You better of not had anything to do with this,' Tony was saying, as he cuffed his younger brother round the back of the head.

Jack's windows were boarded up. His front door'd already been replaced, wood for metal this time.

'Fuck off, Tone,' Lukas was whimpering like a girl.

Tony looked up when he saw us.

'Well, did you?' he said, pushing hard at Lukas until he stumbled and fell back onto the pavement.

'No,' I said.

'Not been robbing up at Brown-Town? Giving them reason to come back here for a bit of revenge?'

'No way.'

'Better fucking not be,' Tony's said, rolling up a grollie in his throat and nose, and firing it towards us through a curled tongue.

He nodded to his Crew-boys – 'C'mon' – and they were on their way leaving the three of us looking at each other.

'Where's Jack?' I asked Lukas.

He was getting off the ground, all puffing himself up now that big brother was gone.

'He told Tony to fuck off when we got here. Went back inside.'

'So it was definitely Brunos?'

Lukas nodded.

Then he said:

'You know what this means, don't you?'

'What?' Ziggy said, flicking down the butt of his joint, and screwing it into the ground with his boot.

'It means we've got a way to get in the Crew...' Lukas said.

He was always going on about this, man. Spent his life worrying about how to get on the end of big Tone's cock.

Me, I wasn't so sure I even wanted to be in the Crew. I mean, everyone was a Crew-boy at some stage, but I was happier hanging outside all that shit and not getting myself too involved.

Ziggy, well he was browner than some of the Brunos from Brown-Town, man, and I wasn't so sure that he'd be all that welcome in the Crew (ha! ha!).

'I don't know, Luke...' Ziggy was saying.

'Come on, man,' Lukas interrupted. 'We go and kick some twat in Brown-Town. Tony's got to let us in.... even you, Zig.'

I was standing, staring at Jack's door, thinking how what they'd done had to be worth a kicking. My head was doing cartwheels from Ziggy's skunk. I hadn't eaten for a day and a half. I was feeling tight, and now I'd got it running round my brainless brain, I was starting to like the idea of getting up to Brown-Town and causing some serious trouble.

'All right,' I said. 'As long as we're doing it good. I ain't going up there to mug someone's nan. We'll make a proper mark.'

Ziggy laughed.

'Fucking right,' Lukas said.

Three horrible, little cunnies, weren't we? We deserved everything we got (ha! ha!)

Seven

'Where the fuck 'ave you bin, Pete?'

This is Lukas's Mum, hanging in the frame of their front door. Fag barely lit, stuck to her bottom lip with spit-glue.

I'm just realising what a complete mess she is, when I remember that I done her the year before last. One night when I came round to see Lukas and he was out dealing.

Jesus Christ, I think (whoever that is). You know, with a real jolt. *Jesus, Pete, what were you thinking?*

'I've been about...' Which of course, I haven't been.

Come to think of it, I don't know how long it's been since I came off the weed and hid myself away. I know it's been at least a month since I got the belt. *Has it been six since I've seen Lukas?*

'Lukas is banged up.'

'What for?'

She laughs. A wheeze. A wind instrument with cancer.

'He stuck Ziggy with a knife, didn't he.'

She's saying it like it's fuck all. Like it's nothing, man.

'When...?'

And I suppose it is nothing. I mean, nothing that wasn't always going to happen, back from those days when Lukas was getting madder and madder and Ziggy more and more stoned.

'Three months ago.'

We're stood there looking at each other.

'Where *'ave* you been?' Her eyes are narrowing.

'Why the fuck'd he do it?' I'm asking, ignoring her question.

She snorts, something like a laugh.

'Someone said he'd caught Zig chasing down a white girl for a bit of his kind of fun... Maybe it was that?'

I can feel her staring at me. Then she kind of picks herself up and shakes herself down. Throws the steaming fag butt out onto the concrete in front of the house, almost taking half the skin off her lip with it. Sort of straightens her hair, half-heartedly.

'You wanna come in, Pete?'

She's Lukas's Mum. Probably not much more than thirty-five, but looks fifteen years older than that. I can see her, crystal clear, all ravaged and held together – I dunno, like she's made of pipe cleaners or something. I can hear the breath rattling around in her lungs, all blocked little bronchioles filled up with solid black tar. You can almost hear the crackle of those tumour cells as they split and re-divide.

And the smell of her, man. That's the worst thing.

I don't remember *that* when I was letting her bounce away on top of me, no way. Every crease of skin that hasn't been opened up to sunlight or water, I can smell. Her teeth and what's between them. The clothes that haven't been washed, thick with must and stale sweat.

'No.'

'You got anything?'

'No.'

I walk away... just leave her, stuck to the door frame, watching after me.

Round the corner, Jack's shop is shut up.

I sit on the crazy-paving dried-up mud at the rec, and wait for a couple of hours for him to open up, not sure, even if he does, that I want to talk to him.

I'm feeling all fucked up in the head.

This is what it's like, I keep thinking, *when you can think*. (I keep thinking that I'm thinking, so much so that it's like some sort of whirlpool with me spinning around in the middle). No wonder I've spent most of my life pumping myself full of whatever's to hand to stop this. Better to be brainless, when thinking is this much hard work.

Round and round and round. Like I'm going crazy, man. Lukas, his Mum. Me boning his Mum. Lukas, all of us, that night on Kensall. Lukas killing Ziggy. Me getting knifed and losing my lung. Me in hospital with the nice brown boys. Lukas knifing them dead cos of them knifing me. Me finding the belt and getting a nice silver scar round my middle to go with the one on my chest.

Shit I even think about my poor dead sister, Debs, and I haven't thought about her for the longest time.

And suddenly, of course, I know what I have to do.

I have to go home and put the belt on.

Go home and put the belt on, Pete.

Get that belt and the dogstar buckle under your skin.

This is what I have to do.

I won't take you through the whole thing again. How I go home and wait 'til it gets dark, 'til Ken has passed out in a Special Brew stew. How I leave the door of my bedroom open just enough so I think I'll be able to open it when I've got no hands. How I leave the back door of our maisonette open too.

How I think that the pain couldn't be worse than last time, but that it is. Maybe worse, or maybe it's pain mixed with fear because I know what's coming.

How it feels like I've exploded in a ball of fire. And how I wake up, covered head to foot (or should I say head to tail) in a thin crust of ash.

And there I am.

Four-foot, mouth full of teeth. Still Pete. But this time, without the shock, the panic, the hysterics. This time I'm going to find out what this all means.

What am I going to be able to do with this?

How fast can I run?

How strong am I?

Am I going to be able to hear better, smell better?

Will I... ?

Enough fucking questions!

This is how it plays that first full night as a dog.

Shit, did I ever make the right decision.

Eight

It'd just gone four o' clock in the morning.

Me and Ziggy and Lukas, we got out of the Links by scrabbling over the wall on the West side, the one that was supposed to keep the Crew-boys and all us good white folk (ha! ha!) away from the other gangs that ran our part of town – the Brunos, the Malis, the Slavs and the Greeks.

We were stoned and pissed fit to bursting with laughter, and as we were making our way along, we had to stop here and there so that one of us could suck all that laughing back in, in gulps. What was making us laugh most was the balaclavas and the black face paint – well, apart from Ziggy – around the eyes. Lukas, who used to look at the pictures in too many comics, wanted to stop and make some bat ears out of card to stick on the top of his head, but me and Ziggy managed to beat that one out of him.

'Shut the fuck up...' *we were taking turns in whispering and cuffing each other round the back of the neck.*

We were on Kensall Road in Brown-Town.

We had a target thanks to a streak of brown piss called Raj who tapped Ziggy up for gear once in a while. The main gang in Brown-Town, the Bruno-boys, didn't do drugs so Raj used to come Links-way for his fix. Zig figured that he might be able to tell something about who did what to Jack.

The last time Raj paid Ziggy a visit for a stash, I picked him up and made it quite clear with use of my fists that he was going to tell us what we wanted to know about the hit on Jack or he was going to see some time in hospital for his trouble. Raj was all wide eyed and look mate I'll tell you everything I've heard, happy to do you a favour on account this being where I come to get my gear. Druggie's always talk, man.

We were outside one of these really smart Bruno gaffs on Kensall. Right where Raj the bossed-out fuck told us to come. It was a corner plot, end of terrace – the smart ones always were – with the front all paved out and a railing fence and a fancy metal gate. One gift was these brown types didn't like dogs so there was no mutt to deal with, barking or yapping, and waking everyone up.

There was no moon but the whole place was lit up with a kind of yellow hum from the street lamps. We were going to have to get this done quick and make a break while everything was still confused, because if we were chased there wouldn't be anywhere to hide until we got back to the Links. And that was a good three quarters of a mile dash through enemy territory.

So what was the plan?

You mean we had one?

Yeah of course we had a fucking plan. In our fucked up and fucked out little minds, we were little geniuses for causing trouble. We loved to make it all more complicated than it needed to be.

I mean, we could've popped a couple of windows and crept around in the dark and put our hands on something someone was really going to miss. Hurt their pockets and all that.

That would have been Tony's style, how the Crew did things back then. Nice, quiet, cold revenge.

Yeah, well maybe it was because Lukas wasn't too much like his brother that Tony'd been putting stops on him joining the Crew.

We got our idea for this plan from Diwali, right?

Crackers and fireworks all night. We'd remembered one day talking to Jack about back when the Brunos'd first started arriving around the Links, how the fireworks for Diwali had scared the shit out of his old mum when they kicked off, and everyone had come out onto the streets thinking we were at war or something.

Me and Ziggy still had a box of rockets we'd nicked last year, and

Lukas had his beloved Zippo (fake) and half a can of petrol. We were going to light up the terrace like a Christmas tree. By the time it all kicked off, and all the Brunos'd run out onto the street screaming and gnashing their teeth, we were going to be well off out the end of the terrace and back to the Links.

What could go wrong?

Well, now you come to ask the question...

Three things:

First: Lukas was a twat.

I mean, we knew it already, right, but that night we realised just how much of a twat he was. Round the fucking twist. So instead of setting some nice little smoky, scary fires on the trees and front fences and in the rubbish bins like we'd agreed, Lukas started posting fire through the letter box of every house on the terrace. A spurt of petrol and a ball of paper or cotton wool or something lit with his Zippo. He was a regular postie, going door to door, before Ziggy and I even realised what he was doing cos we were too busy setting up the rockets ready to go.

Second: it was a terrace on a dead-end street.

So the only way we had out was the way we came in. If we'd been to school and thought about using a map and properly planning our night of fun and fire, we most likely would have given some thought to this. What was our alternative getaway plan, then?

Third: the police arrived.

All right, all right. I'll hold my hand up on this one. Track back to Ziggy saying:

'What about the rozzers? This ain't the Links ...'

And me saying: 'They won't give a shit, we won't even see them. This is Brown-Town, what do the coppers want with helping out the browns? They'll just think it's a turf war between the Brunos and one of the other gangs and leave well alone.'

It turned out they <u>did</u> think it was some kind of gang war and that *was exactly why they decided to come and get there so quick. And all these rozzcars screaming to a halt at the end of the terrace suddenly meant we'd got no way out.*

By this time, the street was on fire, choked with smoke, and the rockets started going off like gunfire. The rozzers had arrived at the end of the road so we'd no way of escape. And the first of about half a dozen long haired, white-eyed Brunos was crashing out of his front door with a knife held high looking for someone to stick it into.

These are the moments, aren't they?

Something took right over. There I was, and there were Lukas and Ziggy, hunted to ground, surrounded and no place to go.

Suddenly not feeling so stoned and prone to laughing anymore.

I mean, what the fuck do we do?

What the fuck do we do?

We bolted for the nearest hole.

Of course, we were lucky. So much so that when we talked afterwards, breathless, smoke-haired and sweaty, we began to conjure up all kinds of ways to explain it.

Me, I don't know.

What are the chances that one house on the terrace on the other side of the road would have its front door open – wide open?

What are the chances that whoever lived there wasn't at the door, or anywhere else for that matter?

What are the chances that the back door was wide open too?

And that the back garden – we'd never even considered this, it being in the opposite direction to the Links and us not having heard of such a thing as a map book – what are the chances that the back garden would be separated by a rickety fall-down fence from the Grand Union Canal that snaked its way from the Broadway to London?

So here's the slow motion set piece for you.

Yeah, I know, no-one uses slo-mo anymore, so let's call this retro. This was the nineteen eighties after all (ha! ha!).

Me, roaring at Lukas and Ziggy.

Ziggy and me heading straight to this open door from across the road. Lukas following behind.

Police sirens, lights spinning.

Rockets exploding like staccato gunfire.

Smoke, thickening, drifting across the road.

Ziggy and me making it through the front door, Lukas close behind.

Screaming, angry shouts, fire engine sirens.

The house suddenly dark and still.

Then let's pause for a moment:

OK so the other boys didn't see it. Or if they did, they didn't say anything. And fuck, at the time I wasn't really sure what I saw.

What with the noise, confusion, adrenaline burning through my veins screaming at me to get away, get away.... and out of my head on all I'd puffed and drunk.

But in a second, less than a second maybe, as we raced through the house, from the hall into the kitchen at the back where the door onto the garden was open, I saw something.

Something in the front room.

Just at that point, as much as I was shitting myself about being caught by the police, or worse by a gang of Brunos with daggers....there was suddenly something I knew I should be properly scared of. My guts dropped a mile and a half and at the same time I was gulping for air and swallowing my own puke.

Something staring at me.

A shadow.

A pale shadow... somehow that.

The shape of something...

Something white...

But I couldn't make out what...

Then we were out the back door, and the silence was over. The rockets were firing, and all the shouting and the sirens were back.

Me, Ziggy and Lukas were over the fence and just kept running and running.

Maybe no-one saw where we went. I could believe that from the rozzers, they were still at the end of the street. But not from the Brunos. They were hot on our heels but for some reason didn't follow us through the house.

We didn't stop running until we got back to the Links, a three mile or so round trip. Every bit of me was ready to explode, my lungs were like sawdust from the smoke. We pulled off our balaclavas, spraying sweat, and looked at each other's black and streaked faces.

'Lukas, you could have killed us you twat.'

Then I was the first to laugh. And we laughed for what felt like half an hour, all smoky and sticky on the outside, and smoky and sticky on the inside too.

Nine

This is what it's like to be something else.

Everything about being you, about your body, what you've learnt without thinking from the day you were born – *everything* – you can forget right now.

You've got a flat head, and a nose you can see that stretches what looks like a foot in front of your head.

A nose that can smell, *really* smell. I don't just mean smell the curry that Ken's microwaved for his tea. I mean me smelling like you can see. Smells that have their own shape, size and colour.

Like later. Later I'm chasing someone. I know who he is, I know what he smells like. Hunting him down on the Estate the Slavs own. This geezer's a mile and a half away, but as he's running I get the full reek of his shitting himself because he knows I'm going to catch him and knock him down and kill him.

I can see his scent. Little tiny dots of him, spinning in the air, drifting in all the places where he's been. Scattering around like pollen, and he's a flower racing away through the night. That's how you smell.

Your arms and legs feel really messed up. I'm not on hands and knees, I've *got no* hands and knees, although in a strange way I can still feel where they are. I'm literally standing on the tips of my fingers which are pads and my nails are three inch claws, which, unlike on a real wolf, are sharp enough to cut neat parallel trenches across a face or a chest. My knees are somewhere up at the top of my back legs, and what was my ankle is something like a backwards knee to me now. The first time I properly used these legs I was falling around all over the place... like you see the baby steps of a leggy fawn just after it's born on one of those programmes on TV.

Having a tail is the weirdest thing, man.

You wonder what the fuck a tail is for, of course, until you're tightrope walking across the roofs on the Links and you've suddenly got what feels like an extra arm keeping you balanced.

And I'm naked too. Totally butt naked, but covered in fur and a thick skin which means I never feel cold. Like the idea of cold just doesn't register. Cold doesn't exist.

Hearing is the same as smelling. I know what I can hear because I can *see* it, I can see where it is. If you're hiding round the corner from me, underneath a car say, I can hear every silent breath you take, I can hear the blood thundering its way through arteries and squeezed back to your heart through your veins. Everything I hear I can see. So you don't need to hide, you just draw the whole thing out and put me in a bad mood because I've got to reach under the car to get you (ha! ha!).

This is the new me, baby.

Once I've changed, and I've ridden the wave of panic, I calm down. This second time though, it still takes some effort, I can tell you. Me telling Pete to chill, man, bring it down, breathe deeply through those fuck-off jaws and out through that wet black nose. *Repeat after me, Pete, you have nothing to be afraid of.*

It's everyone else that should be shitting their pants (ha! ha!) not you.

I stand in my room, let myself suck and spew air, let my wolf-self do the good job of cooling me off.

Right. Now to get outside. Let's see what we can do!

It's a job to get the door fully open. I have to kind of nibble and bite at it until I get a slight grip with my teeth and pull it open. Just like you've seen your dog do, right? It's dark on the landing and of course – oh yeah I forgot to mention that – I can see in the dark much better than I can when I'm Pete. But this doesn't stop me from getting my four legs tangled up together and taking a tumble down the stairs.

Another advantage of living with someone who's permanently drained is at times like this – you know, you've just found out you're a werewolf and you fall down the stairs because you're not used to your pins yet – you don't wake anyone up. Ken snores and farts his way through it all without moving a ripple of fat.

The back door I left wider open, so that's just a nudge with the old nose and I'm out.

The night air on the Links is yellow with street light, clogged with the exhausts of so many twenty-year-old cheap Japanese imports, full of cigarette smoke and rubbish that's been shoved out of back doors in bags and never collected, dog shit, chips cooked in fat that hasn't been changed since the sixties and curry swimming with the same grease, ladled straight from the pan.

I can taste weed in the back of my throat, something that reminds me of sex and something else that reminds me of death, a body rotting somewhere unfound, I'm not sure whether it's human.

All of this carried across my nose on a gentle, slightly gusting breeze. *Wild is the wind, right?*

A quick geography lesson about the Links:

Our little maisonette backs on to a heath where people take their bulldogs to shit, a patch of long grass and gorse bushes littered with supermarket trolleys and stashes of porn hidden by the kids who sit in packs wanking rather than going to school. There's a strangled stream running across it that really only exists to carry drinks bottles and plastic through an arch beneath the outer wall and into the nice river that better people try to enjoy way outside the borders of our land of crap.

Now I'm considering with my Pete mind (inside my wolf body), that if I can get over the back fence – which, by the way, is twenty feet of vertical chain-link (the same all the way along, put up by the council in the seventies when they still listened and people were sick to death of being robbed by junkies clambering over the pickets) – so if I can get over the back fence, I can practice being a wolf on the heath.

First the fence.

I walk... well I suppose really I'm padding... down the garden. Thing I notice straightaway – I don't make a sound. Not that I'm making a real effort to be quiet or anything. It's like these feet – paws – are made of rubber or something. They're moulding themselves round every tiny bit of grit or twig that I step on as I go... not a crunch or a snap, nothing.

The fence is going to be tricky.

It's held up by twenty foot pylons. Solid. The chain link is the stiff kind, thick-wired, designed to blunt bolt cutters. At the bottom of the fence the wire's been concreted into the ground, so no real chance of digging a way underneath.

Of course, later, I'm going to find that I can slash my way through something like this. But these are early days, right?

Right now, I'm still thinking about things the way Pete does.

Can I jump it? I'm asking myself, and not feeling very much like I can. *What about climbing it?* And this seems a bit more likely because this is what Pete would have done.

But in the end I kind of half climb, half jump, and it takes four times before I finally get over. The first couple I just fall off the fence, half way up, the third I get messed up in a tangle of claws and tail and take another tumble trying to get myself out. On the fourth, I'm out.

Now I've got an acre and a half of heath to run around in.

Ten

A week after that night in Kensall it wasn't feeling quite so funny.

To tell the truth (ha! ha!), I'd forgotten all about shitting myself in the empty not empty house off the Bruno terrace. I was too busy lying on clean white sheets in hospital, eating three meals a day and seeing if I could get a rise out of one of the cute nurses or another. Sure, my popped lung was giving me some serious grief, but this was a fucking holiday camp, man. I'd never been so well looked after in all my life.

It turned out the two Brunos that took a blade to me were a few beds up just along in the same ward. Don't ask me their names, I can't remember. But they were a nice couple of fellas.

I was noticing how they were getting lots of their brown friends and family in to visit them every day. And they were having brought in all kinds of stuff to eat and drink that I'd never seen or heard of before. And from time to time, they were getting me to come and taste something or other, and they were well fucking happy if I said I liked it and that.

Neither of them were too badly hurt – just broken bones – so they were out after a couple of days, whereas I was in for two weeks. I sort of missed having them around when they'd left. Now it was just me and a bunch of old blokes, all shitting themselves in pans and crying out in the night. So, by the time I was told I could go, I was well ready to. The food and flirting had been good, but I'd had enough of the ancients letting rip and the odd one dying around me.

'Have you got someone who can come and pick you up?' one of the nurses was asking me as I've got up and out of bed and dressed myself. A fucking hole in my shirt with dried-out blood round it. Nice.

I was turning to her and laughing.

'I don't think they've noticed I'm missing,' I said, and then she was laughing too, thinking I was joking and all.

'Don't worry about me,' I said, and then I thanked them for all their hard work in looking after me. And I reckon this may be the first time I ever had anyone to thank for anything.

Then I was out of the ward and down the stairs and through this fucking labyrinth until I found my way into the entrance hall, and there was Lukas sat in one of the chairs, staring at his feet.

'Pete!' he said when he saw me. 'We're in!'

It was the first thing. Not, how are you mate or any of that shit.

'We're in what?' I said as he got up and followed me to the sliding doors at the exit.

'We're in the Crew!'

Fucking bonzo, I was thinking.

'And me and Ziggy got those bastards that did your lung,' he was going on, running round me like a fucking puppy as I was walking down to the bus stop on the main road.

'What do you mean?'

'We got them when they came out. They were standing out the front of the hospital, waiting to be picked up. Me and Ziggy got blades from Jack. We fucked them up good and proper.'

I stopped dead, looking at Lukas.

He'd shaved his head, I thought. He'd got the Crewniform on now too. Drainpipes and Docs and all that. He was a proper Crew-boy.

I stopped dead and just looked at him.

Then:

'Well,' I said, 'at least they didn't have too far to take them to the morgue.'

Lukas laughed. Me, I got this sharp pain in my chest as we hopped onto the bus back to the Links.

Eleven

I'm not sure when it is that I realise I'm hunting.

It's pretty quiet. No-one really comes here at night now. Used to be one of the places we'd come and puff and fuck but these days things have got a bit more dangerous, haven't they?

Fewer and fewer people like to be out too long after dark, leaving the streets to the gangs, the dealers and the junkies. So the heath is quiet.

I'm more aware of the little bits and pieces of life that haven't been choked to death by bad air or bad food they've found. Nothing much – just the odd rat, a squirrel, maybe a mouse. Animals who've made a home in the city, and we all of us have to find a way to survive.

So here I am:

Running around getting used to these legs. Sniffing around the grass and the junk, doing the 'seeing' bit with my nose and my ears. The trouble is, I'm getting a bit bored of this already.

I start thinking, *well, this seems OK. Why don't I have more of an explore around the Links?*

There's an alley further up my road that cuts through from the heath back onto the road. From there I can get into the guts of the Links. I know it's badly enough lit for me to be able to creep around without being seen, just like I suppose the old boy had.

What I want is to see (another!) person. What's bubbling away underneath, while I'm rolling around in the mud like a fucking puppy, is the thought of how absolutely fucking terrified I was when I was Pete and the old boy wolf followed me.

I start to think that I want to see that look on someone else's face (ha! ha!).

And if I'm really going to work out what the fuck to do with myself now I can do this, I need some action. *What can this body – all this gear that I'm wearing – what can this do?*

Ok, I'm getting pretty good at the four-foot thing now.

I lope (see? Me a wolf, loping) through the brush and up towards the alley, slowing sharply when I realise that there are voices. I'm still getting used to the old see-hear thing so I'm not sure quite how far away the voices are. They aren't on my street, I know that for sure. I can hear they aren't and I know they aren't too, because no-one ever comes to our street this late (or early). Maybe they're one road back. Anyway, like I say, voices.

I recognise one of the boys from the Crew.

Martin I think his name is. He's all right, not one of the worst, if you know what I mean, but quite happy to give a black a good slapping and laugh about it, a dealer on the side (did his own gear as well as the Crew's) and a taste for young girls, the younger the better.

It isn't clear what he's saying, and I can't tell who he's talking to. Just something from the rhythm of the conversation makes me think he's dealing. The upsell swing. Yeah you think you want grass but what you really want is brown. Texture like sun.

Through the alley. Across my street (I'm right, no-one there). Into Lovell Road which is behind mine.

Low on the ground. Silent. Barely breathing.

This is just like one of those fucking wildlife documentaries you see on TV. Just wilder (ha! ha!).

I can smell them now.

Martin: smoke (weed, a coke tipped fag), booze (fucking martini or some other sweet-shit wine), unwashed, Lynx (yeah man, bet that makes him a real magnet for the chicks).

The other person: a girl. She smells nice. A hundred ways of nice, with just a nasty tang of an after-smell of all of the stuff that girls on the

Links stink of. She'd do and all that. After all, a lot better than Lukas's Mum. And I start to wonder, as I creep through the half-light, skirting down the side of the road, *when exactly was the last time that I'd rutted with anyone?*

Martin's saying:

'Aw babe, don't be like that.'

And she's saying – in a heated sort of whisper:

'Don't aw babe me,' mimicking him, 'you shouldn't have fucking gone with Julie Anstell, should ya?'

So it's a different kind of deal. He's looking for some snatch.

'It wasn't like that...'

'Well, what the fuck was it like, you fuckin' wanker?'

She's getting louder now. Verging on the hysterical. The kind of thing where you know that if he isn't going to get any warm and wet, old Martin's going to look for an excuse to bomb out.

'Come on babe...'

'You come on. She's a slag. She's the fucking Links bike and you had to get your little dick dirty wiv her didn't ya?'

'Hold on...'

'Piss, off Martin. That's the last time-'

It's right at this point – I remember it very clearly, because it takes me as much by surprise as it does them. I'm getting quite absorbed in their barny and wondering how it's all going to work out.

And I've completely forgotten myself. It seems so long since I've really seen people, been amongst people. Right at this point, she stops talking abruptly, because *she's* seen *me*.

Martin, who has his back half-turned towards me, just stands staring at her. And she stands staring over his shoulder at me.

Just for a second. Maybe less than a second. Everything is

completely still.

Then she screams.

It so takes me by surprise (I'm bound right up in their little domestic) that I almost shit myself. Just in the instant, I'm looking around thinking – *what the fuck has she seen?*

Then I realise she's seen me.

Afterwards, of course, I'm dead proud. She absolutely pisses her knickers. It's a real fifties horror scream. All blood-curdling and shrieky. I've totally scared the crap out of her!

Then, all instinct, I'm on her.

What I'm *trying to do* is go 'shut the fuck up' and quieten her down. What I *have done* is knocked her onto the floor and taken a big enough chunk out of the front of her neck so that she's kind of gargling and blowing blood-bubbles, rather than screaming.

I've got the good red stuff pissing out of her all over my fur. I've got her kicking and beating at me with her skinny arms and legs. So I just twist and pull, dude, and then she's not pummelling me anymore.

In the time it takes for all of this, Martin (the hero) has headed off at a pace and is onto Lake Drive.

So there's me, and I'm looking at the girl – and thinking that all I've had to eat in about six weeks is that bag of fish and chips and she's all nice and warm and about the closest I'm likely to get to a hot meal for a while – and then looking after Martin.

All right, fuck!

I'm not going to get any peace to eat the girl anyway if Martin starts running and yelling and getting the whole Crew out after me.

So I leg it up the street. It's got to be less than a minute before I catch up with him. He just keeps on running, too out of breath, too sharply suddenly sober to scream. All I can do is bat him on the back to knock him over.

(I lashed out, your honour. I didn't know my own strength.)

He flies forward onto the patchwork tarmac headfirst and the force of the fall takes half his face off. He catapults over himself and ends up on his front about fifteen feet further down the road. His head's at this funny angle, and one of his legs is kind of twisted under him like the joints have been knocked out of it.

I'm pretty sure he's dead.

I'm still for a moment, out of breath myself, actually. Well I guess I've still only got one lung, right?

What the fuck am I going to do with these two?

I can't leave them like this, lying out on the street. Especially the girl. She *really* looks like she's been attacked by some kind of animal (ha! ha!). Who's to say that the rozz won't come sniffing around for something like this? Not out of concern for the Links, you understand, but out of worry that whatever has done this might get out of the Links and do some hurt to more respectable people.

I find something out that night.

I'm just about big enough, and strong enough, to carry a seven stone girl. But not a twelve stone bloke.

She I pick up in my jaws somewhere around her skinny middle and make fairly short work of taking her onto the heath and dumping her under a stunted little tree at the back by the wall.

Martin, I end up dragging off of Lake, through Lovell and onto my street and down the alley. All the time he's making more and more of a mess. Little bits of face keep falling off and I can't do anything else but drop him and go back and lick or chew them off the ground and eat them, tidying up his mess as I go. Fucking horrible bits of hair are the worst.

Now I've got both bodies on the heath. I can't leave them here. So I decide to dig as big a hole as I can, and bury them in it. But not before I've had a quick chow down on the girl, while she's still warm. You know, for energy, for the hole.

It's not easy digging something big and deep enough for two adults, but I'm clawing away at the earth like some fucking Golden Retriever until I'm about three feet down. This is knackering, man. My arms (front legs) ache like fuckery. I'm covered in dust and mud, absolutely filthy.

Her, I manage to nudge into the hole. Martin I have to bloody pick up again – the fat bastard – and as I do, taking him by the waist, I manage to half-drop him again, ripping the back pocket off his jeans and spilling a wad of notes onto the grass, some of which start to drift away in the wind (which by now is getting a bit wilder).

I bundle him into the hole.

Next, I kick back the dirt I've dug out and trample it down as much as I can. Man I even go to the trouble of trying to put back some of the turf I ripped off when I dug it. With my mouth. With my fucking mouth!

Then I pick up the cash (or most of it). First the wad, then some running around chasing the notes that've blown about. All of this, again, in my mouth.

The sun's started to rise. There's that blue-purple haze hanging over the Links now, whatever's poisoned the air colouring the light.

The job I've done is as good as it's going to get. I'm one tired, mumma-fucking beast. I limp across the heath with sore paws and a mouth full of muck, blood and moolah, clamber over the fence, back into the house and, shutting my door behind me, collapse – wolf-form – onto my bed.

Twelve

'I'm bored.'

Come to think of it, I'd been bored for a long time.

It'd been a while since me and Ziggy and Lukas set fire to Brown-Town, since I got stabbed and put in hospital and since Ziggy and Lukas got revenge on those that did me. Not so much had happened since. We'd spent too much time like this – at one of our places on the Links, skinning up, chatting less and less, zoning out.

'Well let's go and look for some trouble,' Lukas said.

He was sitting on the sofa in the corner trying to cut another tat into his forearm. His arms and chest were a mess, I'm telling you. All badly drawn daggers and skulls and shit. He'd been a loose cannon back when we were kids. But now he was getting proper psycho. He could get punchy with a lamppost, man...

'I'm bored of looking for trouble,' I was saying back to him, and then he was looking at me grumbling something about the Brunos again. I swear he'd taken me losing the lung and all much worse than I had. He was a ball of anger.

'Hey Lukas, it's me that can't fucking breathe.'

Ziggy was in the corner like he always was, sat at the little table, hunched over his papers, tobacco pouch and tin box of gear, skinning up.

All three of us were pranged, like we always were.

Lukas was going on and on about some Greeks we gave a kicking to last week, and how we were in the Crew and we were keeping the Links white. And you're watching this wondering whether the stupid fuck had *noticed what colour Ziggy was. (Well later he did, right? (ha! ha!))*

'Stop going on about the Crew...' I was saying. 'I'm bored of that too.'

Ziggy was laughing to himself. He hardly said a word these days, only taking the occasional break from skinning up and puffing to join in on some of the ultra-violence or hunt down some girl or another.

'What's your problem?' Lukas was getting worked up again.

Then Zig was telling him to calm down, relax and get into the weed chill.

And Lukas was pulling on the next joint and muttering to himself.

What was the point of the Crew anyway?

Little kids went nicking – like I used to – would get a cuff round the head. Someone smashed up the wrong car, they got their front windows stoved in. Someone raped someone else's sister, the Crew caught up with him and spent half an hour stripping him down and giving him a good taste of the same with the wrong end of a baseball bat. Someone killed someone, which happened from time to time (well it was that kind of place), they got hanged from the lamp post on the rec.

All the dealers got what they needed so they could give the druggies what they needed, and creamed a bit off the top, so the Crew got what they needed.

A brown or a black or any other kind of Nonglish stranger ended up somewhere close to our streets and the Crew made sure they didn't make that detour again.

And that's mainly how it'd been.

Later on there was a little bit of prostitution. Something edging towards what you might call (dis)organised crime – extortion, that kind of thing. But mostly the Crew weren't all that bright (present company excepted of course), and they didn't want to rule the world.

They just wanted the opportunity for a little bit of swagger in the tiny world they lived in.

That's what Lukas was lapping up.

Ziggy was liking the protection he got when he'd chased down a girl and given something to her she didn't want.

Me?

I didn't know what I was doing being part of all this.

'I'm bored.'

I was bored.

So I was closing my eyes and letting the good stuff drag me away somewhere better. Lukas and Ziggy disappeared, and then, eventually, so did I.

Let's face it, I'd spent too much time on the Links as part of the Crew, like this. Too much weed; too much cheap booze; hanging round in different people's shit-flats; never seemingly eating anything; never really talking about anything; never actually doing anything except nick and fight and fuck.

There had been the occasional turf war to lighten things up.

Minor stuff, really. Why would the other gangs have wanted anything to do with us when they had their own turf and the whole of the rest of London to fight over? We were walled in and the rest of the world was walled out.

One of these turf wars had been caused by a rumour that went round about a girl called Vicky Tomlin being raped by a Mali when she got in a minicab after a night out in the Bush. Not that we gave a toss about Vicky at all, but we'd got the bus (yeah I know, we'd bussed it to our gang fights) down to the Bush and'd had a bit of a punch up with some Malis. We'd given out and taken a few fat lips, until some of the proper Mali boys'd turned up with guns and we'd legged it out of there. No-one had got hurt that bad and it'd turned out that Vicky had been lying anyway. She'd later dropped a pale faced baby and moved off the Estate to live with a Slav named Gregor. But that was her story.

So that day, sat with Ziggy and Lukas, stoned off our rocks.... maybe it was the last day like that.

Because now things started to hot up.

And it was all about drugs.

Everything was getting cheaper. So people, like people like us, could start to afford stuff they'd never been able to get their hands on before. But where they'd been buying an eighth of rocky and making it last a few days or even a week, now they were buying by the hit. Enough coke for a night out (or in), something stronger maybe sir. And the more that people started buying this way, and the more people started buying, the tougher it got to keep hold of the trade routes. The Crew were like the old colonials, man, manoeuvring their canoes laden with exotic goods through the dangerous swamp and offloading all this addictive shit to the natives.

And of course everyone wanted a piece of the action.

The Crew'd been doing things the old-fashioned way.

Buying in bulk from some dodgy Ragger, and selling it on at a margin on the Links. It wasn't long before the Slavs (Gregor and his mates) were getting stuff in so cheap, and so much of it, that the druggies were getting off the Links to buy direct from them.

And this was hitting Tony and the Crew badly in the pocket. And at the same time all the other drug-dealing gangs were hitting each other in the pocket or being hit in the pocket.

So things just got nastier.

There was a guy who was set alight with a car tyre round his neck and a dressing made of petrol slung all over his clothes.

The Greeks started hitting on the Slavs' patch, there was a pitch battle, and, so they say, about twenty ended up dead.

Some dealer, can't remember which gang, got his hands cut off.

And one of the other gangs went after the family of the chief of the Malis so they could replace khat with crack on those streets.

Everything got cranked up a few levels. It was like the whole of West London'd been put on a grill and heated up, tension ready to burst.

This was about when Lukas killed Ziggy, remember?

Ziggy was wiping off his cock after one of his chase-downs in the alley down by the north wall, when he turned and saw Lukas watching him.

'All right Lukas. Long-time no see, man.'

And Lukas just pulled out a knife and stuck him in the guts with it. Someone said that Lukas cut Ziggy's dick off, but I don't go with that. He was fucked up but not that kind of fucked up.

But that was how it was now.

One or two in the Crew like Lukas were well up for it, but, to be honest, a lot of the boys didn't really have the heart. They were part of the Crew for the kudos, the cheap weed and access to some of the half-decent muff on the Links. The occasional bang-up with another gang was the price they paid.

But a full-blown war?

No thanks.

Me. I could take or leave. I was partial to a bit of the ultra-violence. But I was becoming preoccupied now. Things'd started to play on my brain, and these things were making it a bit difficult for me to concentrate on politics and war.

Thirteen

What wakes me up is me puking up.

Eyes, throat, nose, all stinging hot with my own stomach acid.

There are few things worse than waking up this way. It sets a bad tone for the whole day. I shut my eyes and try to squeeze the blistering pain out of them. What is it about your eyes being sore when you puke? How does the puke get up there?

I lay on my side, everything a blur. Arms and legs hanging over the side of the bed. Each breath searing a cut into my one decent, working lung.

As I said, there are few worse things than waking up puking. But you know what, this is one of them. Not only am I waking up this way, but – once my eyes clear and I find myself staring at the puke-pile I've just deposited on the carpet – I realise I'm waking up looking at a pile of half-digested human. The first thing that catches my eye is a tit – or to be more accurate a chunk of tit. Nice milky-white has gone grey, the rosy nipple a kind of off-green colour. But definitely a toot.

I throw up again. This time more of a mess of flesh than anything else.

Rolling onto my back I lay gasping. I have to get up, go to the toilet for some water. It's a real effort to push myself up off the side of the bed and get to standing. A hand on each wall of the corridor to steady myself, then into the toilet and I collapse at the sink. Half-kneeling, hanging on to the bowl, splashing water onto my face and into my mouth, and coughing and spitting up bile.

Finally, I get to looking at my face in the mirror. *Blimey, I look much better than I'm feeling. How can I feel this shit and look that together?*

Then something occurs to me.

I'm looking at my face.

Pete's face.

But I went to sleep as the wolf, right? With the belt on still, underneath my skin. Did I get it off in my sleep?

Then I run my hand down over my belly and bend my head down to see myself. I still have the belt on inside me. I can feel the dogstar buckle under my skin.

I've got the belt on, but I'm in Pete-shape.

Right, I'm thinking.

Well, how the fuck does this work now?

Fourteen

Like I said, things started to get nasty.

The turf wars were hotting up, where all the posing and the talk was turning into action. It'd always been dodgy going outside the Links into the Nonglish areas around, but now it was downright dangerous. We were walled in with nothing to keep us busy but more booze, more drugs and more shagging.

The Crew were less worried about lording it around the Links and more worried about getting their own drugs in and keeping the other gangs' drugs out.

So the Links was changing too.

A good fight used to bring everyone out of their houses to watch and cheer and laugh. Now it meant closed doors and silence. The old'uns stayed in, scared to come out because some drugged up skank might rob them for their pension. The nicking that was going on was more often than not accompanied by some serious violence, just for the fun of it. The weed that was coming in was potent to blow-your-mind levels, coke was cheaper than a packet of fags, and crack even cheaper. And there was more besides, with the Crew putting all their effort into making sure they got it in through the walls.

Me, I was getting more and more paranoid.

Especially at night.

You didn't get much of a chance to be on your own when you lived where I did, but on the odd occasion when I was alone, I started to get this...I don't know... panic...

I didn't know what it was. Sort of felt like I was inside a box and I couldn't get out. Like my arms and legs were tied up tightly and I couldn't move. Like I was completely powerless, and anything... anything could happen to me and I'd have no control.

It was just making everything worse.

I was round at a guy called Dean's – one of the Crew. We spent an evening drinking Thunderbird and burning zoots like they were going out of fashion. At about three in the morning, I got up, my head like a flying saucer hovering twenty feet above me, said g'bye to Dean and made for the stagger back to my place.

The Links was dark. Black except for the cloud of orange light that hung above it coming from the lamps in the streets outside our walls. We didn't have any street-lamps now. Ours were broken (who hasn't played climb the lamp and pop the bulb?), either that or someone'd decided to switch the electricity off at night on our streets.

I started to see the air disperse into tiny spinning crystals, the way I often did if I'd smoked too much of the good stuff.

And then suddenly I got this rising feeling of... fear (I suppose it was)... all heart clenching and making me short of breath. I picked up my walk to a jog. The night air cleared. I was swinging my head around from one side to another.

What was there?

I didn't really want to look behind me. I got that feeling in the centre of my back, a kind of burning, tingling, like someone'd thrown something at me and it was about to hit.

I made it back to the maisonette, and fumbled with my keys. There was silence except for me fucking about trying to stick the right one into the lock. Then I was through the front door and slamming it behind me.

A muffled, 'Shu' fug up,' from Ken, and that was it.

The heart slowed, I could breathe off my lonely lung.

Calm it, okay?

This kind of thing was mainly happening at night. Mostly when I was out. A couple of times I woke up in bed, wide awake, listening.

Thinking: what's that?

What is it?

Where is it?

And eventually I'd drift back to sleep with visions of splintering glass in my head.

So I dropped off puffing, which believe me was a major step at the time. Here I was off the weed for the first time since I was about eleven. Everything starting to become clearer than it'd been for more than ten years.

Now, you're a clever sod, aren't you?

You're putting two and two together, like you was taught to at school (poor me never was, see?) and making four. You're thinking, why isn't this stupid twat making the connection between all this so called paranoia and the night in the house on Kensall Road? Well before you get too far ahead of yourself, remember that I've made your job a lot easier by cutting out a lot shit that happened in the time between.

Shit like:

One or two proper shack-ups (some even lasted for a few weeks – all nice girls (ha! ha!)).

About twenty eight one night stands (yeah, man, I was, and am, a good looking bastard, and the birds round here used to put out for nothing!)

A pick'n'mix of morning after pills.

One abortion (that I'm aware of).

A couple of minor altercations with the cops (including almost getting banged up for something I didn't do, honest (ha! ha!)).

Too many breakfasts of toast or crispy rice or some such shit. Pot noodles, Super Noodles and Vesta curries.

Hours of my life spent crapping, pissing, wanking, sleeping.

And other such.

And during this period I wasn't even remembering the house on Kensall.

OK it was a good story. But it was one of a hundred in my little skank life and not standing out for any particular reason, although undoubtedly sending a chill down my spine once in a while when I did give it a thought. So it wasn't at the top of my mind.

Not until now.

Now was the moment I had another one of these crazy panics on my way home. But this time it wasn't me stumbling back from a night of puff and smoke, it was me walking home – sober ladies and gents, stone and cold fucking sober – from an evening bored shitless while everyone else got mashed.

Me, I was running scared from the paranoia and the more people kept saying to me, 'Pete you pansy, just have a drink and a puff and you'll feel fine,' the more I was feeling like a white-out even though it'd been a few weeks and there couldn't be another ounce of the good stuff left in my system.

I'd got the burning in my back. I'd got my heart banging away in my chest. The ol' sphincter acting like he was going to open wide up and just let everything slip out nicely. There was puke in my throat. I'd got it all as I stood near my front door and strained to see something in the dark and haze across the road.

Nothing.

Nothing to see.

Oh, but I could hear it now.

Deep. A rush of air, in and out. Something of a scraping growl.

Nothing to see but something was there, I just couldn't make it out.

Then the tiny coil of muscle at the base of my backbone gave up, and everything I'd eaten in the last forty-eight hours spilled a chunky stream into my shorts.

'Who's there?' I was shouting.

Then I turned and opened the door, and as I spent the next thirty minutes scrubbing my clothes and myself in the bath, I was all: What the fucking fuck was that?

And as I was dipping and dunking myself and gritting my teeth, the memory of Kensall Road started banging around my head.

I thought: I'm getting a gun and I'm going to fucking kill that thing whatever it is.

And: I know where the fuck it lives.

Fifteen

Well... you want to understand how it works?

This is it from here-on in.

What I learn over the next few months is:

One: the belt doesn't need to come on and off. I don't need to rip myself half to pieces each time I want to turn back to Pete. The belt just stays where it is, round my middle, under the skin.

I just have to learn how to change backwards and forwards. For three months I keep myself to myself. In my bedroom, trying to work out how to do it.

And what I work out is this: I'm (mainly) in control. What does it, I don't know how to explain it. I have to sort of channel everything about myself through the belt to that dogstar buckle stuck inside my belly button...

You know, I don't really know how I do it. I mean, how do you swallow? How do you shout? How do you blink? How do you shit?

Two: the change itself is pretty much the same. Maybe a little less violent, a little less heat and light. But similar.

I say I'm mainly in control, because there have been one or two occasions when I 'm not.

For example:

One night I'm asleep in bed. I haven't tried to change for a few days. Too knackered, just staying at home, watching a bit of TV, kipping. Man, before this I've been up almost every night for a month running around the Links, practising at being the big bad dog, and now I'm needing a rest. Suddenly, I'm waking up at the start of a change, and I realise that I've been dreaming about changing and that must have set me off. I could have set the bed on fire, man! As it is I *just* stop changing. *Just*. So that's another thing I learn. I can stop it if I need to.

There's another time when I decide to go out Pete during the day. Just for a bit of light, really, more than anything else.

I'm thinking I'll have a dander around, maybe go to the shop and get some things to eat and drink, hide them in my room away from Ken. I've gone off the Links because, even though it's dangerous, I don't want to be seen around. There's a shop in the West part of Ealing we've gone to sometimes. Enough of a run-down shit-hole of a place – Indians – that means we can get away with going in. They won't press the panic button as soon as we walk through the door (ha! ha!).

I go in and the guys that run the place are jabbering away and I can't understand anything they're saying, and then one of them sort of points at me and laughs. You know I'm not in the mood at all for this kind of shit. I'm tired and fucking grumpy. Then they all laugh again, this time like they think whatever it is that someone has said is *really* funny. And they're all looking at me, and pretending not to at the same time. And suddenly I feel myself heating up, and before I know it the smoke's started to lift from my skin. And this has wiped the smile off all of their faces. Before it gets out of control, I leg it out of the shop and stop the change from coming on.

Who's laughing now you motherfuckers? Just don't make me angry... you won't like me when I'm wolfie! (Ha, ha, ha!)

Three: there's definitely more of an urge to change at night than during the day.

And when I do change at night, I get a real fucking urge to sleep all of the next day. It's absolutely knackering, but at the same time it makes me feel... just full of beans, man. Just fucking fantastic. Really ready for anything.

Four: the more time I spend changed, the better I get at being changed.

It's difficult to tell because I've never timed myself but I reckon I can run at least twice as fast with four legs than two. I can jump clean over the fence at the back of our maisonette. Everything's sharper for Pete the wolf than for Pete the one-lunged ex-druggy.

Ch-ch-ch-ch-changes.

Five: it hasn't escaped my attention that no-one seems to give a shit about Martin and his bird disappearing.

I spent half an hour the next early evening tidying up the pit I buried them in. And then I spent another half an hour counting through Martin's stash. There's a hundred and forty quid. More money than a deviant like me has ever seen in one handful. Sure, I can't get the dirty taste of him or his money out of my mouth, but I can't help thinking that Mart's cheap jeans and the wild wind have blown Pete a very particular kind of message.

I can't keep knocking off dealers on the Links, for certain. But what I can do is pursue a career in robbing dealers in any of the other twenty or so walled-in shit heaps in and around London. No-one would miss them, or no-one would care. The rozz never goes into the Estates. Fuck me, I'd be doing the world a favour getting rid of Martin and his kind. And every one of them is full of a few tens of cash, especially if I get at them late at night when they've done their rounds, and before they head back home or straight to the kingpin to hand in the wad and be left with their commission.

So six: all of a sudden Pete has a new career. Armed robbery, fang and claw. I'm going to be a rich man.

So what am I going to do with the money? Who knows?

I'm not going to be able to spend it – bar a few quid a week on staying alive. I don't go out much (not as Pete), I don't have any friends. Fuck, I've only managed one bunk-up since I got the belt, and I had to call that off sharpish when she started asking questions. Ziggy's dead, Lukas will be banged up forever, I'm pretty sure that the Crew have forgotten about me (probably thinking that I'm wasted in some crack den somewhere).

I can't suddenly reappear to the world with neck and hands full of bling. And apart from that, what the fuck would I do with money? There's just this vague idea of making a few quid, stashing a few quid, then what to do at some point will become clear.

Number seven: there's just the first shadow of a thought... for the first time in my horrible, shitty little existence, it starts to occur to me that I might not end my days on the Links. That one day, I'll be getting out (like no-one else I've ever heard of).

Sixteen

Next day I went to Jack.

'A gun?' he said, looking even older now than when we were kids.

Bent further, almost in two. Lines cut deep into his face like knife scars. His teeth and gums like they're rotting off the front of his face.

'What for?'

'Come on Jack. What you think I want a gun for?' Playing it a little cool. I'd never touched a gun in my life.

Jack nodded slowly.

I was thinking there was no fire in his eyes anymore. The door to his office that had always stood open was more often than not shut these days.

'All right. Come back the day after tomorrow.'

I was filled with a kind of madness. An urgency. In my head, I had this feeling now that it was me or this thing, whatever the fuck it was, or this thing or me. If I didn't blow the hell out of it, it was going to rip me apart, I just knew it.

I was being hunted.

OK, keep up with me now because we're moving a little faster.

Jack got me the gun. I can't tell you what kind of gun it was. All I can say is that it's the only one I've ever held from that day to this. I had it kind of stuffed down my trousers, although I was a bit conscious of a story I'd heard from one of the Crew about an African lad who'd shot his own dick off in doing this same thing.

I was taking my life in my own hands going down to Brown-Town with the way things were. So I waited 'til late and dressed in black – all over from boots to hat – and went round the back way along the canal. The same way we came in reverse when me and in-prison Lukas and dead Ziggy lit up Kensall Road like a bonfire.

It was fine going along the canal. Only one direction, no way to get lost. Just pitch black except for a slight shimmer on the water. Every splash, twig-snap, rush of wind through trees, every noise I was jumping like a baby. My fingers kept making their own way to where I'd jammed the gun and I kept having to tell myself not to blow my cock off like the Afro boy did.

Now I was at the back of the terrace on Kensall. I knew this because it was the first row of houses. Everything else until then was park-back or running through the industrial Estates that bordered the whole area.

Except I couldn't tell which house was the house.

Shit, I hadn't thought about this.

I'd seen the place from the front for about ten seconds before we bolted through the door. After near shitting myself inside I didn't take anything in about the garden at all. There was no way I was going to recognise it.

Fuck.

The fence had been down before, but it'd been a long time and someone had obviously put it back up because all the houses were walled at the back. I could just about make out the houses over the top, but this was three o' clock in the morning, there was nothing to see.

Then really faint, I heard a cry.

Cry is the best word I can think of, but it wasn't quite that. A sort of moan, a release of air. It sounded tired and... sad. And although it was hard to tell which direction it was coming from, as I jogged further up the terrace along the walls, I could see a tiny glimmer of light inside one of the houses.

The back door of the house looked open.

I forgot the gun and scrabbled over the wall.

I forgot to shit myself, even though I knew straight away that this was the house.

There was someone inside. Someone had given out that cry.

Along the garden path and to the back door.

Through this and into the house.

A pale shadow of the memory of that first night flew in front of my eyes. The fireworks like gunfire, the smoke, the flash of knives and that white shadow of something in the house. For a moment, I panicked, stopped.... should I get out, back into the garden? Then I saw where the light was coming from. The front room. Where I saw whatever I didn't really see before.

So this was the room (light provided by a single candle) which stank. Of piss and sweat and fuck knows what else. I was almost retching and holding my hand over my mouth as I was looking in.

Brown patterned carpet like old people have.

Curtains at the window drawn, scruffily.

Wallpaper in swirls.

A small black table in the middle of the room, on which the candle.

Sofa set behind the table being the only other piece of furniture.

On the sofa, a figure.

To be exact, an old boy, naked.

When I'm saying old, I mean really old.

He looked dead. I didn't know why I thought this but I did. And that he'd just died and that the cry I heard was his last.

And hanging over the back of the sofa was what looked like a belt.

I was standing there for some time, taking all of this in, forgetting the smell of it.

I hadn't been expecting this. I was thinking all gun fight and gore. End of me or end of my losing my fucking mind. But what I got was a little terraced house with a bare front room and what looked like a dead geezer with no clothes on.

And a belt.

After some time, I want to say it was half an hour but who knew if it was longer or less, I stepped into the room.

It was the belt.

What the fuck do I know? Why didn't I just walk back out of the house again? Whatever was here that other night wasn't here now. Whoever this old boy was, well, he wasn't going to do any talking. There was nothing for me to fight and no-one for me to shoot.

But that belt.

I leaned over the old boy's body – half expecting his eyes to open like some kind of fucking zombie – so I could get a closer look. The belt hung over the back of the sofa, and all I could see was the brown-skin leather, stippled and crease-ripped.

What was it about that belt?

I reached out a hand to touch it, breathless, silent, nothing but the pounding of my heart and my one-lung dead and still, empty of air. Gently, I took the leather between my fingers and thumb. It felt... soft... not like leather (or fake leather at least) that I'd touched before.

Soft like skin.

And then, like I couldn't help myself, in the stink and the shivering light, late at night in that house with the old boy laying there, the dark night outside, and feeling inside of myself in a way I couldn't explain, fixed there until I did... unable to move until I did... like that... I just lifted the belt from the back of the sofa.

As I pulled it upwards, I felt the weight of a metal buckle that had hung down the back of the seat. Released, the belt swung towards me and the head of a dog, or maybe it was a wolf, on that star-shaped buckle seemed to snarl in the flickering candle light.

I folded it in my hand and ran out of the back of the house and home.

Seventeen

So the routine goes like this.

Like I said, there's something like twenty or so walled-in Estates like the Links around London. I've known about some of them – the ones in West London – before. I find out about the others as time goes on.

I do a lot of creeping about in the dark – quite a lot on the tops of roofs now you come to mention it – listening to what people are talking about.

So I pick an Estate and play a nice game of hunting for a week or two. Working out who the dealers are on the Estate, what their routes are, what their routines are. Even the most fucked-out junkie dealers have a routine. They're organised to make a round, and the only way they can make it day-in day-out, week-in week-out, is to be methodical, man.

So I'll be doing all this with a hunter's eye, you know. I'm not stood there with a note-book taking down times and places, I'm a dog studying his prey – every detail I need scratching some kind of imprint on the wolf side of my brain.

A lot of times, I just catch the bus where I'm going and find somewhere nice and dark and quiet to change, where I can leave my clothes and come back to when I want to get Pete-shape again. Sometimes, if I'm really in the mood, I change at home and make it across London and back dog-ways.

Sometimes I rob and kill, sometimes just rob.

It depends.

It can depend on who I'm hunting.

Like, I'm following this guy for a week. Over on the Marchwell

Estate. I think his name is Cheddar or something like that. I only listen and take notice enough to work out what I need to know. It isn't long before I take a real fucking dislike to Cheddar. He's one of those real smart-arsed swanky twats, a fucking strong sense of his own importance – you know what I mean?

He likes to give anyone shorter than him a good slapping, most of all girls who are shorter than him. King of his little kingdom of shit and needles.

So this is what I mean when I say it depends...

You think I'm going to say that I kill Cheddar, don't you?

That I'm going to take great pleasure in slicing him open and ripping out the filling? No man. What gives me a buzz is cornering him on his own late one night, pinning him down and ripping out his pockets until I find the fat splash of cash I've been looking for, then letting him go and explain to his boss where the money has gone (oh, he's pissed and shat himself from the sheer fucking terror of me, 'please don't kill me, please don't kill me' all in a high-pitched, whiney kind of voice).

Oh, Cheddar's boss is much nastier than me. A proper big cheese.

They spend three days dispatching the little bastard, and when they've finally done him, they literally hang him out to dry so all the other little wheeler dealers can see what happens if you made off with the boss's doolix.

It depends on whether I need to eat.

Sometimes I'm hungry and other times I'm not. And even if I'm hungry, I have a look at what I'm robbing and that looking can take my appetite away. I might be a dog, but this dog doesn't eat just anyone (ha! ha!).

It depends on other things too, like....

Screamers. All, 'Ah! Oh! No! Please no! Help! Help!' Yah-dee-yah-dee-yah. Oh, just shut the fuck up, will you! A couple of times this happens and I bat a head clean off the shoulders – which I have to admit to finding quite funny. You've never seen a dog laugh, right?

Heroes. All, 'You're not 'avin' me you fucker!' And fists and boots and butting heads. Just don't make things worse. You're asking for a game of knockabout, and that's all going to finish with tiny bits and pieces of you splattered across the tarmac. There's no place for heroes in this story.

But you know what, most of the time I am happier just robbing.

So after some time of this, I start to over-hear conversations about myself. Not much, just whispers, people speaking under their breath because no-one wants to be the one who actually says – 'here, apparently there's a dirty great fucking wolf thing on the prowl that's knocking off dealers, I do hope I'm not next on the list'.

I've become a rumour. Nothing more really. But I'm on the register. Cool, yeah, in some ways. But in others it begins to bother me.

With a little bit every week to see me by, I'm building up quite a stash of money.

The more I do this, the better I get at watching out for the dealers with real cash. These are the guys who are one up from the junkies going door-to-door selling. They're the collectors – on the big rounds on the bigger Estates, there are collectors who work half a dozen or so dealers, pulling in the money a couple of times a night, presumably so the dealers don't get tempted to go AWOL like they thought old Cheddar had. We never had collectors on the Links, don't think the Crew are bright enough to think like that. Anyway, the higher up the chain I go, the louder the mumble gets.

One time I even hear two collectors on a walled-in in North London chatting about something I've done down south of the river. So they've heard.

That morning (OK, OK, after relieving my two fans of all their cash and dumping their bodies in one of the choked little rivers that snakes down to the Thames) I make my way home and after I've changed back I sit on my bed and count up my money.

In eight months just about, I've got together nearly five grand. Five grand.

Might not sound much to you – you posh bastard – but you can't begin to imagine how much five grand is to someone like me.

One more big hit, I'm thinking.

Bigger. Push the total right up. One more big one, then Pete can get out of here.

'Where to?' you ask. *No fucking clue,* Pete answers. I have no clue where to go. I mean, where do dogs go when it's getting a bit dangerous on the rob round home?

Eighteen

So I brought the belt back from the house on Kensall Road. I laid it over the back of the chair in my bedroom, just like it was laid over his sofa. And I didn't touch it.

For three days, I just sat on my bed looking at it.

First, I was wondering: how much can I get for it?

The buckle was the thing.

This dogstar.

To my robbing eyes, it looked worn out, beaten up, and worthless. All the things of value on the Links were bright, shiny and new. But I was thinking I remembered someone saying once that rich people like old things, the older the better. Maybe the dogstar belt was worth something. Maybe Jack could fence it for me...

And then I got to thinking I didn't really want Jack getting involved, as he got me the gun and everything and he might've started sniffing around for more information.

Second, I was thinking about chucking it away....

The belt itself was made of leather, soft skin of some kind but it was tatty, busted up and a little bit shitty. It had a strong, musty, sweaty smell.

Come on, if I'd found it in any other circumstances, I'd have left it where it was. On the first day when I sat there staring at it, I couldn't really work out why I picked it up at all.

I kept my head down. I was pretty sure there wouldn't be any fuss about some old boy, stinking of piss, dying at home in his chair. But what if someone started asking questions? What if, somehow, it all came back on me, and I was sitting here with his belt in my bedroom?

But at the same time I was thinking, this had something to do with whatever it was that'd been following me. And it occurred to me, as I gnawed away at my nails and wished that I'd never given up on the ganja, that whatever it was might be pissed off that I'd nicked this belt.

Next, I was starting to think like this:

Something about taking the belt made me feel...I don't know, <u>weird</u>, man.

I'd got it for a reason. Right?

So it was three days, two and half Pot Noodles and not much else. Three days of sitting there staring at the belt.

Into the third day, I began to get an urge to try on the belt.

I don't know where this urge came from.

Maybe it was some sort of test. Maybe the belt didn't want any old person putting it on. It was patient. It watched me watch it, until it decided it could trust me.

Maybe it was like this: the old boy chose me. He was following me about to suss me out. He wanted me to go to his house. He wanted me to find him there and take the belt.

Then after I got it, the belt had to make its own mind up. It was sitting there looking at me as much as I was sitting there looking at it. Then it made up its mind. Yeah. I was just the kind of lowlife, violent, screwed up fuck it was looking for.

The belt chose me.

At first this urge wasn't that strong. Just the idea came into my head for the first time: what if I tried it on?

Until that point I hadn't even considered wearing it. It was shitty, dirty, like I say, it stank.

Once the idea was in my head, though, I couldn't get it out.

I jumped off the bed and started pacing around my room.

'Put the belt on, Pete.'

From downstairs, I could hear Ken banging around and farting in the kitchen. The TV was beating out a game show drumroll through the ceiling of the lounge. It was dark outside, I realised, it must have been about ten o' clock. I hadn't seen a soul for three days, and I was pacing round and round my room wanting to put the belt on and not wanting to put the belt on.

'Put the belt on, Pete.'

Probably about an hour. Maybe more. It was probably about an hour that I'd been stomping around like this. I was talking to myself. Mumbling.

'Put the belt on, Pete.'

I was thinking: this was just about putting the belt on, right?

That was all.

I hadn't got a clue what was going to happen.

It was just a belt.

'Well put it on then.'

So I did.

I went over to the chair and picked up the belt.

I could see as I did this, that there was a metal clip at the other end of the belt. I could see that this would fit on the back side of the dogstar buckle. This would hold the belt on.

Without thinking I took off the T-shirt I was wearing.

'Skin to skin, Pete.'

I'd got the buckle in my right hand and the belt was swinging gently by my side. Reaching around I caught the clasp end of the belt. Now I'd got it horizontal like, at waist level, behind my back.

'Put it on, Pete.'

Slowly then I brought it round me until the two ends met over my hairy little scrag-hole belly button. It took a few seconds before I could feed the clip through the metal loop on the back side of the dogstar buckle and then they were fixed together, and I let go of the belt with my hands.

Suddenly, I realised how hot I'd been.

My skinny chest with its lightning-white burst-lung scar on one side was all damp with sweat. I opened the window, stuck my head out to get some air that, in these parts, passed for fresh.

A moment of calm.

The Links was still – not silent, I could hear voices, a car backfiring somewhere, music, Ken's game show – but... I don't know... like there was thick fog hanging over it or something, so that all the sound was dampened, as if someone else was hearing it, not me. The same with how it looked, like a grey veil'd been swung in front of it. And the usual smells of smoke and fumes and shit were muted.

Then, like an axe through the head, out of nowhere, the pain came.

The first feeling was of the belt getting tighter.

It was constricting round my waist like a fucking snake.

Fuck me, it was hurting, it was starting to make it difficult to breathe. I was gasping for air, holding on to the windowsill with one hand and desperately struggling with the buckle – trying to undo it – with the other. It was so tight I couldn't get my fingers behind the clasp. The belt was cutting into my skin now. There was a ring of my fucking blood around the edges of the dogstar.

The leather strap had sunk into my skin so it was flush, it was becoming part of me.

I was scrabbling in a panic at the buckle, trying to get my fingers under that dog's head. My nails were all over the edges of the belt trying to find a place loose enough for me to prise it off.

I couldn't breathe. I was doubling up in pain. My waist was a mess *of blood.*

All around, there was a deep cut in line with the top and the bottom of the belt, and my skin was hanging over it.

A final convulsion and the tightening stopped.

Then I was watching as my own skin healed over the top of the belt. Just like that.

Just like fucking that.

My blood was drying up. I'd got a long scab round my middle. Then it was all flaking off and leaving a scar beneath.

This had all happened within a minute.

I was catching my breath.

Heaving hard and trying to get some air into my one-lung.

All I could think was that this fucking belt was inside me.

It was <u>inside</u> me!

I could still feel the line of it round my waist. I could just about see it, and around my belly button I could make out, faintly under my skin, the dog's snarl on the buckle.

'Breathe, Pete, breathe...'

OK, OK, I'm trying to get in control of this trip.

I've got to get control.

Then all of a sudden, I'm like... boom!

And I'm hurting again, and falling and bursting into flames ....

Nineteen

So what's the big one going to be?

Oh, you're way ahead of me, aren't you, you clever sod? You're thinking back to Cheddar and his boss and how I mentioned that that wasn't the end of the story and all. Well, you're right. It isn't the end of the story.

Let's just put that one to bed then, shall we?

We'll start with an action shot:

It's early evening. Just starting to get dark. Rain. Pete's running through the Marchwell Estate in South London. The streets are deserted, except for Pete and the three men who are chasing him.

Me: (*panting, running*) Fuck off, ya dirty bastards....

Pursuer one: (*running, and hacking badly, black and dirty lungs from too much puff*) You're fuckin' dead, mate...

Yah-de-yah-de-yah.

All the way through the Estate until Pete runs round a corner into a dead end. The camera spins round him (like they do in fancy science fiction films) until it's fully focused on his face and he winks, grins, then puts back on his terrified face and comes to a halt, turning towards the three muppets coming after him.

Pursuer two: Got you now...

Pursuer three: You're going to fuckin' get it for making me fuckin' run like that...

Me: Please, no... look, I didn't mean it... I was just kidding around...

Pursuer two: Too late, buddy, you're fucked....

Me: *(suddenly very serious)* It was me that robbed Cheddar's stash.

Pursuer two: What...? *(confused, incredulous)*

Pursuer one: That ain't true, Cheddar nicked his own wedge...

Me: No *(shaking head)* I robbed him and he got the blame for nicking the money himself...

Pursuer two: Fuck off... *(advancing)*

Me: Who's afraid of the big bad wolf, eh?

Pursuers one, two and three stop for a moment.

Pursuer two: You're coming to see the boss...

Pursuers jump Pete and knock him to the ground where, after some kicking and stamping, he lays still.

Of course, I'm not really out, but I am laying there nice and quiet. I chuck in the occasional groan, you know, to make it all seem more realistic. The truth is, I'm realising, that none of what they do seems to hurt all that much. *Fuck me, this belt is making me invincible.*

They pick me up (drop me a couple of times while they're trying to) and sort of load me across their shoulders between two out of the three of them, while the third one does a lot of grunting and huffing and nothing to help.

I get hauled across the Estate – they put (throw) me down three or four times, a couple to rest and once for a fag break – and end up being bumped up the stairs onto the first floor of a set of crap-heap flats. Even with my Pete nose and ears, I can tell there are more people hanging around. Probably minders, some of the collectors, some whores maybe (I can taste something in the air like muff). After knocking, a lot of mumbling and to-ing and fro-ing, they dump me through a door and I lay on the floor with my eyes shut trying to make up my mind when and how I'm going to leap into action.

Then there's a voice.

You always know the boss's voice. Just the same as the Crew. Just the same as Lukas's brother. All swagger and cigarette smoke. Voice full of the sound of itself. Confidence, man. Knowing you rule the roost. That's what it's all about.

'Are you fucking serious?' it says, the toe-end of a boot under my neck trying to lift up my head and see my face.

'Are you three fucking serious bringing this heap of shit to me?' The voice has moved away and turned on my pursuers. There isn't much of a response, probably a fair amount of shuffling feet and staring at the floor.

The lights are on in the room. I can tell through my eyelids, a kind of yellow halo. Four of them standing around me. There are clearly more in the flat, as well as the ones outside. And there's a smell permeating everything. A stale, green stink – not suffocating, not that obvious, but running through everything, catching at the back of your throat if you let it.

It's the smell of money.

'Answer me, you fucking retards.'

I half open an eye and I can see – through the legs of the voice – into what looks like the kitchen, where there are two faces counting money into a bag. There's a lot of it. It looks like more than my five grand, a lot more. *Just let them pack it up for you, Pete, nice and neat into the sack. Make it much easier for you to carry away in your dog-mouth. Good boy, Pete, just be patient. Let them count. Every dog will have his day.*

The voice has stepped in and has hold of one, two or three, I can't tell which.

'... he.... he... said he was to do with Cheddar's stash disappearing...'

'Fuck off. That skank ran off with his own stash...'

'He... said he was the wolf...'

'What the fuck are you talking about?'

Rumours of my existence are yet to reach the ruling classes.

Some shaking and slapping round the head goes on.

'I said, what the fuck are you talking about?' The voice, again, getting really wound up.

Pete stands up.

'He's talking about me.'

You know, I said earlier that the first change was the money shot. Now I'm not so sure. Maybe we should rewind to that first night when I put on the belt. Maybe all you get to see is a flash of light and a little bit of smoke. Maybe you do it the way those real cheap werewolf movies do it and just show a shadow changing shape on the wall. Who knows? I'll leave that to cleverer people than me. Anyway, the reason I'm changing my mind is because this is the fucking money shot, man.

There's a heartbeat, a moment in time, where everyone just stands around staring.

It's shock – that jarring effect where the natural line of movement is broken. No-one knows what's going to happen next.

It's like that right now.

I stand with my back to the front door of the voice's little money house and bring on a change.

Oh yeah.

I make the heat rise. I make an explosion of light and flames. I'm feeling this change like I haven't before. Pain to fucking love, this is exquisite pain. Eyes clamped shut but all the while sensing their fear. Their disbelief. From two feet to four.

Then this is how it happens:

Fire. First the curtains smoking.

'What the fuck?'

Panic. Falling over each other to reach the kitchen door. One, two and three, and the voice. I'm on them all. They're flattened, sprawling.

'Off me...!'

I crack the a back. Head down and jaws open, find a neck, rip the head back to snap it. Too hard and pull the head clean off. Spit and cough to release it.

'Help...!'

I'm on top of the voice and one, two or three, can't tell which, there's too much blood. Voice struggles out from underneath the other. Staggers to his feet. I pound the other one's back. It cracks too. He's bent in half backwards. Still alive, can't speak, just twitching like broken clockwork. Voice runs into the kitchen. The monkeys counting the money are already up, backs against the wall, nowhere to go. Flames hitting a roar. The whole lounge is burning. Sparks from the change set it off. Smoke in the kitchen, voice and the monkeys coughing and retching and pleading. My frenzy of teeth and claws and the three of them are torn apart and bits of them are sprayed all over the kitchen. Pieces of people spattered on Formica worktops, cracked tiles and door fronts. Black, thick air. Dog-me picking up the bag between my teeth.

Then I'm racing through the flames and exploding out of the window, showering the junkies and whores down below with glass. And that's me, making my escape with a bag full of sixteen (sixteen, sixteen) grand.

It's all boom... boom... boom... and there's the trailer voice-over: 'Dogstar...' Certificate 18 (ha! ha!).

SCARY MONSTERS

Twenty

My eyes are glued shut. I've got pain in my head like shattering glass. My whole body feels battered and bruised, like I've done ten rounds. I'm gagging, man, I can hardly breathe. I don't know where I am, I don't know when this is, and I hardly remember *who* I am.

This whole thing is fucked up.

OK, hold still, Pete. Let me get hold of myself.

First:

I'm rubbing and unpicking my eyes until I can just about open them. It's all a blur, they're feeling raw and roasted, and my brain's not receiving.

I'm lying here blinking and trying to peer through the gloom. The goggles can just about see but the head can hardly make sense of it.

Have I been asleep?

Am I still asleep?

The thumping, crushing pain in my skull says no. *No, Pete, you're not asleep. You're wide awake and in suffering mode, mate.*

So where am I?

It's like I'm thinking out of tune. All TV fuzz and ghost pictures.

OK.

I'm on a wooden bed. More like a board, hinged on one side and on the other held horizontal by a chain at each end linking up to bolts in the wall. There's no blanket or sheet, no pillow.

One thing I'm sure of, I ain't never been here before. I'm guessing I'm not going to remember how I got here either. Something telling me I didn't get myself here and that maybe I was out already when I arrived.

Suddenly, I'm realising I'm cold. Freezing in fact.

This place is like an ice box.

I feel like I've got a two vodka bottle hangover. I'm dehydrated. Dry as a fucking crisp. And now I'm shivering my skinny arse off too.

Over the side of my board-bed, I can see that I've been sick on the floor. Ah fuck, I'm covered in my own puke. Got it all over myself. *Just be thankful it's too cold to smell it, Pete.*

So another thing I don't remember is puking.

Man, my eyes are so dry. Sandpaper and salt. My head's just hurting. I'm feeling around it and... shit... there's a lump like I've been given a serious crack on the side of my skull.

Add that to the list.

Feels like whatever hit me broke a couple of teeth as well.

My chest is sore, I can just about see looking down, there's a bandage wrapped around me, brown-stained, and looking like it's ready to fall off, not wound tightly enough, not dressed all nice like when I was in hospital.

It hurts to fuckery to look down so I lay back on the bed and take a gander around. The room's dimly lit, and now I can see that the light's coming through the bars opposite the bunk I'm lying on.

That's not a good sign, is it? Being behind bars and all.

Through the bars, I can't see much, apart from a flickering light-bulb hanging from the ceiling in the corridor making not much light, and maybe there's more bars on the other side of the corridor, and so maybe, I'm beginning to think, I've found myself in prison but one not like Wormwood Scrubs where I'd been before, for a few months.

There's not much else I can make out.

I can't hear much either. Some far-away noises, I can't tell what, maybe a door slamming, maybe distant footsteps, but nothing I can really get my ears around.

Where the fuck am I?

How the fuck did I get here?

My head is too fucked to give me any answers.

All I'm getting is some flashes of something or other but I can't tell what it is, or how long ago it was or even if it's got anything at all to do with me being here.

All I have is a bad feeling I've been here longer than is good for me, and that there's got to be a reason why I'm here, and that when I find out what it is I'm not going to like it.

Then a thought hits my already banging head with a bigger bang.

Oh fuck.

I'm wondering why I feel so.... I don't know.... so *blunt*. At first I'm thinking it's got to be the smack on the head. But suddenly I'm thinking, *no, Pete, that it ain't.*

I haul myself up to sitting (almost) and take a good look at myself.

'Oh fuck!' This time out loud.

This doesn't look good.

It doesn't look good at all.

Right round my middle, where my nice, neat scar used to be, there's more of the useless mess of bandage. I'm scrabbling to pull it off. And underneath, just another mess of dried up blood and bits of ripped flesh, all half-healed, crusted over, brown-stained.

A band that goes all the way around.

And I can feel it now.

Where my belt used to be, with his dogstar buckle underneath the skin, is nothing...

I'm blunt, because I've been blunted.

I don't know where I am, or who brought me here, but what I do know is that they've ripped out my belt.

Whoever these fuckers are, they've taken my belt.

Twenty-one

SCENE: *A badly lit, whitewashed, stone-walled room. In the middle a table, on each side a chair. On one end of the table a tape recorder.*

ACTION: *The door of the room opens and two men in uniform bundle Pete in and drop him into the chair on the far side of the table.*

(I get to say something really witty here, you know, like a movie action hero does. Maybe like, 'I'm going to kill you when I get out of here...' And the boys in uniform laugh but I'm winking through the camera at you, because you know Pete won't let you down (ha! ha!)).

Pete sits in the chair silently, visibly in pain.

One of the uniforms leaves, the other stands next to the door. Another man enters the room. He's carrying a kit bag which he places under the table (clever bastards like you will recognise this as the bag of cash I had between my teeth when exploding out the window on my last and final job). *If Pete recognizes the man, he doesn't show it.*

(Of course I don't recognise him. I've not long woken up with my head still splitting on a bed-board in a prison cell and realised I've been cut open and robbed of my belt (and, it turns out, my money). My guess is as good as yours.)

[The man's name is COBB]

Cobb sits in the other chair opposite Pete. He mumbles something through his moustache as if to himself, and presses the record button on the tape recorder.

COBB: Please state your name for the record...

(What the fuck is this? The Sweeney?)

PETE: (*silence*)

COBB: (*sighs, pauses*) Please state your name for the record.

The two stare at each other.

(Look, I've been in these kinds of situations before. Don't say *anything*. Whoever this geezer is, something's telling me he hasn't got my best interests at heart, right? Oh yeah, I remember what's telling me: the fucking knife cuts right round my middle and the empty pockets of flesh where my belt should be.)

PETE: (*after some time*) Peter Smith.

COBB: (*sighing and pulling a pack of red Marlboros from the inside pocket of his crumpled jacket*) So what's your real name?

(Oh, he's sharp, this one, isn't he?)

PETE: (*again, after some time*) Smith.

COBB: (*rolling his eyes and then cupping a hand to light one of his cigarettes*) How did you come across this?

He reaches into the kit bag and pulls out Pete's belt. It's covered in dried blood.

PETE: (*silence*)

COBB: Come on, where did you get it?

PETE: (*silence*)

COBB: (*getting angry*) This is going to get boring, and I really don't like being bored ...

(Well, whoever he is, he's got a copper's lines. Nothing I've not heard before.)

PETE: (*stares back*)

COBB: Look, I don't know where you think you are, but you're in a fuck of a lot of trouble...

The two men stare at each other. Then after a long pause.

PETE: Whoever you are, go fuck yourself...

(Yes, I'm so cool! This geezer is just winding me up. Who the fuck does he think he is? I'm not answering your questions. I want some answers of my own, right? Yeah, fuck you, man, you creepy, greasy fuck!)

Cobb jumps across the table and smashes Pete in the face with a clenched fist.

(OK, not so cool).

Twenty-two

'Hey!'

It's a whisper.

'Hey, man!'

I pick myself up off my bunk, all kinds of pain still.

Greasy moustache-fuck smacking me in the head hasn't made things any better. He really enjoyed that.

I've got no idea how long I've been back in my cell. There's no day and night here, just that flickering light bulb...

'Hey!'

The voice again. Sounds like it's coming from over the other side of the corridor.

'What's Cobb want with you?'

I'm hanging on the bars of my cell and I can just about make him out now, locked in the cell opposite. He's looking at me but not looking at me, all red hair, pale skin and icy blue eyes. His voice is soft, kind of high pitched, not like a woman's but not like a man's either. A whistle with some kind of funny accent.

I can see and smell now he's smoking a cigarette.

'You got a fag?'

He laughs.

'You're a local boy...'

He's starting to get on my nerves.

'Quiet!' a voice from along the corridor, and I see the redhead retreat back into the darkness of his cell. A couple of seconds later a lit cigarette comes flying through the air through the bars into my cell.

OK, I like him a bit better now.

So I'm back on my bunk, pulling hard on the fag and wishing it was something stronger, and chasing memories, trying to piece together how I got here.

Just getting hold of something.

It's here.

Grab back hold of it.

There you go, Pete.

You got it.

It's me recognising her.

Not knowing who she is.

But seeing her and knowing that she's a dog. Not like that, you dick. I mean she's a shape-changer, a werewolf, a dog just like me. I don't know why, but I can tell she is.

Keep your electric eyes on me, babe.

And I know she's seen me too.

She's looking at me, and not looking at me at the same time.

It's six o' clock at night (Waterloo Station), where I've come to stare at the departure boards and work out – if I'm going to escape the Links – where I'm going to escape to. I'm being jostled by crowds of people, spinning, everyone in a desperate fucking hurry to get somewhere else really quick. I'm being brushed against, knocked into, half knocked-over. I've got arses banging into my hips, tits brushing my elbows, hair in my face.

Pete's been hidden away for too long. Just one half-decent bunk-up since I found my belt. My balls are like cow's udders and I'm walking the ol' John Wayne big leggy. Suddenly today, I'm amongst people again. And at least half of these people are reminding me that someone needs to be milking my udders (ha! ha!).

Oh man. It's like being in a sweet shop. All I can smell is pussy. All shapes, colours and sizes. Ones kept nice and clean, ones not been washed for a week. Little beauties that smell soft like the wind, fat buckets that stink of raw meat. Blonde ones, black ones, curly ones, ones with no hair. Ones that have rutted 'til they're baggy like an old hat, others never been used, tight like doctors' gloves. Oh, they're all here.

These aren't the scrag-ends you get on the Links (all right, there *are* a few of those), these are like proper women. Women in dresses, women in suits, big hair, small hair, perfume, stripes, spots, greys, pinks and pastels.

And there I am, caught up in a whirlwind, unable to think about anything else, when I see this face in the crowd.

Just a glimpse.

I know that I'm looking at someone who's just like me.

Mad, right? I mean, I'm in the middle of a station full of people. I've found a belt, and become a dog. I've been massacring drug dealers night-in night-out for fuck knows how long, recently blown some up, and am making my getaway. And I've not once thought about the fact that there might be someone else like me.

I start to make my way through the crowd.

Not sure if I remember that there is the faintest trace of smoke lifting off me at this point. I'm having to push down really hard to stop a change coming on.

I can see that face again. In profile. It's looking at something or someone, can't tell which, I can't follow her line of sight. Just a flash of dark hair, pale skin, black eyes (like a doll's eyes, ha! ha!)

Stay where you are pretty lady. I've got questions to ask you...

'Hey, watch where you're going...'

I've knocked into a geezer in a suit, pin-striped, white hair greased and pulled back from his face. I turn and look at him as I carry on through the press, fire in my eyes (real fire) and he just kind of gets himself together and breaks into the crowd in the opposite direction.

Through the gaggle of noise I try to pick her out, to locate on that particular beating heart and absorb some of its rhythm. Amongst the million scents I'm trying to separate, I look to see if I can identify hers'.

An elbow in the ribs. A crack in the face from a bag that some kid's carrying over his shoulder. Someone standing on my foot and almost tripping me.

The face still in profile.

I'm ten, maybe fifteen feet away. Still a mass of moving bodies in between.

Then the face turns, and the eyes see me. There's an instant of recognition from her too. Two dogs looking at each other in a room full of people.

She bolts.

Suddenly I can tell that the crowd around me has parted. It's all wide eyes and gasps. And...

'He's on fire...'

'Fire... Fire!'

Then there's screaming. Panic in the crowd. People trying to run from me. I've got to get a grip, stop the change from coming on. I'm staggering towards the main entrance. Just about making it out. Smoke pouring off me now as I break out into the cold air.

I can smell her now. It's not a human smell – it's animal, man. I can see the tiny droplets of her scent spinning around in the air, a light trail down the steps and into a tunnel under the station.

Oh shit. The change is coming on, and this time there ain't nothing I can do to stop it.

I've got my kit bag with my money in it, and my clothes on.

I'm in the middle of London, just getting into a tunnel under Waterloo Station.

I'm starting to burn up on the outside as well as the in. *Just got to let it happen Pete. No stopping it now.*

And before you know it, I'm running right after her into the tunnel (all speeding taxi lights, the smell of piss and tramps), stripping right off and stashing my clothes and my bag in the first hole in the wall I can find, and in an explosion of light, letting wolfie come out to play.

Twenty-three

SCENE: *The same badly lit, whitewashed, stone-walled interrogation room. You remember the rest. Pete sitting in the same chair as before.*

ACTION: *Cobb shuffles in, all seventies copper, and sits opposite Pete. Again, he's got the kit bag.*

They sit in silence staring at each other. Neither moves, as if waiting for the other to break first. (You've got it, mate. This fucker's not going to break me.)

Finally after a few minutes (okay, so we'll edit that back to about 10 ten seconds for you):

COBB: So you going to talk this time? *(A softer tone?)*

PETE: (after a pause, just to make it clear that really it's me that's running things here) You got a cigarette?

Cobb throws a packet of Reds across the table, Pete takes one and Cobb leans across to light it. Pete relaxes back in his chair (oh, grateful one-lung, his first nicotine kick since the flying fag from the redhead – how long ago was that?)

PETE: Where am I?

COBB: *(eyebrows raised quizzically)* *(he's turning his head and looking to the fat boy in the uniform standing by the door).* You really don't know where you are?

PETE: *(pause)* I don't know where I am, what this is, who you are...

COBB: *(laughs, then more serious)* First you. Where did you get the belt?

PETE: ... I found it.

COBB: *(losing patience again)* (real anger issues, this one, Jesus he needs to see someone about this) Where did you *find* it? *(emphasis on the find, much growling sarcasm)*

PETE: Why are you so bothered to know about my belt?

COBB: My questions... Where did you find it?

PETE: (like when you're a kid, right, you just get this sixth sense about when it's not the right time to tell the truth. I don't know why, but something tells me right now not to get into telling this dude what really happened). I just found it. At a dump or something... I can't really remember...

COBB: *(scrubbing out his cigarette)* Why are you lying?

Neither of them says anything, then:

COBB: *(clearly making an effort to keep calm)* You're in prison –

PETE: I'd kind of worked that out –

COBB: Not the kind of prison you've been banged up in before.

(At first I'm thinking that's just harsh, man, then I'm starting to wonder whether he knows more about your Pete than he's letting on)

COBB: *(gets out of his chair)* We can't just have our kind wandering around the streets robbing and killing...

Pete gives nothing away.

COBB: *(getting angry again because of Pete's silence)* Come on... No-one knows anything about you. No-one knows anything about your belt. *(spits the word with contempt)* Where did you get it? Who gave it to you? *(laughs at this)* What did you have to do to get it? *(venomous)*

PETE: *(silent, staring)*

COBB: *(making an effort to calm himself again)* (This guy's all over the place, man) I can't help you unless you tell me. You have to tell me about the belt.

PETE: *(stares at Cobb for some time, as if trying to work out whether to open up or not* – yeah right, dramatic effect, there's no way I'm going to open up...) Nothing to tell... *(and looks down at the table).*

COBB: *(sighs deeply)* Look... Pete *(he can hardly bring himself to say the name)* This isn't prison for young offenders. Your social worker and your legal aid solicitor aren't going to turn up and make sure you get off with community service. You're in trouble. Big trouble. You've killed people. You've made yourself known. They'll throw you to the wolves for this if you don't open up –

PETE: *(looks up sharply)* (Maybe, for the first time, I'm realising just how much shit I might be in – beltless and locked up – a skank from the wrong end of things who could easily disappear without no-one caring in the littlest that he's gone).

COBB: *(thinking he's made some kind of breakthrough).* Look, why don't you come and talk to me again... later today. I'm going to give you some time to think about it. You help me, I can persuade them to go easy on you.

PETE: *(nods)*

Twenty-four

'What's Cobb want with you, man?' the redhead says, the same whistle-voice.

Just look back at the fuck, you don't need to say nothing, Pete.

I can see he's getting agitated.

'Come on, man. They'll be back in a minute.'

He means the guards. Mostly one or other of them is sitting in the corridor, making sure we're all nice and comfy in our cells (ha! ha!) and that not too much in the way of conversation is happening between us.

'What you in for?'

I'm scowling, looking past him. These are my first words to the Schiebler.

'Look mate. I don't know who *you* are. I don't know who *Cobb* is. I don't know where the fuck *this* is.'

He laughs again, but humourless, like it's not funny.

'Aw fuck man. What *are* you? You a greaser, right? You don't look like a smoke or a skin-rip. And you're not one of us, that's for sure...' And there's some laughter at that from up and down the cells – other people're listening in.

I'm kind of interested now.

'What the fuck have they done with my belt?'

'What you talking about?' that voice is getting to be more of a whine than a whistle. And the whine's winding me up.

I'm at the bars and I can just about see up and down the corridor now. There are cells on each side, the whole place is just a little brighter because the guards've left the door open – the door they drag me through when they take me to see Cobb.

'Leave the poor fuck alone, Schiebler.' Another voice, deep, guttural, heavy Jock accent not that I'm really knowing what one of those is.

'Fuck you, Douglas.'

And I can hear a third voice, another mess of a mangle of speaking that's telling them to shut the fuck up and stop bickering like women. It's coming from my side of the corridor, further up to my right. And opposite and along I can just about make out a pair of round glasses peering at me through the gloom from inside one of the other cells.

'What's that you're saying, new boy?' It's the redhead again. 'What's that you're saying about a belt?'

'Why is everyone so interested in my belt?' I'm asking as the guard comes back in and sinks his fat arse into the seat.

Why is everyone so interested in my belt?

My question's left hanging.

Chat's over for now. I'm backing off, and down on my bunk again to pick up where I've dropped off trying to get my memory back.

I close my eyes and breathe nice and deep in and out of my one-lung. Here it is again, Pete, catch it if you can...

A funked up rock song video directed by some bloke with a goatee beard, wool knitted beret and white-powdered nostrils about ready to collapse to rotting.

At first it's all taxi headlamp strobes, alternate light and darkness. Then we pass into some kind of service tunnel and we lose most of the light, and it's close-ups on her black hair and face – panting, trying to catch breath, running, glancing behind her. Close-ups on Pete the dog – a guessing game... a flash of hair, an ear, my eyes, my teeth... And as I'm running, you can hear my claws on the tarmac, the occasional spark spinning off them into the air behind me.

Her face. Wide eyes. Sweat in her hair. Running down her temples in streams. Cheeks flushed. Tiring a little.

Me pounding the street. Catching her up. Mouth full of teeth.

I've got to get to her.

We're nearing the end of the tunnel. I can see the street lamps through the opening at the other end. I'm not wanting her to make her way out. I need to chase her down before she gets there – as crazy as I am, I'm not crazy enough to get caught in the open.

The tunnel's full with the animal smell of her. Like tiny lights spinning and crystallising in the thick air. She's spraying it out behind her, and I'm drinking it up. It's driving me crazier. I'm not knowing what I want to do when I get her. I just know she's like me. I *know* it. And I'm too worked up by it all to ask myself why she's running away.

Then suddenly she's gone.

For a moment before I stop, all I can hear is the clattering – like steel on steel – of my claws on concrete.

Then silence.

Her scent hangs in the air. There's no direction. I can't feel where she's gone. But she has. She disappeared a clean thirty feet before the end of the tunnel.

I get on it hard, see if I can put any kind of placement on where she went. I jog up and down the wall of the tunnel. There are a couple of doors but no openings. I try pushing against them both with my nose, then my head, but they're stuck firm.

Fuck. Where did she go?

Then I start thinking:

Did I imagine this whole fucking thing? Am I losing it completely? Here is Pete in the middle of fucking London chasing some fucking ghost. I've thrown away my bag back up the tunnel (fuck, my bag, my money, my clothes) and I'd better be able to find it because otherwise I'm cash free and stark bollock naked in the middle of London.

Must have been all this time hidden away like a hermit. Too much all at once, seeing all these people, all this pussy in Waterloo Station. Overload, dude, I've gone and overloaded myself, some kind of fucking melt-down.

Then I hear it.

Faint.

A whimper.

I lock on. It's coming from above me. Up on my back legs, front paws against the wall, I can see an opening about a dozen feet above the ground, maybe about eight feet across. That's where she is. *How'd she disappear so quick?*

I back up across the tunnel, take a light run and jump. On the edge, barely into the opening, I can see her at the far end of the space, about twenty feet away.

Of course I know something isn't right as soon as I get up there. At least dog-me knows something isn't right. But d'you know what? Pete's still finding it difficult to really listen to what dogstar's saying.

The whole thing, man, the whole thing is a bad case of the dog not listening to Pete and Pete not listening to the dog.

So what I feel is:

Crack.

Being hit on the side of the head with something really fucking hard. Feeling my brain shudder inside my skull. Feeling the change back coming on. Burning up, and then lying there on the cold, damp floor, head reeling, naked, covered in ash.

The black haired beauty is standing over me. She spits at me. A real fucking grollie, rolled right up from a pair of lungs that are no strangers to filterless cigarettes.

'Twat...' she says.

'That's not necessary.' Another voice, gravel, low. I twist my bursting head to see who's talking. A man steps out of the shadows, drops my bag beside me.

I can't see his face. Just a hat, a long coat – maybe a moustache.

Then he's pulling something out from under the coat. And, as I vaguely become aware of at least two or three other figures drifting into the centre of the room, I realise that what he's pulling out of his coat is some kind of gun.

And he shoots me in the chest with it.

Fuck!

I knew there's a reason I don't like Cobb.

Twenty-five

SCENE: *Same, same, same, don't make me repeat it all.*

ACTION: *Same. All macho bully-silence. Yeah, yeah, yeah. (My split-scar is aching me more than ever, I've half a feeling that I'm going to leap over that desk and grab back my belt).*

COBB: I'm thinking that you're partly telling the truth...

PETE: Finally.

COBB: *(spitting this)* Partly...

PETE: Which part?

COBB: The part where you say you don't know who we are. That you've never heard of the Bank. That you didn't know there were others like you.

PETE: Then you'd have that right...

(pause)

COBB: Look.

He passes me a cigarette and lights it, like we're just about to get all chummy and that.

COBB: This is the way things work... There are rules. We've got our own way of doing things.

PETE: *(nodding, not looking like he's listening, more like he's thinking of something else)*

COBB: *(snaps)* We can't have little fuckers like you running round making trouble. Everything's... *(like he's searching for the right way to put it*) carefully *managed.*

PETE: *(glances at the belt)* (Honestly I don't know what the fuck this geezer is talking about. Truly I don't)

COBB: There'd be chaos...

PETE: *(interrupting)* So... how do I get myself out of here?

COBB: You want to talk now?

PETE: I don't want to rot in here if that's what you mean.

COBB: Now you're making sense.

(Pause. Cobb stands up, opens the kit bag and takes out Pete's belt, letting it dangle from his left hand, the dogstar buckle looking at Pete through his fist)

COBB: You tell us how you got the belt. Tell us who you got it from. You tell us all about how you've used it. Tell us everything, and we'll let you go.

PETE: *(stares at the belt)*

COBB: *(as if in answer)* We'll destroy the belt. We'll let you go, and you can go back to your normal life. The one you had before all... this.

(My normal life? Is he taking the *piss*? Oh man, even if I believe for a second that it's true that he's going to let me walk out of here if I cough up the beans, this is *such* the wrong thing to say.)

PETE: Well in that case, I think I'll refer you to my previous answer.

COBB: *(staring at Pete, waiting for his response)*

PETE: Which if you remember rightly was fuck you... and this time fuck you very much.

(Cobb nods gently)

COBB: Well in that case, there's nothing else I can do.

(He gets up, putting my belt back in the bag and zipping it up)

COBB: You're in it right up to your neck, you cocky little shit. This isn't a game. They're going to throw you to the wolves.

(Oh, and just so you know, he really means it.)

Twenty-six

I'm thinking about what this Cobb geezer said. You know, when he was asking me all those questions and I was telling him to fuck right off. He said they were going to throw me to the wolves, and I'm wondering who they are. I haven't even got on to thinking who the wolves are going to be.

But from everything I've seen and heard since I've been here, I'm thinking there are others.

There's a sink and a toilet in the corner of my cell. (*Yeah, I know – nice!*) Lucky I've been brought up a skank or I might find all this just a little bit degrading (ha! ha!). I'm sitting on the bog, and smoking one of Cobb's fags – me having managed to lift a pack and plastic lighter off him before we finished our little chat.

I'm figuring that whatever's going to happen's going to happen soon. That way, I might as well smoke myself through the whole pack right away. Besides, once he realises I nicked them I'm guessing he's the kind of bloke that'll want them back sharpish.

So I'm sitting there, sucking smoke deep into the one-lung and holding it there to do its grey-and-brown work, and I'm feeling just a tiny bit high off the nicotine hit what with no food in my belly and nothing in my blood-stream to speak of. My head's spinning. I've got thoughts rattling round, feeling like they're bouncing off the damp and cracked plaster walls of my cell.

The flickering light-bulb in the corridor is turning shadows on and off, and I'm blowing smoke through them, making shapes. There's my own shadow. On, off. On, off. On, off. And as I'm watching it, it's growing and transforming and then it's my big, black wolf standing up from the bog-seat and climbing through the bars and away to freedom.

You know by now that I'm not much for thinking, right?

I mean, this is all action. No-one's here to learn anything.

It's just occurring to me, as I'm sitting there puffing and pumping out smoke and playing games in my head with what I can see in the half-light, just how much trouble I could be in. Your Pete – oblivious to the world outside of the Links, and the dealing of drugs and the stealing of drug money – has somehow been sucked up into something a bit more serious.

The lucky thing is that I don't know when I'm out of my depth.

Low expectations, man, that's the secret of a happy life.

Lucky that neither me nor anyone else I know ever expected anything of Pete. And look at me now. Banged up. In some serious shit. With some serious sounding people on my back. I'm fucking over-achieving (ha! ha!).

And this is what I'm thinking as I hear the door bang open at the end of the corridor. I was born banged up, wasn't I? I've been trying to get out even before I realised I needed to. All them fuckers happy to live and die on those twenty-two acres of concrete and dog shit and dope that's the Links.

Well I'm not.

So the keys clatter into the lock on the bars of my cell, and as the guards grab me – one on each arm, like – I'm thinking: *you know what, Pete? Even if it ends now. Even if they really do throw you to the wolves, you didn't live and die on the Links.*

Which makes you better than Ken and dear old Mum, better than Ziggy and Lukas, better than Debs, the poor cow. Better than all of them.

And it's for this reason, as they haul me along the corridor, up some stairs, throw open a door and drag me, blinking, into the blinding sunlight, that I'm laughing like I just won at the dogs (ha! ha!).

Twenty-seven

We're bundled into the back of a truck.

A closed metal box with a bench on each side

I say we, because it's not just me that's been dragged out of my cell and out into the real world.

There's Schiebler – the redhead from the cell opposite, the one who tossed me the fag, and kept asking questions. They sit him on the bench next to me. He's too busy whining about the pushing and shoving he's getting from the guards to say much to me.

And I see the short one with the round glasses that I caught staring at me from his cell on the other side of the corridor. The one who didn't say anything. He's looking at me again, and when I meet his eyes, he doesn't look away, just keeps fixed on me, man. Not like he's squaring up to me. I don't know, more like he's sussing me out.

There's a stream of others, brought in one at a time and sat down – with some stray fists and boots to encourage them – on one or other of the benches. I'm noticing that some have their arms chained behind their backs, and some of us don't. And there's a lot of cursing and spitting and growling, and some of it in words that I don't understand which is making me think that half of these geezers are Nonglish, and wondering what the fuck they are doing here.

In between the doors out of the prison and the door into the back of the truck, I don't get much time to look around. The sunlight is harsh, man, after all that time (however much time it actually was) banged up in the half-dark. What I do see is clean pavements, and glass – you know that blue-black reflective glass you get on buildings in movies – and the glass goes right up and up into the sky in every direction. And that it smells so... clean. Like they've got different air here from the fug that we breathe on the Links. I can smell coffee and sweet cakes, and nice-cooked food the like of which I've never tasted in my life. And I'm in the truck before I can get any more.

There must be more than twenty, with most of the bench-space taken. All shapes and sizes, all men, all with this expression on their face that I'm beginning to recognise – looking and not looking at the same time, like they can see things, and see through them and past them. All at various stages of being dirty and sweaty and stinking, I suppose, depending on how long they've been in their cell with only cold water from the sink to wash in. There's two or three who've clearly taken a beating – all black and blue eyes and lumps and bumps all over their heads and faces. And there's even one who they've had to half carry in, on account of his leg obviously being busted and not put back together by nice doctors in white coats.

They bring in what must be the last couple.

The first is the Jock.

He's all: 'Get your fucking hands off me...' in the mangled-up speak I recognise from my corridor.

Although I can see that the guards have got batons, and a holstered gun each, they're scared of him. They ain't manhandling him in the same way they did the rest of us.

And as they push him down into his seat, he makes to jump up at them growling and they take a step back, and then he laughs.

'Fucking arseholes,' he says, pushing at his bush of hair to get it out of his face.

And then these eyes of his move from face to face around the truck:

'Anyone got a drink?' he laughs again.

The last climbs into the truck with some help as his hands are clamped behind his back, but he's not getting any of the harsh treatment. The guards let him find his own space and he smiles, and nods, dark-haired and black-eyed and says something I don't understand, but I recognise his voice from my corridor too.

The truck engine fires up, and the two guards pull the rear doors shut and we can hear them being locked from the outside. Then they take their seats at the end of the benches, guns now slung across their laps.

'Where are they taking us?' I'm saying to Schiebler, under my breath, the growl of the truck engine being loud enough to drown out my words.

'You really don't know, do you?'

'I wouldn't have fucking asked...'

'To the hunt...'

He's not looking happy. Most of the rest of them aren't looking happy either.

'That don't sound good,' I say.

'It isn't,' says Schiebler, and closes his eyes.

Twenty-eight

Not much more than an hour or an hour and a half, and I can feel that the truck is slowing. We've been on what must be a main road for a while – the engine a steady roar – and then we've come off that, and it's been more up and down with changing gears and swinging us about in the back with turning corners.

But now, wherever it is we're supposed to be going, well I guess we're here.

No-one's said much on the whole journey. A few of the boys have slept – or at least kept themselves to themselves with closed eyes – most have been just staring into space or at their feet.

The guards have been chatting a bit as they smoke, but I've not been able to hear what they're saying. Me, I've been thinking about the locks on the outside of the doors of the truck, the metal box we're in and the guns the guards have with fingers loosely covering triggers. I've been half-dreaming about my big, black dog and what short work he would make of all of this: an explosive change would half be enough to blow those doors off, and the teeth and metal-claws would do the rest, and I'd be off and back to where I set out, on my way to somewhere new.

But we are where we are, Pete.

We'll bide our time.

Now is not the moment for heroes.

Remember how you lost the lung, and think about what damage a stray bullet might do to the other one.

So I wait until the truck comes to a stop and the engine's cut.

It's completely quiet.

I mean, quiet like I've never heard quiet before. Not like night time at the Links where there's always something to hear. The hum of traffic, someone somewhere shouting or screaming, a car backfiring, music thudding...

It's the first time in my life I've heard nothing.

'Get up,' one of the guards is shouting at us, as the locks are released on the doors from the outside.

There's a fair amount of groaning and stretching, and then we're getting up and jumping down onto gravel – apart from the geezer with the broken leg, who's half-helped and half-dropped onto it, yelping in pain.

Our guards are joined by a good half a dozen others, all jack-boots and guns and shit and they're forming us into a line.

It's late afternoon now, judging from the light. All quiet still except for our crunching and scrunching on gravel. We're stood in a walled yard – this ain't mine and Ken's back garden in the Links – there's got to be a dozen cars, vans and trucks parked here, all shiny and new like. The yard's out the back of a big old building, grey-stoned with these tall windows (hundreds of them) and a roof like a castle. But it's the sky I'm staring at man. I've never seen sky this big and blue and clear. And with the tiny ounces of bad black wolf-blood coursing through my veins, I can *see* smells I've never seen before.

It's.... fresh.

That's what it is, I'm realising. This is the first time in your life, Pete, that you've breathed *fresh* air.

And we're waiting like this, with me too wrapped up in seeing and smelling and listening to all these things I've never seen and smelled and heard before, when a door opens and out shambles my old friend Cobb, bringing down the tone, man, really bringing down the tone.

'Take them around to the front of the house,' he says to the guards. 'The traps are up. Mr Skeet is looking for things to kick off at ten tomorrow morning.'

Cobb lingers to watch as we're moved off in our line, and I catch his eye. He looks through me, all creases and stubble and thick moustache and I can tell what he's thinking.

He's looking forward to tomorrow.

He's looking forward to seeing my cocky arse fucked.

That's what he's thinking.

I look back as we leave the courtyard through a gate, and catch sight of him shuffling through the door and into the building.

We'll see, I'm saying to myself.

Don't count your fucking chickens.

We end up on what must be the other side of the house. There's grass – I've never seen so much of it – stretching out into the distance, a lake and beyond that, hills and woodland.

In our garden on the Links, we had half a dozen cracked paving slabs that Ken used to call our patio. This place has a patio that's as long as the whole of our street. And more of those long widows, and grey slabs and turrets. Fuck me, I didn't think this kind of thing existed in real life.

And in front of the patio, on the lawn, there are four cages. Big, metal cages, big enough each for half a dozen people. They've got doors that face out over the grass towards the water and the woods.

I'm taking this all in and there's a shout as one of us – a geezer up at the front of the line – makes a break for it, and he's off and running across the grass. There's a crack and he collapses, and I've seen enough gun-play between the drugs gangs where I live to know he's been shot. I look up and see that one of the windows on the second floor of the building is open – must've been open the whole time – and there are two or three figures hanging out of it, and more behind them, and one of them's got the rifle that just shot the prisoner in the back. And there's laughter and some cheers, and then the geezer with the gun – sharp-faced and slick hair – shouts down:

'Get them in the cages, I don't want all the decent bets wasted now!'

And the guards are like, 'Yes Mr Skeet.'

And we're being thrown into the cages – at gun point, none of us now fancying our chances of getting away – and I end up shoved down on my backside in one of the cages next to Schiebler, the Jock, the short-arse with the round glasses and the dark-eyed, dark-haired language mangler with the hands locked behind his back.

Twenty-nine

It's dark now.

I can see just about OK, on account of some light coming from the house, and dim lamps, and the guards, who are sitting along the patio behind the cages, occasionally sparking up a fag.

We've tried whispered conversations, but the guards are less than keen that we pass the evening by chatting. I guess they don't want us hatching plots and all, and a couple of times they've launched pot shots over our heads, so it's mainly been still.

I've got that the Jock is called Doug. That the round eyed geezer is Matt or Matti or something like that, and that the dark-haired one is Sal… 'Sal poot,' he says and laughs, whatever the fuck that means.

Much more I haven't got.

The hunt starts tomorrow at ten, and it's *us* what's being hunted. So Cobb wasn't shitting me, I *am* up to my neck in it.

When I ask Sal why he and some of the others have got their hands chained behind their backs, he just laughs again.

And apart from that we just sit in silence and smoke up the rest of our cigarettes, taking it in turns to help Sal with his.

It's cold enough, there's enough adrenaline pumping around me, and enough noise coming from the house – music and shouting – that I'm not going to sleep. *Something tells me that you're going to need all your strength for tomorrow, Pete. And here you are, not getting your shut-eye. What would Mum say if she wasn't a pile of ash in a box?*

It's at this point when a door opens, and all that muffled music and shouting spills out onto the patio. At the same time, we hear gunning engines and a couple of four-by-fours canon onto the grass and spin round to face the cages. Spot lamps are switched on and suddenly we're lit up like it's day time.

There's a dozen or so blokes coming out, dressed up in black suits, white shirts and these idiot butterfly ties. In the middle of this group, I recognise Skeet – the one with the rifle who cut the escapee down. They've got cigars in their mouths and drinks in their hands and they're laughing and joking, and there's a bit of friendly banter and arguing going on.

Hanging off their arms or milling in amongst them are a bunch of women.

Nice looking ones, you know, all dressed up in fancy frocks and that, but I've seen and smelled too much – lower grade – muff like it not to recognise them straight away as whores, the lot of them. So these rich boys pay for it just like poor folk do. And they're giggling and laughing at the jokes the men are making, and there's the odd hand reaching down into a crotch, the odd kiss and pressing of tits against chests and you can see how all this is going to end. The lot of them are wired too. Most likely coke – I can just about taste it on the air too – and I'm thinking that if there's guns around I want to be a little bit careful that I melt into the background and not say something that might upset someone, know what I mean?

'Who's taking bets?' this is Skeet.

'Let's have a look at them first, Gideon.'

So... *Gideon* Skeet. Come on, what the fuck kind of name is that?

And the group is walking the length of the cages – starting at the other end of the row – and I can hear them exchanging and matching odds, and I can smell the notes that are passing hands.

Eventually, they get to the cage that me and the boys are in. Skeet is sucking on his cigar and draining his drink. He throws the glass onto the grass behind him.

'I'm sad to see you here, Sal,' he says, his voice flat, monotone, like he's not sad at all.

'Well, I should be more careful who I fuck in future...' Sal, laughing again, like *everything* is funny.

'You don't *have* a future,' an angry voice from behind Skeet.

And this geezer is held back by a couple of the others and Skeet turns to him, and says coldly:

'You should have been taking care of things at home, Clay, then maybe your wife wouldn't have ended up with Sal's dick in every hole...'

There's more laughter and a 'Fuck you, Gideon...' and the angry voice stomps off into the darkness.

'... I don't like what's going to happen to you, Sal. You were almost one of us. But I'm afraid until I'm in charge, these are the rules... You want to fuck around, you have to be discrete.' And he grabs hold of the nearest whore and kisses her, while fixing Sal with his grey eyes.

'So this is discrete, is it?'

Another voice.

A woman's.

It's like no-one's seen her coming, but here she is. Suddenly, everyone's quiet. Or maybe it just seems that way to me. Her voice is like crystal, man, it just cuts through. Through the coke they've been doing. Through the smoke. The banter, the giggling of the whores. Through everything.

You take my breath away, baby.

Skeet can't see it. Of course he can't. He's *blind*, man. If he could see, he wouldn't give a fuck about anything or anyone else. But he's blind. Funny how me, a skank of the lowest order, worse than a smudge of shit on the boot of people like him, it's funny how I can see it and he can't.

So here the darkness parts.

And she stands there, looking at Skeet with the whore hanging off him. She's cold to him – I can tell that – but there's just the tiniest hint of a smile on her lips, like she's appalled and just finding it a little bit funny all at the same time.

'Darling,' he says, and just for a fraction of nothing he's lost it before he pushes away the paid-for and composes himself and holds out a hand to her which she ignores.

'Clara,' he says, voice a purr, all oil and charm, 'you're not usually interested in the hunt.'

'I'm not,' she says, '*usually*,' stressing that last word.

She's immaculate, man. I mean, in every way. I've never seen anyone like her before. And – if you understand what I'm saying – it's not that she's beautiful, although she is, it's that she just *has* it. She has everything. She's calm, she *holds* them – they're *all* a little bit in awe of her – but there's something else in those eyes that I can see too.

It's like looking in a mirror.

You know what it says? That something in her eyes?

It says: I've got to get out of here.

And right at this moment.... and even as I'm thinking it I'm thinking that this isn't supposed to be that kind of story.... *but right at this moment, your friend Pete, the friend you have followed from a blind, drug-fucked foetus through the bad and some good times all the way to wolf and probably soon to his death, your friend Pete is knocked down, man. Thoroughly knocked down.*

'And I wasn't interested in *this* hunt,' she goes on, 'until Cobb told me about the one with the belt.'

'I don't know what – ' Skeet starts but she interrupts him.

'It's *him*,' she says, and she's holding me with her green eyes. 'Isn't it?'

Yeah, you know it baby.

You're feeling it too.

'I'm not sure...' Skeet's saying. 'I'll get Cobb – '

She turns to him.

'For once,' she says, 'I'll play your game.' This word she can barely bring herself to say. 'I'll have a thousand pounds on *him*.'

Skeet laughs. He's checking me out me for the first time – my skinhead scrape growing out, unshaven, unwashed, looking in every way like I come from the kind of place I grew up in.

'What... *him* to be the last?' he says, as if she's joking.

Last to <u>what</u>?

'Not to be the last to die,' she says, her voice like a bell. 'To be the first to *survive*.'

He looks confused, speechless.

She smiles at me through the bars of the cage, like she's throwing me a challenge. Then she walks past Skeet and back into the house.

Thirty

There wasn't much sleep had.

The music and whatever else must've carried on inside went on well into the early hours. And then at some point doors were thrown open again, and we could hear running – human feet – across the grass in the pitch black, followed by what sounded like wolf-feet, and that followed by the sounds of the whores screaming and dying way over in the woodland across the lake. Leaving me sitting in the dark thinking that this must be what Gideon meant by being discrete – I guess it's the way that posh folk clear up after their indiscretions, making sure there's no-one left to sell stories to newspapers or cause other such embarrassments.

Once all is quiet again, and I spent what seemed like a reasonable amount of time feeling sorry for all of them that were snorting coke and shagging like rabbits just a while ago, only to be turned into dog food shortly afterwards. Well then I'm wondering for a bit how a runt like me could ever get with a woman like Clara…. and I'm also wondering whether I'll end up dead tomorrow, another mess cleaned up like the whores.

Then before I know it the sun's up, and we can hear movement from the house, and the crackle of cars being driven up the gravel drive and parked in the courtyard. The guards disappear in groups – maybe they're getting fed their breakfast – and there's time when it's just about possible to talk without being threatened with a gun.

I'm overloaded with questions. Weighing down on me, man. But there's so much going on I don't have the energy to work out where to start. Besides, I'm distracted, so I just listen to the others.

'What do you know about these hunts?' Schiebler's asking Sal.

'Only that the Old Man isn't happy about them. He'd prefer it if Gideon did things the old way. But the old ways are dying out...' Sal laughs.

'Better to have a fighting chance in a hunt than burned at the stake,' Matti's saying quietly, a breathless whisper.

'But we haven't *got* a fighting chance,' Schiebler's whine. 'That's the fucking point, right? We *don't* have a chance.'

The other two fall silent.

'I shouldn't be here...' Schiebler's saying this, his voice almost cracking with how much he's feeling sorry for himself.

'You killed someone, didn't you?' Sal says. 'If anything it's me that shouldn't be here. All I did was fuck the wrong piece of arse.'

He's laughing so hard at this, and from the look in his eyes reliving the memory of it, that I'm finding myself laughing too.

'What's our chances of getting out of this alive?' I ask.

The laughter stops.

'You heard it,' Schiebler says. 'No-one's ever lived through a hunt before.'

'It looks like Skeet's lady sees things differently,' I say, but maybe feeling a bit less confident than I sound.

'She's just pissed off at him for all the fucking around,' Schiebler says. 'She doesn't believe you'll make it any more than *he* does...'

Cheery fucker.

'So, why don't you lot make the change? Go dog-form and fight?'

'Why don't *you*?' Sal says, shaking his chained hands so I can see them behind his back.

And just then, our nice little chat gets interrupted.

The suits from last night are back, this time all tweed and brown trousers and shoes. Gideon Skeet is there at the head of them. Then right after come four more, but these are stark bollock naked, striding out, man, as if they don't give a shit.

Skeet's calling out to Cobb who's arrived at the scene from the back of the house.

'Fetch the cars round.'

And I can tell, from the look that Cobb gives him, how much he hates Skeet and all the other whore-slaughtering, coke-snorting bastards. And me, I'm thinking – *as much as I've got scores to settle with Cobb – we've got something in common there.*

A few minutes later, a couple of open top four-by-fours tear up the grass and stop in front of our cages. Skeet climbs up into the one driven by Cobb. The rest of his gang – the ones with clothes on – get into the other one.

The hair on the back of my neck is standing up.

This is it, I'm thinking. *The hunt's about ready to go.*

'Murderers and thieves,' Skeet says, standing on the seat of his four-by-four, so as he can get a good look at us all through the mesh of our cages. 'It's time to pay for your sins.' And he laughs like he's made a really good joke, and sits down.

'Whenever you're ready,' he calls over to the butt-naked boys. 'Take some breakfast if you need to, but make sure you leave plenty for the chase.'

I can smell fear now.

Up and down the cages, there's the stink of it.

Each of the four rude-boys stands in front of a cage.

'Hello, ladies,' says the geezer who takes up stand in front of ours.

It's Clay. The one from last night. The one whose lady Sal was caught boning.

'I'm dying to eat you,' he says.

I'm thinking how this seems to be directed at Sal more than anyone else, especially when Clay winks at him and laughs.

And then he reaches his right hand over his head. He's grabbing at his top lip – the whole of it, like, the whole of the top of his mouth, and starting to pull upwards, so's I can see his white teeth and red gums. And then, he starts to scream, and he really wrenches, and with one last tug and a roar, he's torn the skin from his skull.

Thirty-one

At first it's all blood and noise, man.

Like he's ripping himself apart, top down.

And then I can see the wolf-hair matted with blood and the teeth growing and sharpening, and as he tears at his skin, he's turning himself inside out and I'm realising that although he's a man on the outside, there's a dirty great wolf on the in.

This must be why Sal's hands are cuffed. To stop him doing the same.

Fuck, this is starting to look really bad.

The trap's opened on the first cage, the one at the opposite end of the row to the one we're in. We can see half a dozen figures race out of it and start making their way as fast as they can across the grass.

All four of Skeet's boys are almost wolf-form.

Next one, another five boys this time, racing across the grass.

Let us the fuck out.

Skeet's boys are still bloody, and still shaken by the change, but now they're wolves. Yellow-eyed, grey. No match for my black beast, but more than a match for a bunch of unturned running men.

They're ready to hunt.

The next trap.

This time, although two make off quick out of the cage, there's the geezer with the broken leg and someone's stayed behind to give him a shoulder, and they're kind of staggering across the lawn, three-legged.

The first of the dogs is on them.

There's laughter from Skeet's four-by-four, and from the other one with the rest of his mates in.

'That's cheating!' one of them's shouting out, and the others are thinking this is really fucking funny, and they're all clinking glasses and cheering on that dog. It's got hold of the one with the cracked leg, and the other geezer's pulled himself out somehow and has started tearing away towards the lake.

A second dog arrives, and they start fighting over the broke-leg, one at either end, pulling and growling at each other, while he's screaming and struggling to get away, and then we can hear a kind of pop that echoes against the wall of the house and he's split in half and each of the dogs drags his bit away by ten feet or so, then settles to chow down on it.

Another howl of laughter.

And some more popping, but this time of corks off the bottles of fizzy piss they're drinking in the four-by-fours.

So <u>this</u> is breakfast.

Our trap opens.

We've got to be fucked.

Except Skeet is shouting, 'He's getting away', and pointing at the boy who's made a run for the lake. He's dived in, maybe thinking he'll escape by swimming for it.

The two spare dogs – including Clay-turned, who should be keeping an eye on us – race after him. Lake-boy's doing well, out far enough that the water's nearly up to his shoulders, and then he's launching himself in and his arms are curling over his head in a crawl.

Go on, my son. You can make it.

But then Clay-turned and the other dog get to the lake's edge, I can't tell which is which now. One of them is splashing in after the swimmer – with Skeet and his gang cheering on – and manages to grab hold and turn him, and he's half-drowning as he's dragged back to the shore, and the other dog joins in with all the ripping and rewrapping.

He had his chance and took it.

It didn't work out, poor fuck.

And we've seen *our* chance, and we're on our way, all five of us together looping wide round the dogs still feeding, muzzles red with fresh blood, tearing up those bodies with teeth and claw.

Thirty-two

Fuck, I haven't run like this since I was a kid.

We're across the smart lawn, and then on to rougher grass, heading towards trees. They're thick enough to stop the four-by-four crew getting through in their jeeps, but the dogs won't have a problem.

One thing at a time.

'Over there!'

I can hear Skeet, he's shouting at the dogs, and although I'm running too hard to turn around, I'm betting that he's pointing at us this time. And if he's at the dogs, telling them not to forget that there are five more after-breakfast snacks for them to chase, I'm also betting they'll be onto us soon.

Got to get to those trees.

I'm at the head of our pack, I can feel the others just off my shoulders either side. Sal finding it hard to run with his hands cuffed behind his back, and he's cursing using words I don't understand. Doug is puffing like a train, coughing 'fuck' on every out-breath. The other two are a few steps further back, Matti silent, Schiebler panting a kind of whistle, in between muttering to himself about the shit we're in.

Almost at the trees.

'Go on!'

Skeet again, and this time I turn my head, and see one of the dogs let loose whatever bones he's gnawing on, and break to a run, heading straight for us.

Fuck.

If he catches us in the open, we're fucked. Or at least one or two of us are fucked. Maybe he'll get that ginger fuck, Schiebler. Maybe the dog'll get him first and give the rest of us some more time to get away.

I can't hear the dog yet, he's got a few hundred yards to make up. Skeet and his boys are roaring at it. They don't want us to make the trees. They want us to get caught out in the open. So they can watch. I'm thinking, *Skeet's going to enjoy seeing me torn right apart, I'll bet he's going to get Cobb to drive over so they get a nice close-up on that.*

Everything's on fire. My legs, my heart slamming away in my chest. My head fit to burst. I can hardly breathe.

Almost at the trees.

Now I can just about hear the dog's feet pounding away on the grass behind us. It's growling as it runs.

'Come on!' now it's me shouting at the others.

No way am I going to give Skeet the pleasure, man. No fucking way.

'Come on!'

And then Sal goes down.

He's hit a ruck in the grass, and he doesn't have his arms to balance or his hands to break his fall. I slow, see Schiebler pass me, realise the others've stopped.

'On them!' Skeet's shouting, the jeep circling and roaring its way towards us, gaining ground on the dog.

Me and Doug grab a shoulder each and drag Sal to his feet.

We all three stumble, and Matti's joining in and somehow we don't fall.

Then we're running again.

Back up to speed.

We're almost at the trees.

I can hear the dog's breathing now, like saw cuts in and out, in and out. Fuck I can almost hear the blood pumping through its veins.

And then suddenly we're in.

The sun disappears.

All the sounds of the four-by-fours, engines gunning, Skeet shouting, the dogs, all of that suddenly muffled. It's grey, and almost still.

Back through the trees and on the grass I see the dog break its run and come to a stop before it hits the woods.

The last thing we hear before we head deeper into the dark is Skeet:

'What are you fucking waiting for? Get after them!'

Thirty-three

It goes on like this:

Sprinting over the leaf-litter.

Picking up Sal each time he trips and crashes to the ground.

More and more fucked, knackered and wanting to stop, but knowing we can't.

Headed fuck knows where.

Catching something of a noise of the dog or dogs further back which we know are hunting us down.

Thinking, *no matter how far we get, it ain't going to be far enough.*

And I'm trying to direct us deeper into the trees, where it's darker and maybe harder for the big beasts to get to us. We're getting cut and torn by brambles and low-hanging branches. A couple of times we get to a dead-end, such a thick matt of undergrowth we can't get through, and we have to double back and find a way round.

But we're still just running and running.

My one-lung's stabbing heat in my chest.

My eyes are stinging with sweat.

Part of me is thinking back to that time when me and Ziggy and Lucas ran all the way back from Brown-Town, stinking of smoke and fit to burst.

And, with that, I'm almost choking on laughter.

Running and running, Pete.

Aren't you tired of running?

Which gets me to, *fuck this*, and coming to a stop.

I bend in half, hands on my knees and breathless, and shake my head.

And to myself and any of the others that want to listen I say:

'I'm not fucking running anymore.'

Thirty-four

The rest of them stop further along.

At first they wait, uncertain, as if I'm going to kick on again.

I stand up.

'No,' I say.

'No, what?' Doug says.

'I'm not running anymore.'

No-one says anything.

Then Schiebler:

'So what *are* we going to do?'

'I don't give a fuck what *you* do but I'm not running...'

'Come on,' says Doug. 'We stick together....'

'OK, so we stick together. We stand and fight,' I say.

'You think I'm going to be able to fight in these?' Sal says, laughing and holding his hands up behind his back.

'You think any of us are going to be able to fight?' Schiebler's in a panic.

'I thought all of you were dogs?' I'm saying. 'Doesn't that means it's dogs on dogs?'

'We don't have what we need to make the change,' Matti says.

Neither do I as it happens.

'And you'll wait three days for him to,' Doug glances towards Schiebler.

Fuck me.

A fine bunch of useless fucking werewolves we are.

'So we stand and fight anyway...'

'We *can't* fight them. Not like this,' Schiebler's rattling away in that whistle-voice he's got. 'They'll tear us apart.'

Like they did the others. We're all thinking the same.

I'm staring at him.

Staring at all of them.

They're staring back, asking themselves what I'm going to do, wondering what they're going to do.

It's Matti who talks first.

'OK,' he says.

Schiebler just about has a fit, man.

'What do you mean, OK? You're going to stay here and get ripped to pieces?'

The two of them look at each other.

Then Matti says, 'We carry on running, we'll get caught and killed anyway. I'd rather stand and fight like he says.'

'You're making no sense –'

'Me too.' That's Douglas interrupting.

'We're fucked one way or another,' Sal says laughing again. He's enjoying this.

'My advice,' I'm saying to Schiebler, 'is that you fuck off.'

'Who the fuck are you, man – ?'

We're just about to step up to a proper argument (which, by the way, I would have won fist-style) when we both hear it.

Oh shit.

We're still.

The others have heard it too.

They're all tensed up. *That's it. There's definitely nowhere to go. Not now.*

I'm waving a hand to tell them to get down, and we're easing ourselves onto the ground. We've got to have been heard. If the wolves that're chasing us are anything like as cool as my belt-dog, well of course we've been heard. And we've been sensed and smelled too, and whatever's doing the listening and sensing and smelling is on its way and looking forward to a five-course chow-down.

Through the trees, now, I can see it.

It's been tracking us neat and tidy, waiting for its moment.

How the fuck are we going to get out of this?

They tore the other boys apart, like rag dolls.

What chance've we really got? I'm asking myself as the fucking thing breaks cover and charges towards us.

And then you get:

The thundering of its paws through the undergrowth.

The chainsaw growl of it.

The teeth, as long as my fingers.

Yellow-eyed.

Grey fur.

Nose and mouth stained with the blood of its kills.

It's got me in its sights.

It's coming for me.

I close my eyes, waiting for it.

As I do this, I realise I'm feeling... I don't know... *OK*.

It's like I'm *cleaner* being outside.

I might've lost my dogstar belt, but no way am I feeling as blunt as I did when I was locked up in the cell. Everything's starting to... I don't know.... *sharpen up*.

Blood starts thundering its way round my body. Whatever's left of that big black dog inside me is coming back to life. *Here doggie, here!*

I'm in the zone, man. Ready for what's coming.

Oh, you'd better be, Pete.

And for a second, before it hits, all is calm. Its claws tearing up the ground, the growl rising to a howl, the beat of its heart, its breathing, the shouts of Sal and Doug and Matti, and even Schiebler's screaming. All of this is silenced.

And I can see and hear, in that moment, just like wolfie does. I'm a man, but for a split-second I can feel the world like my dog.

Come on, you fucker.

It's diving through the undergrowth.

Mouth gaping.

Coming straight at me.

Come on, you fucker.

I'm reaching around myself, on the dirt.

Not sure what I'm reaching for.

Something I've seen. Something I've sensed.

Come on, you fucker.

I can feel its breath on my face it's so close.

I can smell it, I can smell the blood of the boys it's already killed.

Come on, you fucker.

Then my hand closes over something.

It's a branch.

A broken branch.

Three feet or so of it, a couple of inches thick.

Come on, you fucker.

And in that moment of calm before it hits, I've got hold of that branch.

I've pulled it up in front of me.

As the wolf slams into me, jaws open wide, I've slammed the branch into its throat.

And on collision, we're catapulted backwards through the brush and trees. We're spinning, locked together, branches and leaves whipping and tearing my skin until we hit dirt. There's dust and grit spraying behind us, and eventually we stop.

Thirty-five

Quiet again.

Except for the sound of my one-lung dragging in air.

I'm alive, I know that much.

And nothing's hurt too bad, at least no more than a few scratches and that I'm going to get the mother of a bruise across my chest where it hit me, and this and the fact that the wolf is lying across me means it's hard for me to breathe.

I'm just getting to thinking, *Is it dead? Have I killed the fucking thing?* when I feel it move, a kind of shudder and a cough and it's spitting out bits of splintered wood, and then twisting itself round and trying to get up off me, and staggering as it does and almost falling back down.

And I'm lying here all quiet thinking, *I thought I had you, you fuck,* then it makes it up onto four legs, still unsteady, like, and slowly turns its head until it sees me, flat out on the dirt. Its face starts to crease up into a growl, and these lips draw back and I'm looking at the size of those fucking teeth, mouth full of blood, some of its own and some from the boys it's chowed down on, and these yellow eyes are pinning me down.

Fuck.

And then *bang.*

From behind it, there's shouting, and it doesn't have time to spin round before they're on it.

Three of them I can make out as I'm shuffling away across the dusty ground, my chest fit to bursting, and there's Doug with what looks like a dirty great stone, and Matti with half a fucking tree trunk and even Sal, hands still cuffed, but he looks like he's using his boots, and all three of them are on the wolf – *nicely set up by me, you understand, all weak and not knowing what's hit him already* – and they're clubbing and kicking and smashing at its head, and its legs have buckled and there's flecks of blood and fur flying, more and more of a fury of it, and eventually it collapses under them, but they keep at it and I have to yell at them to stop.

And again, 'Stop!'

Doug's lifting his stone, red-faced like he's been painted.

'Stop!'

Doug staggers back, and Matti and Sal stand down too.

'It's not dead,' Doug says.

I get myself up – *fuck I'm sore* – and walk over to where they're standing now, looking down at it.

Schiebler comes out from behind the trees, I clock him staring at the mess of a wolf and then up at me and the others.

What the fuck do you mean, it's not dead?

There's a low moan coming from the mash of its dog's head.

'Let's finish it...' Doug says, chomping right at his bit, ready for some more stone-smashing.

'Wait,' I'm saying.

'Come on,' Matti says. 'We need to get set again. There'll be others here soon.'

So we carry on with our stand, see if we can take out the other three of these fuckers. Yeah, well maybe. But they're hard to kill, I'm saying all this to myself, *and I'm not sure I'm fancying our chances doing this three more times.*

'How do we get out?' I say.

'Out?' Schiebler says.

'Out, yes, out, you dopey fuck.'

This tangle of blood and hair at our feet is still whimpering, but then the sound of that disappears under something else like splitting and cracking. Its fur tears in a long rip along its back, and underneath there's more blood and muck, but underneath *that* is what looks like human skin again.

Fuck me.

He's coming back to man-form.

The rest of them are less interested. I guess they've seen it all before.

Me, I've got to watch this.

The dog-skin and all its hair are peeling back, like, and there's more human under it – body and arms and legs – and the wolf-face splits, and a man-face is being sucked back into itself, but swollen and blackening because it's been beaten so hard and in less than a couple of minutes, with all the wolf fur seeming to fall away into nothing, I'm staring down and realising this is Clay... the one after Sal, who must've been tracking us to make sure that he would be the one to do the punishing for what Sal did with his wife.

His eyes are closed, and I can hear the moaning again, but this time sounding more like the kind of moaning a man might do than that what a dog does.

I look back up at the others.

'Like I said, how do we get out?'

'Well we could make it to the perimeter,' Matti's starting to say and I'm zoning out of his chat about getting to the edges of the Estate somewhere and trying to make it out over the walls.

'What are we going to do with him?' Sal says, and Doug makes it clear what *he'd* do in putting a boot to Clay's head and threatening to do it another time.

Me, I'm thinking back to this story I heard once about a bunch of Malis who got taken by the Slavs (during some gang-fight or other) and brought back to their Estate for stringing up and some good old fashioned torture before dispatching, you know, for teaching of a lesson.

And how somehow the Malis'd got free. Maybe the Slavs were drinking too much of that gut-rot liquor of theirs. But whatever it was, the Malis had grabbed someone important and got a knife to his neck, and all the Slavs had stood back. They let the Malis walk right of out the Estate.... just let them *walk* out of there, man, blade at a throat, without no-one touching them for fear of a cut and a slice and this top-man spilling his blood everywhere all over the tarmac.

'We take him with us,' I say. 'He might come in handy.'

Schiebler's just about to disagree.

'Shut the fuck up,' Sal says before he can open his mouth.

'Good, let's get him up and get going.'

Thirty-six

Clay's not that happy about coming with us, but he's too beaten up and covered in blood and dirt to put up much of a fight... nothing that isn't cured by a sound couple of slaps across the head from Doug anyway.

'What about him changing?' Sal says, still steaming because, although we've tried to knock the cuffs off with stones, his hands are still pulled straight behind *his* back.

Good point. Who knows how long before he's going to feel chipper again?

'Break his arms,' I say.

And although Schiebler starts to protest – *again* – the words aren't hardly out of my mouth before Doug's getting stuck in, pushing Clay back onto the ground and sticking one boot in his face to stop him screaming, and using the other to crack bones.

It's a fucking mess.

But after what Clay did to those other boys, and what he tried to do to me, I'm not much worried about losing sleep over it.

When done, we pull him up again. We've got nothing to cover him with, so he's arse and balls, and his broken-up arms are hanging and swinging all rubber, just like his dick – it's kind of funny, to be honest. At least for the first half an hour or so, and then the joke wears off. Now, instead of running and running fit to burst, we're walking and walking, fit to having had enough of this shit, and I'm starting to wonder whether I should've let Doug have his way and get his boots to do the talking, in other words to say goodbye to Clay.

Matti's leading the way, peering up at the sun each time we get into a clearing, and mumbling in that almost-no-voice of his about which direction we need to go in. Me, I've got no clue. Give me streets and concrete and I might have a chance, but every fucking tree looks the same. We could be going in circles for all I know. All that's clear is we don't seem to be going deeper and darker, the woods aren't getting any thicker, and at the same time they aren't getting any thinner neither, so maybe that means we're heading parallel to the edge of the trees, rather than further in or back out. Parallel, and towards the wall where we'll climb right out.

So as I say, it's going like this for a while.

And I'm noticing that we're making a lot of noise, what with us having to half-drag Clay and all. But amongst the foot-dragging and crackling of dry leaves and scuffing of dirt, there's other kinds of sounds out there in the trees. Then Matti and then the rest of them have heard it too.

Fuck me.

We're being tracked, and this time there's got to be more than one dog.

We stop and I'm raising a hand to get everyone to shut up.

'They'll have you...' Clay says, spitting bubbles of mucus and blood.

I'm just about to shut him up too with the back of my hand when there's a crashing of dried leaves and twigs in amongst the trees. Then another, but this time over to the other side of us. And then some more, getting closer.

'Why they making so much noise?' Schiebler says.

They're coming towards us from deeper in. I turn and look in the other direction, we've started to drift towards the edge of the wood. Through the trees I can just about make out the open space, grass, and maybe I catch the sound of an engine gunning.

Another crash, and now we can hear a low growl too.

One, two, yeah, there are three of them. All three of the dogs circling, moving in on us.

'They're driving us out,' I say. 'They want us in the open.'

'What the fuck're we going to do?' says Schiebler, whining.

Closer.

And I can hear, more clearly now, the sound of an engine from out on the grass.

Three sets of yellow eyes, lit like lamps in the darkness between the trees. Trained on us, unblinking, and three sets of low, chugging, chainsaw growling.

'Well,' I say. 'We're fucked if we stay in here...'

'... and you're fucked if you go out...' Clay says, a bloody rasp.

'We'll see about that,' I say.

I'm looking around, and thinking.

There are bunches of small trees, shooting up, trunks not even as think as my wrist, a tussle of leaves at the top, only about as tall as me. I get hold of one, and using my foot to hold it still at the roots, I bend it until it snaps.

'Give me a hand,' I say to Doug.

Together we pull the thing apart, and we're left with a four foot pole with a sharp end where it spilt. It's strong enough.

I take the pole and hold that sharp end tight under Clay's chin.

'We'll see...' I say again '.... how much they want you to live...'

Thirty-seven

Then with three dirty-bastard dogs behind us, we're making our way through the trees and we're blinking into the light again. And right as we do this, there's an explosion of engine noise, and there's grass and dust blown up like smoke and one of the four-by-fours shudders to a stop just twenty or thirty feet ahead of us.

We stop, and the dogs stop too, just inside the trees, watching to make sure we don't try to make a break for it back into the woods.

The dust settles.

It's the jeep with Skeet in, Cobb driving.

Skeet stands up in the back and Cobb climbs out.

He's got a gun.

Me, I'm pushing my tree-spear right up into Clay's throat, and he's struggling to breathe and trying to get those rubber arms moving in spite of the pain, but Doug's got him too. Matti and Sal are either side, and I can sense that Schiebler's falling back behind us.

It's all quiet for a minute.

Then me:

'Let us go,' I say. 'Or he gets it...'

And I jab hard enough at Clay to open up a cut in his neck.

'*Does* he?' Skeet says.

Cobb pulls up his gun onto a shoulder, but I can tell he's going to have to wait until he's told what to do.

It's quiet again. Camera close-ups on each of us, that kind of thing.

'I've got to give it to you,' Skeet's saying. 'This is a first.'

Behind us, the wolves are bristling, threatening to come out of the trees and at us, getting ready to finish what Clay tried to start.

'No,' Skeet calls out to them. 'You boys had your chance.'

Cobb's staring at me, that gun pointed right at my head.

Just give me my chance, I'll bet that's what he's thinking. *Just let me squeeze the trigger and put an end to this little fucker.*

But instead:

'Give me the gun,' Skeet says.

Cobb looks up at him questioningly.

And this *really* pisses Skeet off.

'I said *give it to me*.' This time he shouts.

Cobb drops the rifle from his shoulder and passes it up to Skeet, butt first.

Skeet takes it, swings it round and holds it up, squeezing it against his face and closing one eye. He's pinning me down with the other, looking right at me, the barrel of the gun so fully fixed on my face it seems to disappear and all I can see is the black hole at its end, ready to let loose a bullet that's going to split Pete's head right in two.

'Let us go,' I say again.

'Do you honestly think I'm going to let you walk out of here?' Skeet says.

'If you don't, he's dead.'

I've got Clay so tight now he's gagging with the lack of air and the pain of his arms and his beaten-up head.

The dogs behind are rumbling out a growl, standing down but tense. Thinking they might still get a moment.

Skeet pointing that gun at me, and then he says:

'I'm sorry, but it just doesn't work like that.'

And I hear a crack as the barrel of the gun seems to explode.

Thirty-eight

Clay's head bursts like a wet balloon.

Aw, fuck me.

There's blood, skull-splinters and bits of brain all over me.

The crack of the gun and the slap of the bullet's knocked me down; Doug's tumbled with me. I've got the weight of Clay on me again, this time man rather than dog, and I'm pushing him off and pulling me out from underneath him.

And at first I'm thinking that Skeet meant to shoot me and missed, got Clay by mistake and I'm lying there waiting for the next bullet to hit – but this time for it to hit me – then I see Skeet let the barrel of the gun drop.

Silence.

I can tell Cobb's shocked by what he's just seen.

The dogs behind aren't making a noise either; they're properly stood down now.

Then:

'Useless fucking idiot,' Skeet says calmly. 'First he lets you fuck his wife, Sal, and then he lets himself get....'

And he doesn't even finish this part of what he's saying but just waves an arm towards us.

'What kind of fucking dog is that?' he says after a time.

He holds the gun out for Cobb to take back.

'Can the dogs have them now?' Cobb says quietly, not looking at Skeet.

Well, we gave it a shot, right?

We took our chance and almost made it.

Skeet looks across at us, from one to the other.

'No,' he says, sitting down. 'Tell the boys to get changed back, the hunt's over.'

'... and them?' Cobb says.

Skeet pauses.

'Take them back to the Bank, put them in the cells. I'll work out what to do with them later.'

Thirty-nine

Fuck me.

I reckon you'll need a bit of a break from the action, right? I know I do.

Give me some time to catch up with myself.

So you go and get an ice cream and a can of fizzy pop.

Well go on.

Fuck off then.

But make sure you're sat back down before the film starts again.

INTERMISSION

Schiebler, the Werewolf: we kill the things we love

Go on, ask him...

Come on Schiebler, don't be shy.

He's got plenty to say when it comes to whining about what we shouldn't have done and what we should have done, instead of what we did and didn't do. But suddenly, he's not so chatty.

What's that? 'Fuck me'?

You wish, you ginger twat.

Now play nice. Or we'll show them your arrest report.

Who did you kill, Schiebler?

Why did you kill her?

Cat got your tongue?

Well, if he won't I will.

I like a good love story (ha! ha!)

Schiebler's a nice middle class kid from some little town, somewhere Nonglish – Holland, I think he calls it.

He grows up a dog. A proper born one, a *werewolf*. The real deal, he says in that whistle-voice.

Yeah, well.

Give me my boom-change any day of the week.

One time we'll have to sit down with a bowl of popcorn to watch Schiebler change, for a laugh.

'Hey is that hair growing out of your ear, Schiebler?'

'Yeah, give him an hour and he might crack a tooth!'

We'll give up after a couple of hours, and he'll carry on screaming and sweating and breaking his bones for another six. *Eight* hours all in all. Like giving birth to yourself, Schiebler says – and then the same to get back into man-shape. Sod that. He might be the real deal, but I prefer being a fake. No wonder the real shape-shifters are the ones who shift shape least often.

So Schiebler doesn't spend much time dog-ways...

When he does make the change, well he makes for a brown, foxy (sharp-nosed, don't get carried away) looking thing. He's a two-foot, not a four-foot, and we all take the piss that he's got something a bit like a kangaroo. You really want to piss him off, call him Skippy.

He's an odd fuck (you've noticed, right?). I put that down to the mongrel Dutch-Deutsch background. His old man was a kraut, a real stiff-arm – you know the type – perfect as camp commandant. Got hunted down and shot in the sixties by some of those who hadn't enjoyed their stay with him back in the day.

Left little red head at home with Mummy, all whining and pining and howling at the moon late at night on the dykes outside the little town his family lived in.

He was the smart kid at school that no-one liked. (Why doesn't that surprise you?). He went to a neat little college with normal kids, and those normal kids used to beat the shit out of Schiebler, and Schiebler used to take it. Yeah sure, he'll tell you now that he bit back hard, but I can tell he's talking crap.

He was the smart kid at university (apparently it's like school for big kids too scared to go out into the real world) that no-one liked. Spent all his time with that nose stuck in dusty books, studying some, and then some more, and even more after that. He manages to keep on studying for years, like he's never going to leave.

Until one day he meets a nice girl with glasses who likes to do the same.

No-one's ever liked him before. He'll tell you he was all loved up and that. Maybe, maybe not. For my money, it's much more to do with this being the first (and only) time he's been getting his dick wet on a regular basis. One day, when she comes back home after going away to visit family, anxious to see her flame-haired love (for Schiebler's sake, let's make her a babe in the flashback scene), she finds him half cracked on all fours in his little studio flat, and starts screaming and hollering (... yeah, of course she didn't know he was a dog), and she just won't fucking shut up and she's getting to running down the stairs and out onto the street, all fucking hysterical, and before he knows what he's doing, Schiebler's broken her neck to make her quiet.

It's tragic. Isn't it? So I'm all solemn about this, and *definitely* not laughing when he tells me.

After this, Schiebler turns himself in.

Let's say that again.

He turns himself in.

And that way, he ends up in Cobb's cell, and spends a few months feeling sorry for himself and not being too bothered that he's going to end up dead – until Pete steps in and gives him a new lease on life (ha! ha!).

Sal, the Skin-rip: chasing tail

SWITCH TAPE TO PLAY:

A shaky picture, crackle round the edges. Then Sal, staring at the camera with those eyes, a smile tugging at the corners of his mouth.

'I don't need sex. I just like it,' he says, through a puff of smoke. His voice is a crunching, deep bassoon, lubricated by the constant presence of a brown cheroot. He raises his hands – which are cuffed together and held by a chain to his waist – to pull it out of his mouth, so he can speak more clearly.

'Are these really necessary?'

'You're a skin-rip. Of course they're necessary,' says a voice off camera. It sounds like Skeet.

Sal nods.

The voice again: 'So you confess to your affair with Emma Biggs?'

'Wasn't it you who walked into the office where I was having her over the desk?'

Sal makes those eyes of his.

'What do you think, eh? You saw us. Me dog-form fucking away at her from behind, and her – all woman – screaming at me to fuck her harder. We must have done it ten or fifteen times. You think that's an affair?'

Sal laughs and blows balls of smoke at the camera.

'You know, all the rich girls like it that way. They prefer dog to man every day of the week. Why do you think that is?'

Silence from behind the camera.

'Hey, are you getting off on this?' he asks.

'This is *Emma Biggs*. Her husband's Clay Biggs. He's on the Bank's *board*, for God's sake.'

'Maybe if Clay could make it dog-shape once in a while and give her some bone.... Well maybe she wouldn't have come to me.'

'Sal,' the voice again, but this time softer, 'this isn't looking good for you. Clay's not going to take this lying down – '

'Ha! It runs in the family – '

'He wants *blood*.'

Sal shrugs as though he thinks this reasonable.

'You're one of us, Sal. But I can't protect you any more if you go on like this.'

'So I'm supposed to fuck whores like you and your crowd, Gideon. To pay for it rather than give it to women who really want it?'

Silence again.

'Who's making the judgement?' Sal says, after some time, eyes glazed as though reminiscing.

A sigh from off camera.

'Lakeman,' says the voice.

A pause.

'Oh,' says Sal and laughs hard at the memory of Mrs Lakeman bouncing around on top of him. 'Well, it looks like it might be my turn to get fucked.'

Then he laughs harder still.

Doug, the Greaser: once upon a time, there was a real boy

Just like me.

Except that where I'm getting tumbled up in a Sink in London, Douglas is doing a good, clean job of growing up surrounded by trees and grass in Scotland.

 His dad is a minister and his mum stays at home and looks after him and his sister, and he goes to school like a good boy and does his lessons and all that malarkey. So far, so nicey nicey.

Except that for Doug growing up, big bad wolf was his dog-collar dad in the black suit, who liked to rule their little house with a rod of iron and a fist that could crack skulls. All three of them – wife, son and daughter – got their regular feast of it.

And this goes on for years, and Doug, although not very bright to start with, is growing bigger and hairier (and maybe stupider) and is starting to think that maybe he should start giving back some of what he's been getting.

One day he does. And he likes it.

He *really* likes it.

Dear old dad swaps cream teas and cucumber sandwiches for hospital food, and Douglas decides it's time to skip town, and see what he can do with his new-found taste for fists and boots.

He ends up in Glasgow, working at the docks during the day and pissing it up in the pubs by night, finding a use for those great fucking hammer hands he's got.

But one night he picks on the wrong (right) guy.

Douglas don't know it, but he's met the only dog sad or mad enough to be in Glasgow. Doug's sunk a dozen pints of piss, and he's looking for someone to give it large to, and there's a geezer minding his own business in the corner of the pub, smoking rollies and staring into the bottom of a Guinness pot.

'Wha' fuck yoo starin' at?' Douglas starts and blah, blah, blah... and the geezer's got up and said something like he don't want any trouble, and tried to get past our Doug to the door. And, you know how it goes, Douglas pulls him back and takes a pop, and keeps going at him and at him, pushing and pushing until the geezer blows. So this geezer cracks a bottle of grease, starts smearing his hair and face with it, at the same time as taking hold of Doug and throwing him through the pub door out onto the street.

Doug's out and on the floor and on his arse, so full of beer he's going to burst like some Jock balloon. All a blur. Then...

Well, Doug can tell you:

'Fuckin' face on him. These black eyes. Half man, half wolf. He leaned down, and roared at me, and that was enough. I fuckin' shat m'sel'.'

He did. Shit himself, I mean.

Sat on the street filling his trousers with a pile of beer-black shit, where his ring piece has just waved goodbye.

And a second after that picture is taken, the geezer is a greased-up wolf-man, legging it off down the alley. Like he said – he didn't want any trouble. Douglas is all shit and sweat and sober and going back in the pub to clean himself up.

No-one's been harder than Doug since he last caught one of Dad's whippings when he was a kid. Not until now.

So after a week of hiding away like a pussy, Douglas decides to do something about it. He sobers up, jacks in the job at the shipyard, and spends the next three years trying to find himself a way to dog.

Let's skip forward a few pages in the fairy tale...

Here's Douglas, looking more sober, a little older, a lot hairier (the full beard and the long hair now), sun-leathered face and tombstone teeth, tattoos on the insides of his forearms (dogs, what else?), standing naked to the waist.

Looks like he's in a tent... lit by candles, you know, orange and yellow flickering and all that shit. There's an old woman with her back to him mixing something up in a wooden bowl. She's doing the whole ub-abud thing, pausing every once in a while to sprinkle or drop something else into the bowl. You get the picture, she's some kind of West Country witch. At last after three years' searching, Douglas has found the way to be a dog.

She turns and offers the bowl to him.

His hands are shaking.

This is the closest Doug ever gets to having a tear in his eye.

He takes the bowl and puts it down on the floor next to him. With care, like he's handling a baby (not that that's ever going to happen, ha! ha!).

She's gesturing to him, saying something.

The crusty kecks come off, and here's Douglas bare arsed and naked. Then he's dipping his hands into the bowl and taking handfuls of grease and rubbing them all over himself. When he's completely covered from head to foot, shining now in the candle light like a polished turd, he stands, twinkle-blues shut tight and arms pointing straight to the ground.

We see the muscles in his arms and legs and chest start to convulse. We get the tearing and cracking sounds as his bones and joints begin to change. It's difficult to tell on account of him being such a hairy mother already, but we think we see more curling hair appear, stop-motion, like moss all over his body. He visibly grows by a couple of inches. His eyes glaze over black, and his mouth opens to roar with the pain and we see extended canines.

And then it stops.

He stands there for a moment, still breathing hard. Maybe waiting for a second explosion of change and pain.

But nothing happens.

Here's Douglas. A little bit taller, a little bit hairier, with black eyes instead of blue ones, and looking a little bit like he's spent the last six months doing some serious weights, and with teeth a little bit longer and sharper. But still, here is Douglas.

'Is that it?' he says quietly to the witch.

She looks embarrassed and shrugs, and goes to get on with clearing up the mess she's made making the grease.

'Is that fucking *it?*' This time, he shouts. He sounds kind of pissed off.

The witch starts to babble. She's nattering nervously. Clearly suddenly worried that she's got a six foot six, humourless Jock half-dog in her tent who's not over-happy with the service she's provided.

'Grease can only make you the wolf you are... it can only *release* what you are, nothing can change what you are....'

You get the picture?

Good old boy Doug doesn't.

He's got the grease he's been looking for since that night in Glasgow, only to find out he makes the kind of wolf that looks better in a boiler-suit in black and white circa 1940.

Oh he's pissed off for quite some time.

That's what gets him back into drinking and fighting.

But old Doug finds the one advantage of being a non-dog dog is that he can be his wolf self wherever he goes and, to be honest, no-one really notices much. He can walk around in London without standing out from the crowd.

By day he sleeps, and by night he goes out to fight, financing his drinking by following suits down back streets and relieving them of their wallets. And it's all that boozing and brawling that eventually gets him arrested.

Matti, the Smoke: moonlight robbery

Cut to Matti.

He doesn't say much, and when he does say something, he's so quiet sometimes you hardly hear him. Perfect American English except for the occasional odd intonation, and a kind of gentle rush of air through his teeth when he pronounces an 's', making him sound breathless when he speaks. Matti's around five ten, although for some reason he appears shorter. He has pale hair, pale skin, pale, nutty coloured eyes which you can barely see behind the glasses he wears (these are real eighties style Deirdre Barlows, right?). He dresses preppie – always pin-striped trousers, a V-necked jumper, white shirt, always the same.

So... cut to Matti.

He coughs and looks, embarrassed, at the camera.

'You want me to...?' He motions towards us.

'Yes,' says a voice off-screen. 'Just look at the camera, tell your story, whatever... walk around if you want. Whatever makes you feel comfortable.'

'Oh OK.' He pauses. 'It's that I thought maybe I could-'

'Just fucking get on with it!' Another voice off-camera. (That's me (ha! ha!)).

'All right. Sorry.' (Clears his throat). 'Okay.' Then everything in a matter of fact drone like he's at a job interview. 'My name is Matti Sandhorn. I am thirty-two years old. I come from [...] in Finland.' He pauses. 'I don't know what else to say...'

'Tell us what Finn women are like to fuck!'

Lots of 'ha, ha, ha's off screen. That was obviously Sal, all animal growl, and chewing on the wet end of a cigar.

'Aw stop with this shit,' Schiebler's voice, 'let him get on with it. Not all of us have a dick instead of a brain.'

Sound of Sal laughing.

'So what you got instead of a dick, then?'

'You *are* a dick!'

Matti sits there, waiting for Schiebler, Doug and Sal to stop bickering.

Cut to Matti's mother. She's speaking with this really thick and gloopy Finnish accent, half singing half talking, but making it sound sad, man, like she's going to cry.

MUM: Matti was a normal boy.

(Matti, man, what is he a poodle?!)

MUM: He was a good boy.

(She shakes her head)

Cut to DAD (vodka-glazed eyes and red-raw cheeks): He was a little shit.

Cut to MUM: I hoped that when he got his dog-skin, that this would settle him. I hoped this... I don't know. Matti is just different to the other children.

Cut to DAD: I was in two minds about giving him his skin when he turned sixteen.

Cut to MATTI'S SCHOOLTEACHER: (forgettable type in his sixties, stripy woollen jumper and facial hair) Any time he was in the room, something would go missing. I don't think that boy was capable of looking at anything without wanting to appropriate it.

Cut to DAD: Elma insisted. She thought it might change him... but it didn't. Once he got his skin... once he became a Smoke... it made him a better thief than he already was.

OFF CAMERA: What do you think it was that made Matti Sandhorn a thief?

DAD: How do I know?

Cut to MUM: He was such a good boy...

Cut to SCHOOLTEACHER: If you want the truth... he was just born that way. Some people are. On his first day at school at the age of seven, he stole the headmaster's wallet.

OFF SCREEN: What did he do with it?

Cut to SCHOOLTEACHER: Nothing. He just kept it. He didn't even touch the money.

Cut to DAD: He's never done it for the money. He does it because he likes it, that's all.

Cut back to Matti – the rest of the gang still bitching at each other in the background – the faintest of smiles on his lips.

Pete, the dogstar

And then there's me.

Well you've got my story. And it ain't finished yet.

So let's get back to it. Take your seats, ladies and gentlemen (ha! ha!).

The intermission's over.

Forty

It's late the same night and we end up back where we started.

The five of us, I mean, back in our cells. Underground – I get to see this time that, it being less bright sunlight and more evening street-lamp glow, this prison we're in is down underneath a glass tower that seems to go on up forever, and that this tower is surrounded by other towers not seeming to go up quite so far.

We've not spoken, on account of the guards in the back of the truck like on the way out (blah, blah, blah) but when we get back to our cells they fuck off for a bit and leave us alone to chat through the bars across the corridor.

'So what's going on now?' I'm saying.

There's silence.

Sal is rubbing his wrists, and stretching, his arms being all fucked up and sore and raw from the chains which they took off when throwing him back behind bars.

'Who knows?' he's grinning like he can't wait to find out.

'One thing's for sure,' Schiebler says, fretting like he always seems to. 'If we were fucked before, we're totally fucked now.'

'What? More fucked than being hunted down and killed by Skeet's dogs?' This is Doug. 'At least we're alive.'

'We're not *supposed* to be!' Schiebler, sucking nervously on a cigarette. 'We're *supposed* to be dead. You're not *supposed* to be able to do what he did to a dog. No-one's ever fought off a dog – not with their bare hands.'

'I think you'll find we all had a part to play in that...' Doug says, turning his fists and staring at his knuckles, smiling.

'Cobb is going to want some more time with you. This time he might not play so nice,' Schiebler's stabbing that cigarette in the air, the red end glowing in my direction.

'... We all had our part to play in that except you... you fucking yellow-dog,' Doug says to Schiebler.

Then just like that, they're laying into each other, Doug into Schiebler and then Schiebler into Doug, all 'fuck you, you whining Dutch cunt' and Schiebler's slanging back calling Doug a 'grease-boy' and Doug is shouting something about at least it doesn't take him three hours to change and that Schiebler's dog looks more like a kangaroo than a dog, and more some...

And I find myself not listening anymore.

I can just see Matti's round-glass eyes staring at me through two sets of bars, before I go and lie back on my bunk and shut my eyes, closing out the row that's going on, with Sal, now, telling them both to shut the fuck up and me – knackered, really knackered after last night's no-sleep and all the running and fighting today – falling asleep.

When I wake up, it must be much later. The only sound is Doug's snoring, airways clogged from years of whiskey and cigarettes. I've really been out for the count, that black sleep where you're nothing. Coming to is like being sucked back to life from dead.

I'm just about closing my eyes again, ready for some more when I hear the door at the end of the corridor open. There's talking in low voices, I recognise Cobb's voice straight away, and then that the other one is Gideon Skeet – playboy whore-killer.

I shut my eyes, pretending to be back asleep.

'Where is he?' Skeet's saying.

I can tell they're outside my cell now and they're talking about me.

'What do you know about him?'

'You're interested now?' Cobb shoots one back.

There's a pause.

'What do you know about him?' This time, a harder edge.

'I gave my report to the Chairman.'

'Well I want you to give it to *me*.'

There's another moment of silence between them. I can hear Cobb pulling out and lighting one of his Marlboro Reds.

'We don't know much. He wouldn't... talk. He's a thug, a small-time criminal. He got hold of this belt somehow and he made some mischief around the Sink Estates, killing drug dealers and stealing money. It was *contained*...'

'Why wasn't I told about him? The first I find out is my fucking wife making bets on him...' Angry, trying not to shout.

'I told you, I reported to the Chairman.... your *father-in-law*.'

'You should have reported in to me *too*.' Really angry.

Silence again, apart from Cobb's pulling in and blowing out smoke.

Skeet's calmed himself down. 'I want some time with him now. Wake him up. I'm sure I can make him talk.'

I hear Cobb move himself between Skeet and my cell.

Cobb: 'The Chairman's called a meeting of the executive board tomorrow evening. The Bank will deal with it.'

Skeet: 'What the fuck has this got to do with the Bank?'

Cobb: 'They're not happy with the risk to business. They'd rather the problem was properly sorted.'

Skeet: 'Without finding out more about this belt? He made a mess of Clay with his bare fucking hands, for Christ's sake, and he wasn't even wearing the belt...'

Cobb: 'Exactly. With respect,' although there's clearly none at all intended, 'the board weren't happy about the way you handled things...'

Skeet: 'I'd have handled it differently if someone had told me about him...'

Cobb: (quietly) 'Like you handled Clay Biggs...'

Skeet: 'He was as good as dead. As far as the Chairman and the board are concerned, he *was* already dead....'

Cobb's silent; I can almost *feel* them staring each other down.

Cobb: 'My recommendation to the Bank will be that the boy is killed and the belt destroyed.'

Skeet: (seething, almost losing it) 'This is *fucking ridiculous*! You can't make a decision like this. Cobb, I want to talk to him now, and I want you to bring me the belt...'

Cobb: 'I can't,' he says it calmly, I can hear the fucker trying not to smile. 'I'm under orders from your father-in-law. The boy and the belt are to come before the board tomorrow afternoon... and he was very specific about not allowing you any contact.'

Skeet: 'Fuck my father-in-law!'

Cobb: 'Maybe.... But it's him I work for.'

There's another pause.

Skeet: 'Yes,' quieter now. 'But he won't be in charge forever, Cobb.'

And I hear him turn and walk back up the corridor and out through the door.

Forty-one

I bet you know what an executive board is.

At this point, I don't even know what a *company* is. The only company I know is the company I keep and that's not the kind of company that nice people like you keep. And fuck knows what the *Bank* is. You think anyone on the Links has a current account?

So this is the first boardroom I've ever been in.

Note to myself: when the book's published and made into a movie, and when the movie's a worldwide hit, when everyone's doing the dog, then I've got to make sure I get myself a room like this. Very fucking fancy.

I've been cuffed and slapped about a bit by the guards (don't fret it, they'll get theirs). And the boys in my corridor are all 'where are you taking him?' and that – I think they like me, man (ha! ha!) – then I've been dragged down some stairs and along a couple of other corridors and into this boardroom.

It's bigger – this one room – than our whole place on the Links. It's got wooden floorboards and panelled walls, great big framed paintings of fat blokes in shirts and ties, all in all looking like it cost a fair bit of money to put together. More money on decorating that room than I've ever had in my life, most likely.

And in the middle is this long table – more wood – and sat round it, in leather chairs, is a bunch of smart looking people in suits.

There I am, standing, hands in cuffs behind my back (just like Sal was yesterday, although it's not as if *I'm* going to rip some skin) and there *they* are, sat staring at me. And I'm noticing that there are two empty chairs, and thinking that one is the chair where Gideon Skeet would normally be sitting but for some reason he's decided not to turn up for this one, and that the other would have been for Clay Biggs who, bad for him, swallowed a branch and then a bullet instead of swallowing me.

Standing to one side is Cobb.

Next to him... oh, yeah... the foxy chick from Waterloo Station. She's looking good and I can see why I gave her the chase – all Miss Jones, crisp collars and a bra two sizes too small so her tits point up at the pictures on the wall. I make sure of the slightest little wink in her direction. *Aw, come on babe, no smile back?*

There's another woman but she's sitting at the table. She I don't throw some Pete bone to. She's got iron grey hair and a look that could wither your bollocks, and she smells like medicine. The rest of them round the table, the men, are pin-stripes, old boy style, lacquered hair, close shaves, ruffed ties, all that shit. A couple of them I recognise from back at Skeet's country pile – but scrubbed up, like.

Every one of them's turned towards me.

Every one of them's got this look on their face. A curled lip, like you're looking too closely at something you'd rather not step in.

Then I realise I can feel the belt.

My belt, the dogstar.

Cobb's got it with him.

He's carrying my bag and pulling out my belt which he puts down on the end of the table. He speaks first.

For a minute, I can hardly understand what he's saying, his voice is gravel from all those Reds and muffled by that greasy moustache of his.

The geezer at the end of the table holds up his hand:

'You can address the board.'

'Yes, sir.'

I'm guessing by the way that Cobb is almost on his knees with his tongue out ready to insert into a sunless spot, that this must be Gideon's daddy-in-law, the Chairman.

'We brought him in,' he motions at me, 'three weeks ago. He'd come to our attention because he was working some of the Sink Estates, stealing cash from drug dealers. The occasional kill.'

'But he remained contained?'

'Yes. He worked several Estates, but only ever inside them...'

There is some gentle laughter at this point. Not the kind of laughing you get when people find something funny. More a release of tension – oh OK, he's only been dogging around in the Sinks, well at least it's just the under-class he's been chowing down on then, we can all breathe a sigh of relief, can't we?

'We captured him at Waterloo. He had money. He was leaving.'

There's silence.

'What do we know about him?'

'Little,' Cobb says. 'I mean, we know enough about him, but we don't know where he got this, and we don't know what it is.'

He pushes my belt across the table and the Chairman picks it up, like he doesn't really want to touch it, like it's dirty.

'And then...'

'He was taken to Goldsworth, for one of Mr Skeet's hunts.' Cobb lets his gaze move across to one of the empty chairs momentarily, then back to the Chairman. 'He survived the hunt....' Cobb falters for a minute.

'But Clay didn't ...?'

Cobb's silent, as if he's going to say something, and one of Skeet's boys shifts in his chair, then: 'No, sir.'

Oh, I get it. I'm taking the rap for Clay, am I?

'And he...' he nods towards me, 'was in human form?'

'Yes, sir.'

There's a ripple of something like shock around the table.

The Chairman takes the belt-buckle with loose hands and looks closely at the dogstar.

'And you don't know where he got this?'

'No, sir.'

'Or where it comes from?'

'No, sir.'

There's some murmuring around the table.

Cobb starts to say something else.

'Go on,' the Chairman says.

'I don't think he knows much more than he's letting on. There isn't much more we can... extract from him.'

Well that's a relief.

'And what about finding out more about this?' The Chairman holds up the belt.

'Mr Skeet is strongly of the view that it should be examined...'

'I'm aware of Gideon's interests,' he cuts Cobb off. 'I want to know what you think.'

'I think it's dangerous.'

'Go on.'

'It's my opinion that the boy and the belt represent an unnecessary risk – to you all, and to the Bank... to business as usual.'

'Thank you.'

The old boy places my belt back on the table. Carefully.

'Gentleman, and lady,' for the medicine-woman, 'you know I prefer to keep things simple. And that I don't like risk. I also know that the world is changing, and that Gideon is increasingly frustrated that we won't... can't... embrace that change.'

'This Bank is more than one hundred and forty years old...'

He glances up and scans the paintings.

'And we've been successful because we've kept ourselves under the radar, we haven't drawn unnecessary attention to ourselves. I'd be as bold to say that this approach has been very lucrative for us...'

Lots of nods of agreement.

'Perhaps things will change...'

He says this like he's sad, staring at a point in thin air somewhere in front of him.

'But not yet. Not while I'm Chairman.'

He glances back at Cobb.

'Are we agreed then?'

Most of them round the table're nodding again, Skeet's boys a bit more stony-faced.

'You know what to do with him, Cobb. And as for this...' He picks up the belt again. 'We destroy it, and close this matter.'

And as he says this word, *destroy*, I get a sudden, sharp, stabbing pain round my middle, like the belt's being ripped out all over again. I gasp, bend double, then I see the belt stiffen in the Chairman's hands.

Oh shit.

Something's coming.

I'm almost retching with the pain.

Then it releases.

And as the pain lifts – quick as it came – the belt whips out of the Chairman's grasp and wraps itself round his neck. It tightens, and he scrabbles and scratches at it...

'Get it off me...' he's choking.

It's cutting tighter and tighter.

His face is red, man, his eyes are fit to bursting out.

And all this in less than a few seconds.

'Get it off...' he can hardly make the words.

The room's still in shocked silence.

Just for a moment.

Then it's chaos.

Forty-two

Well folks, I really haven't got time to stand here watching you looking at each other with your mouths wide open, I've got places to rob and people to kill.

Ba-da-boom.

Hot from being so close to my belt, the blood's raging, man. I'm pumped. The cuffs round my wrists feel like they're burning up, and with wrench of my arms I split the metal chains and make it free.

Everyone's in a panic, and you've got Cobb and the guards trying to pull my belt from the Chairman's neck, and the harder they pull, the tighter it gets 'til I swear his head's going to burst.

Me?

I'm on the table (real sweet Pete-leap), skidding over the veneer on my knees, and holding out my hands for my belt to come to back to me.

Cobb and the guards are still tugging, and my belt is hanging on, squeezing.... squeezing...

And I'm like: 'Let it go...'

But they're still pulling and it's tighter and tighter...

And me: 'Get the fuck off it...'

Until we've got this crazy tug of war going, with me on one end of my belt, and Cobb and the guards on the other, and in the middle is the Chairman, his head being pulled this way and that, looking like it's going to pop at any minute.

Then *whip* like a snake, the belt slips out of their hands, and off the Chairman's neck, and back to me. Cobb, the Chairman and the guards fuck about falling over each other, and collapse onto the floor.

A kind of gasp goes round the room as if all the slick-back-and-suits've suddenly cottoned on to what I'm doing, but none of them seems in much of a mood to stop me (ha! ha!).

Cobb's shouting, 'No!' like I'm going to listen to him.

Well, to all you skin-rips, greasers, smokes and old-dog werewolves, whatever the fuck all that means... say hello to me – the dogstar...

In one beautiful movement, I've:

Jumped back up on the table.

Ripped off my shirt.

Swung the belt around.

Just before I explode, I can see Cobb, the foxy chick and the two guards... they're starting to pull themselves inside out, just like Skeet's boys did back at the ranch.

The chick (for obvious reasons I'm watching her most closely as I start to burn) rips off her Miss Jones blouse with one hand (by the way, lady, congratulations on those tits)... and with the other hand she's reaching into her mouth and tearing the skin from her head.

And me, as I shut my eyes in the blaze, I just know I'll be changed much quicker than they can be. Then there he is, ladies and gents, my beautiful beast standing four-foot on the table before they've got to cough their insides out completely.

There's cartwheels of spinning fire everywhere. There's screaming, a lot of shouting. There's the smell of smoke now, mixed with the furniture polish and after shave. All the suits-and-boots are trying to make it away from the table.

A couple of them seem to be going into some kind of geriatric change – proper old school werewolf stylie – but at less than a mile an hour. They're nowhere near going to make it to the wolf in time. Some of them are trying to get out of another door at the other end of the room.

I've got to get me out of here.

My big bad dog's got a sniff of clean air. So let's be finding our way up the stairs and out, mate. *What the fuck are we waiting for?*

I stretch my legs (all right, all right, scrabbling a bit on all that varnish until I get my claws ready to pierce holes through the solid wood) and I'm like some heat-seeking missile hurtling towards the door I came through.

Coolio.

I take off a couple of heads as I go. One of the guards (yeah, take that you fat fuck) and a bag of piss and wrinkles in an expensive suit. Sad day for you, Daddy. Man I've got some real problem with authority figures.

Cobb and the foxy lady are still just bags of fuzz and bone (she not so cute with all the fur, I've got to say).

Head down and shoulder barge the door open.

Only one way to go and I can taste these fingers of fresh air amongst all the stale hum of prison stink. The corridor's taking me back up to the cellblock.

Crack!

Through the door at the end of the corridor, up the stairs and... back into the cell block.

Oh, they've heard me coming, the boys.

This is the first time they've seen me four-foot and dog-form and I can tell they're impressed.

'Look at the *size* of him,' Schiebler's saying in his whistle voice.

And I can see the other three standing up at their bars.

I'm just thinking about changing back so I can get some clothes on and get out of this place on two legs, maybe take the boys with me, when:

From behind I hear three skin-rips enter the corridor. Fast at first, on the chase, then suddenly coming to a scratching halt as they see me. I turn to face them, let out a really cool growl, you know, kind of chainsaw pitched down a few notches.

Make yourselves comfortable, boys. This is going to be a hell of a show.

I can tell which is which. Don't ask me how I can tell but I can. The other guard's leading the pack with Cobb and foxy-chick behind. They're going to wait to see what I can do to the uniform before they get involved, I'll place money on that.

They look different from me, similar to each other.

These skin-rips are just like real wolves, bigger, but they do the grey coat, the yellow eyes, same as Skeet's boys, and I'm standing here now watching them watching me thinking that I can have all three of them.

No problem.

Come on then if you think you can take me... Pete's a street-fighter, I've been scrapping in alleys since I could walk. You fancy folk are going to find that I don't play fair. Besides, I've got to get my revenge in for being caught, caged and beaten. Oh yes.

First the guard comes at me.

I can tell he's scared of me by the way he lunges. His heart's not in it. This boy hasn't been in a fight since he last saw his toes. *Oh, I'm going to hurt you for all that roughing up you gave me.*

He comes straight.

It's easy enough for me to move aside and let him glance off me, and I help him along with a swat of one of my paws. I'm turning as he gets back onto his feet, and we lock onto one another. He's trying to grab at my neck with his teeth, so I turn him and lock onto his with mine.

Got you, you fuck!

I pull down on him with all my weight and his legs collapse. I turn him, as he kicks at me and jerks his head to try to break free. He's on his back now. I'm holding on with my jaws just enough to keep him in the lock, but not enough so as to break him. I can see Cobb standing at the end of the corridor, watching... him and the chick just watching. *Not going to come and help then?*

Beneath me, the guard-dog is wide eyed and struggling for breath and there's a kind of rasping whine, the fucking spaniel, as he pleads for his head.

Unlike you I don't take prisoners.

I bite hard into his neck, break the windpipe and cut the jugular and there's blood and bad breath everywhere. Let's leave him to bleed in front of the crowd.

I raise my head and stare at Cobb.

We lock eyes.

From me another deep growl, from him nothing.

Then I'm racing at him and the chick.

The boys are shouting for me. They know what'll happen to them if I don't get them out.

I hit Cobb with full force and his legs buckle under him, but I roll over the top of him and onto my back and before I know it the bitch is on me, snarling and slavering in my face, her jaws snapping, trying to take a chunk out of my nose or my cheek.

I'm trying to knock her off by twisting my body and lashing at her with my paws, but she's got herself wedged in between my front legs and although she's not too big, her weight's enough to keep me down, I haven't got any strength pinned flat like this.

Cobb shakes himself up onto four-paws, and he comes at me.

Fuck, he's going for the belt. I can feel him digging around my stomach with his teeth. *Mind my fucking dick, man, I'll kill you deeed if you touch my dick.* I can get a back leg at him, and I do, knocking him away and taking a slice out of the side of his face.

Now to get the bitch-chick off.

Jesus she's a ball of fucking fury, she really don't like me. Maybe it's time to kiss her back. As she pushes her head towards mine again, I'm too quick. I've got my mouth round hers, her whole muzzle inside my jaws.

It's the lock-on.

She can't breathe.

I clamp hard and I've still got hold of her while I pull myself from under her, and use the strength in my neck to flatten her onto the floor. She lays there straining to get some air, eyes all wide and bloodshot and I can see Cobb standing back, looking at me, not wanting to come any closer because he knows if he does, then I'll break her neck. Snap. *All over darling, we could have been good together.*

Everything's gone quiet now.

The boys are waiting, breathless, to see what's going to happen. People would *pay* for this shit, man.

I growl at Cobb through my mouthful of fur and bitch-spittle. He starts to back off – *yeah, that's right, mate, that's what I'm talking about, back the fuck off and leave me to make my way to the fresh stuff.* He sits on his haunches by the door.

His head hangs and those yellow eyes burn at me.

Chick-wolf is getting desperate for air, starting to twitch. She can't bear the pain of her empty lungs anymore. *Death starting to turn the lights out, baby.*

I'm eye-balling Cobb. He's eye-balling me.

You dare, Cobb's saying through those pretty yellers, you dare.

OK.

'Ave it your way.

I spit the bitch's face out.

She yelps as she rolls away, heaving for air. My teeth have made perfect holes in her face.

That second, exactly at that moment – Christ he must have seen the muscles flex in my face as I started to let her go – Cobb explodes off his haunches and along the corridor towards me.

And right at the same time, I'm launching myself at him. Forget the girl, this is about me and you, you bastard. Me and you and my dogstar belt.

I can see the smells of it all, sweat and fear and excitement, Cobb and his scorching rage. And the girl as well, I can hear and smell her, back in chick-shape, no clothes, holding her blood-smeared, punctured face in her hands.

All the time, the air is getting thinner, cleaner, sharper.

Cobb's grey wolf; my big, black dog.

Then:

We hit.

I roar as I feel his jaws clamp onto my neck.

Turning – an instant reaction – to try to swipe at him with a wolf-fist, I lose my balance and we tumble across the floor, locked together. We bowl into the bars on Sal's cell and the force of it knocks the door clean off.

There's lots of rolling around and barking and snapping and growling, and going at each other, getting each other into a matt of blood. He's got my throat and I'm twisting my head trying to release it and go for his. Then he's digging at my belt scar with the claws on his back feet, and I'm starting to think that the fucker's got me.

Sal's out of his cell, and he's found a set of keys hanging up and is letting the rest of the gang out of theirs too.

At the other end of the corridor, not-so-foxy chick is standing, naked and bloody, in the doorway (*not being funny, but your face looks a mess, babe*) and she's screaming:

'Kill him! Fucking kill him!'

I'm bigger than him, I'm stronger than him, but he's a wiry fucker.

He's getting to me. My one-lung's fit to burst. *Shit, man, I'm out of practice being the dog.*

He's really starting to hurt me.

My belly's opened up and I can hear his claws catching on the dogstar.

We're slipping in pools of my blood.

He's on me, clamped to my neck.

The bitch-chick is screaming.

'You're fucking dead. You're going to fucking die for this.'

And the boys at the other end are shouting too. Telling me to get out.

'Let it go, Pete. He's got you, man.'

Aw, shit, I can't get myself out of this, I'm stuck to the fucker.

Is that what you want?

You want to really get stuck to me?

Well, you asked for it.

I arch my back and pull Cobb towards me in a bear hug as he throttles me.

I'm pulling him right in to me, until we're fur to fur, almost skin to skin.

That's it, you bastard.

Now see how you like this.

And I bring on the change.

This is a burn rather than a boom.

Searing heat.

I'm a-fucking-blaze.

Then Cobb lights up like a candle, man.

I can smell him burning, hair and flesh. I feel his jaws release and hear him screaming, but I keep hold of the fucker until the burn's gone and we're all ash.

We're melted together.

The stench is making me wretch. He's still alive. In a bad way, though. A non-dog would have died, that's for sure.

I peel him off and push him away.

Well that shut the bitch up (ha! ha!).

I'm up.

Doug's thrown me some clothes.

'Well, what are we waiting for?' I'm saying. 'Let's get out of here.'

And we're off and up the stairs and making our way to the fresh air, my one-lung exploding in my chest.

Forty-three

We come out onto the street.

It's where we were brought out a couple of days ago – all clean city smells – but it's evening now, and damp with fog in the air, like we're looking through water.

'Let's get the fuck out of here,' I say to the rest of them.

'Where?' Schiebler says, in one of his panics.

'Who gives a shit where,' Douglas is shouting this time. 'Anywhere!'

This place is empty.

No cars, no-one walking the streets. The air is still.

There's lights on behind the glass in all the scrapers scraping the fuzzy sky. I can hear music and laughter and I can smell beer that must be coming from a pub somewhere round here. There's food too, I can't tell what, my nostrils being trained up to make out fish and chips and curry and Pot Noodles only.

Where the fuck are we now, anyway?

I'm saying this to myself, rather than out loud. With all the things I've had to think about over the last few days – that there's other dogs, that I'm in prison, that they've taken my belt, that they want me dead – well, with all those things to think about I haven't given much thought to *where* the fuck I am.

I mean, this ain't the Links, right?

This is a place for fancy people like the suits back down in their boardroom, like Skeet, like the Chairman, like Clara… and for the briefest of seconds I'm thinking about her and making a promise to myself that our paths are going to cross again before this story's out.

This is *my* City. Where I've been dragged up and made a wolf, and learned to rob and fight and fuck, and I've always known there were smart and rich types, you know from TV and that, but I've never seen where they live and where they work. *Fuck me, they have us well walled in, don't they, these fuckers?*

And then I realise we're being watched ...

Through the fog, there's a pair of yellow eyes, then another, and then more, and that low growl multiplied by who knows how many, and oh crap, here we go again.

We edge our way along the glass wall, away from those eyes and growls, and down the street, but slowly, because they might strike at any minute, and something's telling us that there's more where they came from – maybe even too many for Pete to fight (ha! ha!). And we're doing this when we're seeing more eyes and hearing more growls this time at the other end of the street.

'We're surrounded...' Schiebler doing his thing.

Across the road is an alleyway, and I can see – sense – through the gloom, that there's one of those metal, fire escape ladders hanging down into it, and that if we can get across to there and up the ladder we've got a chance.

'Over the road...' I whisper this so the boys can hear, I don't know whether the yellow-eyed dogs can too.

'Let's go,' Sal says, and him and Schiebler and Matti and Doug are racing across the road, with me hanging back just enough to see what the dogs'll do, and in that moment, the door we came up through – from the prison – slams open again, and there's Cobb, all burnt to shit, red raw, man, still almost smoking from the barbecue I've given him and he turns and sees me, and sees the others almost across the road, and he shouts at his dogs, his voice sounding as though his neck's still on fire:

'Let them go – but not him!' he's pointing a stump of a fist at me. 'I want him *dead*!'

'Go!' I'm shouting after the boys, because Doug and Matti are half stopping to stay behind with me and fight.

'Fuck off, and I'll catch up with you.'

I stare at the yellow eyes and at Cobb.

Which one of you fuckers is going to try it first, eh?

And I can tell that news of me being the only man ever to down a dog has got round quick, because none of these dogs wants to jump cover and try me. *Everyone wants someone else to have a go, do they?*

The problem is, I know that if they *all* break cover – *when* they all do – I am fuckedy fucked. There's got to be fifty of these bastards, all wanting to be the one that takes Pete and his black dog down.

So I'm looking round, along at Cobb and at each pair of yellow eyes hanging in the grey air, and then I'm looking up.

Up.

I get you.

Of course.

It's the only way, right?

And then I turn myself to face my reflection in the glass, and before the dogs can make it to the fight, I'm climbing the side of this scraper thinking I could do with a belt that turns me into a monkey, not a wolf.

Forty-four

You've got me, I'm climbing – Spider-Man stylie – up the side of this fifty storey tower. All blue-black glass and full of office-types looking out the window wondering what the fuck's happening, alarms going off inside and that.

Down below, you can just about see them through the fog, it's Cobb's skin-rips on the streets, and some of them are trying to make their way up the building on the outside, wolf-form, and others are heading back inside and coming for me up stairs. And as well as the alarm, everywhere inside there's screaming and chaos, and I can see smoke beginning to pour out through the doors where we got out, where my change has set fire to something (as well as Cobb, ha! ha!).

You see, there's good news and bad news, right?

The good news, I've got my dogstar belt back. I have my beautiful belt back inside me, cutting through the skin, his wolf's head snug under my belly button where he belongs. And though I'm man form now, I've just had another taste of being changed to a dog, and the strength of it is coursing through my veins, like I'm still on fire, and I'm climbing the glass face of the tower, hand over hand, fingers gripping the gaps between the window panes, as though it were a ladder.

So that's the good news.

The bad news is...

Actually, fuck the bad news.

You know me well enough by now.

You know me well enough to know that, as bad as it looks, on my way up, not down, and being chased by fifty or so of Cobb's dogs, inside and outside the tower... well, you know me well enough by now to know that I'll find a way out of it.

Of course I'll find a way out of it.

Forty-five

Oh, this is fun!

I surprise myself how quick I get up the side of the building.

With my belt back under my skin, I'm strong.

I can smell smoke from the fire, where the sparks flying off my Cobb-hugging change have set a burn going, and those prison cells of ours are going up in flames. I can hear screaming from inside the building – people are still at work, man – where some of Cobb's dogs have decided to go back inside and come up for me, hoping maybe that my plan is to crawl in through a window or something.

Plan?

Fuck plans.

I can hear the scrabbling of claws, and splitting of metal and glass, as others are chasing me up the glass. And the howling and yipping of a whole load more who are waiting down in the street, expecting that I'll lose my grip and take a tumble, and that they'll be able to shred me up when I do.

And then as I get closer to the top of the scraper, I can see more yellow eyes looking down, peering at me from over the edge of the roof. More growling and glaring and slavering and that.

Whichever way I look, I've got Cobb's dogs.

Inside, outside, above and below.

I stop climbing.

Well I can hang on here for a while, but sure as fuck they can hang around inside and up top and on the street longer than me, even if the climbers might have to give in.

So, I ask myself, *what's it going to be then, eh?*

Up and down, there's yellow eyes staring at me through glass.

Yellow eyes below.

Yellow eyes above.

I've got burning yellow eyes dancing round my head, and it feels like it's going to explode.

What's it going to be then, eh?

Explode.

(I can hear the slick producer groan and mention something about the budget).

All this glass. All these eyes.

And me, Pete, a human dog-bomb.

So explode it is.

I take a look around, and there... I can see the boys.... on top of the building with the fire escape ladder, a dozen storeys up.

And I'm thinking that it's... what?... a hundred feet away. Maybe three hundred feet down.

Do you think I can bounce a change off the side of this scraper and make that distance? Do you think I can survive that kind of fall?

Well. There's only one way to find out.

I hang on with my arms, kick off my shoes, and walk my bare feet up the glass until I'm tucked, as far as I can be, into a ball.

A few deep breaths.

Bring...

Breathe.

...on...

Breathe.

...the...

Breathe.

...change.

There's a fizzing roar, searing every cell in my body. It builds to a sonic boom, and I feel myself thrown with force away from the side of the building

At the same time there's a crack like thunder.

The whole glass face of the scraper is held frozen in time.

Just for a second.

Then it shatters into a million pieces, and falls like rain.

And as I'm hurtling through the air, burning into dog-form, I can hear the screaming of Cobb's dogs inside and out being showered with splinters. And then I hit the floor hard, and feel my body break. It's a chaos of smoke and broken glass and gushing blood. And I'm lying there, sensing all of this, but feeling it move further and further away into the distance.

But as it all disappears into darkness, there's the far-away sound of a heart beating – Cobb's heart – full of hatred and wanting revenge, and I know that even if I do survive this, even if this fall hasn't broken me so badly I can't live through it; this is not going to be over until one of us is dead.

HEROES

Forty-six

I'm in so much pain, the voices are hard to make out. Like I'm under water, like the words are hollowed out so I can't grasp what they mean.

I can feel the warmth of fire on my back. My front, facing away from it, is cold, and although I'm lying on something – a blanket or some clothes in bundles – the earth is even colder beneath me. As well as the wood-burn smell of the smoke, there's something else – something that reminds me, vaguely, of this stuff that Debs used to clean our toilet with, back on the Links, back when she was alive, back when I was Pete and only Pete. Without thinking, I reach down and run my hand over the wolf's head under my skin. Still there.

The voices I can hear are beginning to become more distinct. I can hear Schiebler's whining, whistle-voice, Sal's cigar-rasp, Doug's boom and, very occasionally, Matti's calm but breathless whisper.

I remember the fall. From the scraper, with all that exploding glass, and all the screaming and the blood. I remember hitting concrete. And my body breaking.

Who knows how long I've been out?

Everything's been broken. I can feel where the breaks were. My shoulder – the right one – and the top of the arm, the ball that fits into the socket. They were shattered. My right leg too, the top and the bottom bones. And my skull. Along the side of my forehead, and my cheekbone. All cracked, and shattered in places.

But I can tell that it's all been knitting itself back together.

My good dog blood has been pumping around Pete's body and fixing what needs fixing.

It's OK to wake up now. You're mended.

But I'm thinking to lay there and listen to what's being discussed...

SCHIEBLER: We shouldn't have come here...

What the fuck's he moaning about now?

DOUG: Well, *you* didn't need to come here.

SAL: This is the last place they'll expect us to be.

SCHIEBLER: It's still too much of a risk...

DOUG: Not for me, it's not. And not for him either...

MATTI: I have to have my dog-skin back.

SCHIEBLER: You know Cobb will hunt us down, don't you? He won't just give up... especially not now.

SAL: I'm not so worried about Cobb... he didn't look so good last time we saw him (and he laughs).

SCHIEBLER: (he's getting more and more worked up) But we'll be on the run... forever...

DOUG: So what, shall we hand ourselves in? After you. Got a bit of a track record, haven't you?

SCHIEBLER: Fuck you.

They're quiet for a moment. I can hear one of them dragging a stick across the fire, raking up the embers, and then throwing more wood onto it.

SCHIEBLER: (quietly) It's not *us* Cobb's after *really*, is it?

DOUG: What? (beginning to lose it)

SCHIEBLER: It isn't *us* that Cobb really wants.

SAL: So we turn *him* in?

SCHIEBLER: I'm just saying...

DOUG: If it wasn't for *him* we'd all be locked up still. Or worse...

SCHIEBLER: Yes, but...

DOUG: (raising his voice) *You'd* be dead, Schiebler. He saved your life and you want to turn him into Cobb... ?

SAL: (laughing) Are you *kidding*? You're kidding, right?

SCHIEBLER: What about you, Matti? Tell me I'm not the only one thinking this...

All eyes must be turning to Matti. He sighs – I hear the gentle rush of air over the crackling of the fire – and takes time to think before he speaks, like he always does.

MATTI: I am *not* with you. Give him some time to mend, and then he'll know what to do. For my part, while we're rested up here, I will go and get my skin back.

DOUG: I'm with *you*. If you're happy for me to hitch a ride, I'll come with you to score some grease.

It's at this point that I make like I'm waking up, all yawning and stretching and that, then rolling over and sitting myself up. Out of the corner of my eye, I see a look on Schiebler's face, something like: oh fuck, I hope he didn't hear all that, and I'm throwing back just enough of a flicker of: yes I did you fuck, so you better watch yourself.

'Where the fuck are we?' I say.

Schiebler's all nicey nicey now: 'You've been in and out for a couple of days...'

'Where are we now?' I ask again.

'You'd better ask them.' He nods towards Matti and Doug.

'So?'

'We are a three and a half miles from Gideon Skeet's Estate-' Matti starts.

'And these two,' Schiebler interrupts, 'are planning on breaking in...'

'Is that right?' I'm saying.

'That *is* right.' This is Douglas.

Matti says: 'Skeet has something of mine. My dog-skin is part of his collection now. I would like it back.'

Doug: 'And they say he's got enough grease to fill a stadium. I'm planning on going with Matti and getting myself set.'

'Just the two of you?' I ask.

'That's the plan,' Doug says.

'What's to drink? I'm fucking thirsty,' I say, realising my throat is all cracked and dried.

Schiebler tips from a kettle next to the fire and passes me a mug. *Tea. Fucking hell. When was the last time Pete had a cup of tea?* It's hot and sickly sweet, and I gulp it down. I'm going to need more.

'What about Cobb?' Schiebler says.

'What about him?' I snap back.

'He's going to be looking for you... for us,' he corrects himself.

'Let him look. I need some time to think about Cobb.' Last time I saw *him* we had a blazing row (ha! ha!). 'In the meantime, I'm thinking it's a bit fucking rude of you two to fuck off on your own to raid Skeet's pad...'

Schiebler groans.

'What, were you going to let me sleep through it and miss all the fun?'

Sal falls to that chainsaw laugh of his.

'Oh yes,' I say. 'That fucker locked me up in a cage and set his dogs on me. Let me be honest and say I'm bearing a grudge... What were you planning?'

'In and out, quietly,' Matti says. 'Take back what is ours.'

They're all looking at me.

'I think we can plan for a little bit more trouble than that. I'm in the mood for some revenge for the way he treated us...'

But what I don't say is that I'm in the mood for something else. For bumping into that mighty fine wife of his, and seeing if I can't steal something more precious from Skeet than an old dog-skin and some grease.

Forty-seven

Me, I'm ready to go at this thing half-cocked. But I've got something to learn from the gang, even if they seem to have set me up as top dog – the man in charge (ha! ha!).

You see, we're robbers all of us. You know about Pete, scourge of drug dealers all over London, parted of their cash and occasionally their heads. Matti Sandhorn, born a thief, who loves the fun of it more than what he gets out of it. For him, it's the stealing and not the booty that counts. Doug, okay more of a mugger, but even at his level, still all about relieving a man of his things, in Doug's case usually a wallet and enough cash for a few pints and a packet of puffs. Sal, well his thing is stealing other men's women. I just don't see him getting half as much pleasure from poking his own as he does boning someone else's, dirty bastard.

And Schiebler.

Well, you probably wouldn't think Schiebler a robber like the rest of us. But he is. He likes to thieve the joy and happiness out of every fucking thing. As bad a thief as any of the rest of us – if not worse.

This is exactly what he's doing now. Just at the same time that Matti is trying to teach Pete some new tricks.

'If we are going to do this,' he's saying, 'let's do it properly. And that means planning it... Not just rushing in...'

'What you trying to say?' I'm laughing. This is getting to be fun. All those months of working the Sink Estates *alone*, I've never really given much thought to what it would be like being part of a gang. I'm thinking about what we're going to do at Skeet's and I'm beginning to wonder what else we could do – all together, like. A gang of thieves.

Dog-thieves.

Moonlight robbery and all that (ha! ha!).

'... or let's not do it at all...' Schiebler's interrupting again.

Right, I've had enough of this.

I stand up, and let the heat come over me. Just enough, but not so much as to bring on a change. I can feel the first few wisps of smoke rising from my skin.

Schiebler's looking up at me, suddenly shitting himself that he's pushed it too far.

'Fuck off and get in the van,' I say to him.

He starts to complain and I just fix him with a proper look.

'OK,' he says.

He's up into the driver's seat proper quick.

It's pretty fucking ripe in there now, what with it having been a week now since the boys nicked it, and with all five of us sleeping in it, and us being parked in the woods like this, well, let's just say there are five hairy dogs that need to get cleaned up.

Then he's slamming the door shut behind him, and winding down the window, half for the fresh air and half so he can still earache our conversation and throw in a barb now and then.

'Carry on,' I say to Matti.

'I like to get in and out quietly. With no trouble,' he says. 'So we scout the Estate, work out who comes and goes and when, analyse the defences, identify the weak points...'

'No trouble,' I'm nodding, and if I'm honest, this is something that's never really occurred to me before.

The idea is that we split into three. Me, I want to stay close to Schiebler, so I suggest that me and him stick together. Sal and Doug do the same and Matti's happy to be by himself – I'm guessing he's used to doing things that way and he likes it.

Matti's drawing maps in the dirt with a stick and doing his planning things, and I'm losing interest. My mind is wandering thinking about her – and a little bit I'm asking myself what's going on because I'm less interested in what she might look like without the coat and the jumper and jeans and boots on, and more interested in making pictures in my head about me laying there looking at her, pictures where we're talking to each other and I'm listening to what she's saying rather than just concerning myself with warm and wet.

I've got to get out of here.

'So is everyone clear?'

Where the fuck've I been?

'Pete,' Matti's saying. 'Is it all clear?'

I haven't got a clue what he's been saying.

'Yeah, all clear.'

It's beginning to get dark. The fire's burnt down to red and orange embers. My bones are aching with the cold.

'If we're going to be up that early, I'm turning in,' Doug says, and there's a murmur of agreement. I'm gathering that Schiebler's already asleep in the back of the van.

'I'm going to sit up for a bit,' I say.

I'm kicking the coals up into a pile with my boots and putting another log on the fire. I want some more time with Clara.

It's got to be half an hour or so before I can hear that the others have gone to sleep – all quiet apart from Doug's rattling snore. My excuse is that I've just woken up from a couple of days out cold after the fall. I'm wide awake sitting staring at the flames, throwing on more wood, until I get a great crackling roar. And that I'm sitting there thinking about her almost all night, until the fire starts to die down, and finally I drift off to sleep.

I've got to get out of here.

In my dream I can hear the cracking of twigs from the fire. We're all in cages, each one of us. And we need a big bad wolf to break us out. Me, I'm pressing my face against the bars as the wolf approaches, moving from cage to cage, sniffing around and working out who he's going to set free. I can feel the cold metal of the cage against my skin, and there's a voice…

'Don't move…'

My face is hard against the bars.

'Quiet and don't move…'

I'm completely still.

Then it seems that the voice, and the cold metal… they're not inside my dream but somewhere else, and as I glide back upwards – to meet them – I snap into consciousness and realise the metal is the end of a gun, and the voice belongs to a face I've seen somewhere before.

Forty-eight

'Well, hello again.'

The geezer with the gun I recognise from Skeet's house. The voice, well that belongs to Gideon Skeet himself, standing somewhere behind gun-boy. And just as he's saying this, a bunch of his other boys are wrenching open the back of the van. There's some shouting, and Doug's leapt out and getting ready to try using his fists against the guns they've got, when he sees me pinned to the ground with a shotgun at my head.

'Probably not a good idea, mate,' I'm trying to say to him.

It all calms down.

This isn't going to be a fair fight.

Even if I *could* get to dog form before my head gets blown off, the rest of the boys'll be dead before they change. We're fucked.

'You're full of surprises,' and this time Skeet's laughing. 'My father-in-law's in hospital because of that belt of yours. You made a *real* mess of Cobb.' He sounds *very fucking* pleased when he says this bit. 'You've caused several million pounds worth of damage to the Bank's property. You've brought unnecessary attention to us...' *Okay, he seems less pleased at this point.* 'And caused me a lot of work...'

He walks over to where I'm lying. He motions to shotgun-boy who slowly, like he doesn't altogether want to, lifts the barrel of the gun off my face.

'And now you turn up here again.'

Skeet's looking down at me. His face is all cheekbones and glassy, grey eyes. His teeth are grit hard, and I can see the pulse of a vein in his temple. Then the tension drains, and his mouth softens into a smile.

The next thing he's holding out a hand, offering to pull me up. I'm wary at first, but he nods at me.

'Come on,' he says.

I reach up and he pulls me onto my feet. He's strong.

His men have still got the gang held up, and I'm just about to notice that Schiebler isn't there with him, when I spot him standing about twenty yards behind Skeet trying to hide himself in the trees. He clocks that I've seen him, and shrinks back into the shadows, and Skeet clocks it at the same time...

'He did the right thing,' he says.

'Really?' I say.

'This isn't what you think.'

'Isn't it?'

'No,' then as if to convince me, he's telling his men to stand down, which they do although they don't really seem all that happy about it.

'I don't want a fight,' he's saying to me.

'You wouldn't win one,' I'm firing back.

He laughs, but his eyes are steel, not laughing with him.

'Why would I want to fight? You've done me a favour...'

I'm shrugging.

'You don't get it, do you? The old men are out of the way. I'm next in line...'

He's still got hold of my hand.

'Come on,' he says. 'I've got a proposition for you. Come back to the Estate. This time... you'll be my guest.'

I go to pull my hand out of his, and his grip tightens.

'What do you say?' he says.

It's my turn to laugh.

'Well, what the fuck?' I say. 'Why not? We were on our way to see you anyway. You've got some stuff that belongs to us.'

So we're off, out of the woods and onto one of the tracks where there are cars waiting, and the boys are raising eyebrows at me as they come alongside, and I'm making at them as if to say don't worry, I've got this, and then, as I pass Schiebler he doesn't want to look me in the eyes and I smile at him making sure to show him my teeth.

Forty-nine

This time, as we plough up the gravel drive, I get to see the front of Skeet's place. Fancy me, little skank from the Links, dragged up in muck and mud, getting an invite through the front door of a place like this. All mowed lawns, tree-lined paths and bushes shaped into squares, and as we come closer to the house, the size of it, man... I mean, I knew it was big from when we were here before, but from further away – approaching it, like – this is a guy whose house and garden is ten times bigger than the whole of the Links... the whole of *my world* growing up.

We rock up at the front, and this time, we're taken into the house.

Through the front door.

And there I'm staring up and around at all these old paintings, and thick, velvet curtains, and these wooden carvings clinging on to the biggest staircase I've ever seen that goes snaking away upwards into the distance.

Skeet stops us in the hall.

'Thanks to you,' he says, with the steel eyes and the smile that doesn't fit, 'I have urgent business to take care of in London today. I'll be back this evening. I want us to talk then, OK?'

'All right,' I'm nodding.

'In the meantime, get cleaned up... make yourselves at home...' This last bit I can tell he's straining to say it in a nice way, like he actually means it, but I'm smiling back and saying thanks like a good dog. He's used to getting his own way. Whatever he's got up those expensive cuffs, I'll bide my time, and listen.

See, Matti, your friend Pete is learning some patience.

'Show them their rooms,' he says and then he's back out the front door with a bunch of his cronies, and we can hear the crunch of gravel and roar of car engines as they head out and off.

The geezer with the shot gun has stayed behind, and him and this old girl who's appeared from nowhere show us upstairs, and we're walking along a corridor about a mile long, and one-by-one being let into a bedroom. Matti's first, and as they open the door, and he walks in, there's his dog-skin laid out over the bed. The old girl's saying make yourself comfortable, ring the bell if you need anything and they'll bring us up food, and that Mr Skeet has asked – as a gesture of good-will – that we confine ourselves to our rooms until he gets back. Doug's next and in his room – his eyes nearly popping out of that great Jock head of his – there's bottles of what I can only guess is grease by the way he's acting like an addict who's been let back into a crack-den after a few clean months. Then Sal, then Schiebler and finally me.

As I sit down on the bed, and the old girl closes the door, I hear a key turn in the lock.

Prisoners again. But this time with a smile. So this is how it's going to be.

At least it's an upgrade from my last cell (ha! ha!).

The bed for a start. A proper bed, a double (at least) and it's got some kind of canopy hanging over it. And next to it a chair, with a pile of clean clothes on it, which I guess are meant for me. Fair enough. I am pretty ripe with days of no-washing and still all the sweat and blood and smoke from the escape.

There's a door leading off the room, so I pop my head in and see it's a bog with a bath and shower. I can get cleaned up here. But first I need some proper sleep in a proper bed. It's got to have been... what? I don't even know how long it is since I slept in a bed. I'm looking forward to this. Pete's crawling under the sheets and blankets and tucking himself up all nice like a baby and falling asleep within seconds.

And that way, the first I know of anything again is when there's a knock at the door, and then a key in the lock, and a sweet young thing comes in carrying a tray with food and drink on it. I flash her a smile from the bed, and she blushes and puts the munchies down and hurries back out again. I can hear her running down the corridor, all flustered, forgetting that she didn't lock my door again on the way out.

Well, no hurry on my part.

Nosh first, then a bath. Then maybe a look around. I'm sure my new friend Gideon won't mind.

The food's good. I've dealt with that pretty sharpish, and I'm guzzling more sweet tea, and I can feel all of this doing my broken-but-healing-up bones the world of good. Then I'm in the shower, and scrubbed clean, and I've thrown on some of the clothes from the pile by my bed and I'm ready to explore.

Careful opening up the door. Turning the handle all quiet, like, and then I'm checking up and down the corridor to see if anyone's around. *Clear.*

Which way? Well I'm thinking back to the stairs, the ones that looked like they were making their way up forever, and seeing where they take me. There isn't a sound. My dog-ears are just about picking up some deep breathing – must be the boys, all sleeping off their lunch. All five of us knackered after cracking our way out of prison then trying to sleep in the back of a van for days and nights.

Back at the stairs.

I'm noticing now, inlaid into the dark wood, there are these pictures – carved out, neat and tidy – that run up the bannisters. Wolves chasing wolves, racing along higher and higher, and so I decide to follow them upwards and see where they go.

I'm also becoming aware of something in the air.

I mean, I can feel cold draughts running up and down the stairs – I'm guessing you get that in old places like this, currents of air, bringing a chill with them and taking it away. But although you've got the cold, you've also got a core of hot, sweet, heavy air too. The higher I go, the thicker the air gets with a fug of it.

The further I go, I begin to see the smell too, spirals of it moving together, spinning along with the drafts. I feel almost like I'm going to drift off with it, and I have to give myself a talking to and wake myself back up.

It's still completely silent. Like I'm in a vacuum and the rest of the house and the outside don't exist. Nothing here. No human or dog scent, no sound of a beating heart or lungs expanding and collapsing. And all the while that dreamy smell's making its way down inside me.

I'm up the wooden staircase to the next floor, here things open right out, and I find myself in some kind of hall. Fuck me, it's almost hard to breathe, the air feels like water. It's making my head spin.

All around the walls of the hall there are pictures – not paintings, these are made of cloth, sewn and threaded – of dogs and people, dogs of all different kinds: four-foot, two-foot, ones that look like wolves and ones that look more like bears, and ones that are standing right up and wearing armour and holding axes in their hands. There's fighting going on, and people being cut up and bitten up, and spurts of blood (faded and brown) and heads rolling around the place, and swords and arrows and that kind of stuff.

It's weird, man, it's kind of freaking me out.

I'm feeling a tightening round my throat. Like the ghost of being strangled.

The smell, the thick, liquid air, these weird pictures.

'Soon I will come back for my belt.'

What the fuck?

They sound real somehow, but the words are inside my head.

'Aren't you supposed to be in your room?'

A different voice.

Crystal cutting through the gloom.

I'm stuck for a second, asking myself whether I've heard it or not. Whether this is inside my head too.

I turn round.

At first, I can't see her face. She's standing with her back to one of the windows that run along one side of the hall. There's sudden, bright light behind her, as if the sun's come out from behind clouds. She's a silhouette. A perfect silhouette.

She's wearing a dress, and the light's shining through it, and through her hair, so it looks like she's got the haze of an aura around her, and I can see the shape of her dark against it.

Then the sun slips away and my eyes adjust and the silhouette fades, and it's as if she's stepping into the hall through it. She's looking at me and not looking at me at the same time. There's a curl of a smile on her lips. Those green eyes have me pinned down, I feel like I can't move, man…

'I'm just taking a look around,' I say.

'I see,' she says.

This is Pete knocked flat.

She knows it. She had me back that night when I was locked up and she put her bet on me. She knows it.

'You've made quite an impression… ' she comes back at me, after we've stood looking at each other from some time. And just in that, she falters, I see it, even though she tries to cover it,' … on my husband and his friends.'

'Really?' I say.

'So you've come here to talk…'

'I didn't have much choice.'

The smile saddens, and she looks away for the first time.

'That's how my husband…' she searches for a word, '… operates.'

'Is it?' I say.

She brings her eyes back up to mine.

'Yes.'

I've got to get out of here.

'Well,' I'm feeling this and feeling that I'm picking myself up from the knock-down. 'I'm kind of used to doing my own thing.'

She laughs.

'Yes, maybe you and my husband are the same in that respect. Which could make things interesting... I should thank you by the way... for the money I won at the hunt...'

'You're welcome...'

'And I know that Gideon is grateful...'

She's digging me, man.

'That you put my father in hospital...'

She's detached. Seems like her and Dad aren't all that chummy.

'The Chairman, right?'

She nods.

'Not so much me as my belt – didn't take kindly to the idea of being destroyed...'

'Father,' she sighs, 'has a tendency to destroy anything he doesn't understand... or can't control.'

And I'm thinking suddenly back to those Bruno boys, the ones that knifed me and got beat up, and we all ended up in hospital, and how their families were in and out every five minutes bringing nosh and presents and loving kindness. And I'm guessing that Clara's not back and forwards up to hospital to see her old man, and that maybe in some ways she's just as happy as Skeet that he's going to be out of the way.

I'm just about to say something, when we hear that crunch of car tyres on gravel, and I can tell from her reaction that Skeet's back and our conversation is over.

'I'd better get back...' I say.

'To see what plans my husband has for you,' she says, as if finishing my sentence.

I go to make my way down the stairs.

'You don't need to worry about me – '

'I'm not,' she cuts in, just a little bit too harsh, like she does care really.

'I'm sure your husband's got *his* thing in mind...' and here I pause for just a second, 'but I've got my *own* ideas about how this is going to play out.'

There's just a flash of red across her cheeks.

'See you later,' and I'm away.

Fifty

I'm just about back in my room before the knock comes, the door opens and the old girl's there telling me that Mr Skeet is back and requiring my company and I'm all, like, stretching and yawning as if I've been asleep, although I can tell she's looking at me with a raised eyebrow because the door wasn't locked and she's wondering whether it's all an act and if I've been out where I shouldn't be. But she's probably thinking better not to say anything, better she doesn't know.

Skeet's in the hall where I was chatting with Clara. No sign of her, although I can catch the scent of her – just – faintly running through the air.

He's all suited and booted, but he's taking off his jacket and tie and slinging them over a chair, and coming to me and shaking my hand. *Shaking my hand.* Who the fuck shakes people's hands? No-one where I'm from and that's a fact.

There's cuties running in and out laying tables with food and booze, all happening around Gideon but he's acting as if he can't see any of it. They're invisible.

My guess is, if I didn't have a belt and a big black dog with claws and teeth of steel, I'd probably be invisible to him too.

'I have some friends round tonight,' he says to me. 'Some of the lads. I'd like you and yours to join us. We can talk...'

And he breaks off because the room's starting to fill up with his boys and he's off shaking their hands too. I recognise some of them from the hunt, and I can see one or two of them giving me looks like they're not too pleased to see me here. A couple of times Skeet puts a hand on an arm or a shoulder and almost looks at me while he's whispering something in their ear.

Me, I've asked for a beer, and although that asking was met by a blank expression as if no-one round here has ever asked for beer before, eventually I've got some, and I settle into a corner to watch what's going on.

Not long after, my boys are shown into the room.

Douglas starts piling up plates of nosh and grabs a whole bottle of whiskey that's sitting on the side – uncouth, man, you can't take him anywhere (ha! ha!) – the others are a bit more used to polite society. They're neater and tidier, and don't feel the need to stuff their gullets.

We all sit together.

'What does he want?' Schiebler asks in a low voice. 'What's he said to you?'

I throw him a look which says I don't think he's in a position to ask questions.

'I'll deal with Skeet,' I say. 'And I'll deal with you later.'

The ice-blue eyes burn a little then he looks away.

'We could make it out of here, now I've got grease and Matti's got his skin back. We'd be a match for these fuckers,' Doug says, mouth full.

'I know that,' I say. 'I know that, but I want to see what he's got up his sleeve first.'

'He's a tricky,' Sal says.

'So am I,' I smile. And we carry on noshing and drinking.

Skeet's boys are knocking back the good stuff too, and by the look of them, that's not all. There's white lines everywhere and joints being sparked up. I realise how long it's been, and how clean and clear I am since those days. Fucked if I'd ever get back into that shit again.

There's music playing now, and the lights've been turned down, and there's girls – I can smell them as well as see them – all hot and excited with the thought of the shagging and the fat wallets that'll come out afterwards.

A couple of them come over to us. They're absolutely fucked, and I guess they have to be or else they're going to start realising that they're in a hall full of hungry dogs, and the starters have been knocked back, and they're going to be the main course. I say no, nice and polite like. Doug might've given them a go left to his own devices, but for different reasons none of the rest of us is all that interested.

'What the fuck?'

There's a few of Skeet's boys bringing on some kind of change, kicking off with orange burning eyes. But it's slo-mo, man. Like they're going to inch into dog.

'They're old-dogs... *werewolves*,' Matti says over the noise of the music and the boys laughing and the girls shrieking and giggling.

'What d'you mean?'

'Like Schiebler. Old school dogs,' Doug says laughing. 'Problem is, it takes them hours to make the change, doesn't it Schiebler?'

'Fuck you. At least I make a proper dog.'

'Well if that rangy two-legged fox is your idea of a dog, yes.'

And Schiebler's just about to go to back for more with Doug when I shut him up.

'So this is going to turn into hunt, right? Like before...' I say.

At this point, Skeet comes over to cut in.

'Less a hunt, than a slaughter,' he says stone-faced, then he cracks one of his half-smiles. 'You want to talk now?'

'Now's as good a time as any.'

I get up, raising a hand to let the others know that I'm going to deal with this myself. Around the room, there's bottles of grease. *That's what the air's thick with.* And what with the music and the half-light, it's becoming more and more difficult to see what's going on.

We leave the hall and we're off down a corridor, the music and laughter fading, until we get to what must be Skeet's office. He motions at me to sit down, so I do, all nicey.

There's a painting on the wall behind his desk, and he opens it up like a door, and spins a dial behind it a few times, then another door opens – a safe – and he's pulling out a box of something. I've got just enough time, and am managing to peek without him noticing, to see that there's what looks like a pile of cash in the safe, and that he's so keen to fire up he doesn't close any of it properly. He sits down on the other side of this fuck-off big leather desk he's got, opens up the box and starts cutting himself a line of the white stuff.

'My private stash. The best. You want some?' he asks.

'I've given up.'

'Good,' he says. 'Better that you don't.'

He's snorting through a rolled up twenty until his eyes look like they're going to burst out the front of his face. Then he pinches his nose, closes those peepers for a second and comes back to the room.

'So tell me about your belt,' he says, and this greedy look casts a shadow across his face.

You want it, don't you.

'Nothing to tell.'

He wants to ask me more, I know he does. But he thinks better of it.

'OK, however you want to play it…. Then I'll get straight to the point,' he says as he pours us both a drink.

'I appreciate that.'

I'm helping myself to a fag from a box on the table, and giving the grateful one-lung a dark injection.

'What's on your mind?'

He gets up and starts pacing around as he talks, a bit agitated, a little bit coked-out.

'I want you to come and work for me.'

I nearly choke on my cigarette.

'What, all this for a fucking job interview?'

A flash of something dark across his face, then he composes himself. He leans forward across the table, grabbing a fag himself and lighting it.

'I'm looking for a business partner...'

'So what is it you do?' I say.

'It's not what *I* do. It's what you can do I'm interested in.'

'Go on.'

'I'm looking to diversify...'

I must look like I don't know what the fuck he's talking about.

'Look, the old man. The Chairman. His family are dog royalty. They've run the bank for six generations. Nice and safe, under the radar...'

'OK.'

'Afraid of being exposed...'

He slams a hand on the desk.

'Can you believe it?'

No I can't.

'Hiding away. Like... *rabbits* not wolves.'

He's getting really agitated now. Angry, plus all that coke racing through his veins and his brain.

'So getting back to what you want me for...?' I ask.

He fixes me with those steel-eyes.

'You're part of my diversification plans.'

Fuck me, Clara was right. This geezer is used to getting exactly what he wants.

'Thanks to you, the old man is on his way out. There are one or two more I've got to remove before I can take control of the Bank.... move it in some new directions. In the meantime, there are other ways in which we can make money ...'

If he doesn't start speaking English, I swear I'm going to bring on the change and rip his fucking face off.

'I read Cobb's arrest report on you. What you were doing. You know your way around the Estates. You've got contacts into the gangs...'

'I wouldn't say that...'

'More than *we* do. I want to take control of the drug routes. And I want to supply London with grease.'

So this is it. He sees a shaven-headed skank like me, born right on the other side of town, and he's thinking I'm the man for the job. If he read Cobb's report right, he would have got that I was stealing from the drug runners, not working with them. But he won't get it because in his mind we're all the same. If I'd have wanted to be Tony and head up the Crew, then I'd have taken it from him as soon as I got the belt.

Fuck me.

'We'll make a fortune.'

I'm sitting back in my chair, stubbing out my fag in the ashtray on the desk, and I'm thinking: *hasn't this bloke got enough already? What the fuck would he do with more?*

'So what do you say?' he says, without it sounding much as though he's asking me a question.

'It's a hell of an idea,' I say.

And he stands up and holds out his hand again, and I take it. He grips mine like a vice and he's looking right into my eyes, boring into the depths of me. But he sees what he wants to see, laughs and suggests we get back to the party.

'No more work,' he says. 'We can pick this up tomorrow.'

Back in the hall, it's darker and fuggier and full of more laughter and shouting than before, and more than that I can see that Skeet's boys have got to work on the hired help. There's fucking happening before the eating.

We're standing at the entrance, watching it.

He nudges me. 'Make sure you change outside, right? I don't want you setting fire to the tapestries...' and he laughs like he's made a really good joke.

We walk in, and as we do the lights go on. I'm almost blinded.

There's half-turned and full-turned dogs, and amongst them are boys still man-form fucking with the whores, and there's white powder and smoke, and over-turned plates and glasses all over the place. With the lights on suddenly, there's a moment of shock, then one of the whores starts screaming, and some others join in, sobering up real quick.

Gideon rips open his shirt.

'Time for the hunt,' he shouts, then he's ripping himself inside out and becoming a dog.

There's a lot more screaming, and those boys still man-form are doing their skin-rip too. The old-dogs are finally changed into their wolves, and the greasers are making their funny looking man-dogs. The room is fucking full of them.

Girls are pulling on clothes or trying to half cover themselves up, and they're running and tripping and falling down the staircase. The dogs are letting them go, giving them a head start – making it more of a chase.

Gideon's dog turns to me. All yellow-eyed and silver fur.

'I'll be with you,' I say.

And he and his dog-mates start to make their way down after the girls. You can hear the screaming as they race outside, at the back of the house, and as they run and get caught and torn to pieces, and you can hear the yipping and barking and growling of the dogs hunting them down and do the tearing.

I sit down.

You know, it seems to me that me and the Crew – we're a bunch of dirty, low-down criminals, with bad attitudes and bad manners (ha! ha!). Me, I've done lots of things I'm not so proud of. But it ain't that surprising when you think about it, given the shit-hole we grew up in, and the shits who brought us up.

I'm betting that Gideon Skeet's dad didn't cuddle up to him at night like Ken did with me and Debs, and that his Mum didn't puff herself full of junk when he was a baby inside her. I'm betting he's not gone a month without hot water, and a week with not much more to eat than Super Noodles, because the money's been spent on Special Brew and porn mags. I'm betting he didn't have to nick money to buy himself clothes at the market. I'm betting all of that.

These geezers. Every last one of them born with money, and being sent to nice schools, and well looked after, and having all the good things in life.

These posh bastards should know better, shouldn't they?

'What do I say?' I say, half to myself, finally answering Skeet's question. 'I say, fuck you...'

Then I look up and I see Clara standing there, staring at me.

'You were wrong,' I say, getting up and calling to the boys who're all still sitting in the corner having kept clear of everything that's gone on.

'Me and your husband are not the same. We're not the same at all.'

Fifty-one

One:

'You got your skin?' I'm saying to Matti, and he's nodding.

'You got your grease?' and then I'm seeing that Doug's got a bucket-load of it (or what looks like it) where he's been scraping all these little tins and tubs of it and tipping it into a silver bucket what they keep ice and wine in (very fucking fancy).

I turn to Sal.

'Ready?'

He nods.

'And what about you?' I say to Schiebler. 'You still got your bollocks?'

He's suddenly looking a bit green, you know, under his red-top hair, realising the fun's over.

'Look, man...' he starts to say.

'Look what?'

'Look,' his eyes are kind of darting around the group, from one to the other, laughing nervously... 'I was in on it, man, we were all in on it together. I knew Skeet was going to treat us OK, that's why I went to him... yeah, I knew...'

The others are all watching me. Inside I'm thinking this is all pretty funny, Schiebler shitting his pants, and everyone thinking I'm going to tear him apart. So I'm giving nothing away at all.

Clara's got me fixed too.

'Well....' I say, and Schiebler tenses up, getting ready for what's coming. 'You need to work out whose side you're on, don't you?'

He's suddenly all desperate and making out like he's my best friend.

'On your side, man. Of course on your side....'

'You fucked up, didn't you?'

'I did. I totally fucked up.... I'll make it up to you.'

Really?

I don't know what the rest of them think I'm going to do with Schiebler. *Fuck me, it's like they think I'm in charge (ha! ha!).*

'You can make it up to me now...'

He goes from looking hopeful to a face full of nerves and worry again.

'What you want me to do?'

Two:

'It's time for us to go,' I say. 'While these pricks,' a nod to Clara by way of apology for dissing her husband, which she ignores, 'are off playing tea-time with their prozzies.'

OK.

'You...' I turn to Clara, 'are coming with us.'

I grab her by the hand, spin her into my arms and give her a good old-fashioned black-and-white-movie kiss. She struggles a bit, then melts. Close-up on her heaving breasts and all that.

Then...

All right, all right. I'm making that up. Let's start again...

Two:

'It's time for us to go,' I say. 'While these pricks,' a nod to Clara by way of apology for dissing her husband, which she ignores, 'are off playing tea-time with their prozzies.'

She sighs, sounding a bit like I imagine a mum might if the kids are playing up and she's getting pissed off with it.

'You're going to need money,' she says.

Never having had any – no that's wrong, but the only time I have had any it being quickly removed from me by Cobb and the she-bitch – this hasn't occurred to me.

'And transport,' a good point given that our rank van is still parked somewhere in the woods.

'Cars, there's plenty of outside,' Doug says. 'Just need the keys...'

'They're all kept down in the servants' quarters,' Clara says. 'I'll show you.'

'Thanks...'

'Thanks? Don't thank me,' she says. 'I'm coming with you.'

I laugh, and so do Sal and Doug. Schiebler looks like his arse has fallen out the back of him.

'Gideon thinks he's got you. When he finds out he hasn't, he won't be happy,' she looks at me. 'I told you, he doesn't like to lose.'

'Well he's going to have to learn to like it, won't he?'

'Maybe,' she says, her face hardens. 'I don't want to be here while he does...'

'What about money?' Sal says.

I take a long, good look at Schiebler. Until his skin starts to go as red as his hair, even though he's trying not to notice that I'm eyeballing him.

'I think Schiebler's going to take care of that...' I say.

Three:

Me and Schiebler, back in Skeet's office. His safe just a crack open, and a nice pile of notes inside.... *Oh, this is much more than my seventeen grand. It makes my seventeen grand look like a kid's pocket money. Which it was (ha! ha!).* There's a shiny leather briefcase on the floor next to his desk, it's locked so I bash it open and tip out the papers and pens that are inside it. Then I stuff it with as much of the money as will fit in. Schiebler's standing back at the door at this point, not knowing whether to stop or to run.

'Not going to help me fill this up,' I'm grinning at him. His mouth is making bubbles like a fucking goldfish.

'But... but...'

'But what?' I say, a sudden flash of anger. *Remember you stitching us up?*

'It's bad enough us running. Bad enough. But his money... and his *wife...!*'

'It is bad, isn't it? But not as bad as you running *to* him in the first place...'

He's doing the but... but... thing again, and then it occurs to me how I'm going to get Schiebler to make up for what he did.

'Here...' I hold out paper and a pen.

'What?'

'I want you to write him a nice note...'

He shakes his head and starts to back off.

'Write the fucking note,' I say again, smiling, with fire in my eyes.

Four:

We're all loaded into one of Skeet's four-by-fours. I can't drive, remember? So there's no point me trying to kid you that I'm up front jabbing the gas pedal to the floor and spraying gravel in a wheel-spin until we're off and out. It's Clara, clearly, gunning it like a fucking demon out along the drive, and picking up speed so fast, that, by the time the sound of the engine has attracted attention and a couple of dogs have left their whore feasting and come running, we've got to be doing sixty, and even the quickest of dogs (me!) can't keep up.

Five:

Skeet running into his office. Back-changed, man-form, butt-naked and still covered in blood and muck and filth, and seeing the safe, open door and emptied, screaming something and banging his fists and all that, then catching sight of our note, reading that, and losing it in such big time that the big wooden desk ends up match-sticks.

Dear Gideon, it says, *I appreciate your help in getting the boys in. Pete says thanks for the car, the cash and your wife. Best wishes, Anton Schiebler.*

Fifty-two

The street's empty. Totally deserted.

The whole place is quiet, man.

Very fucking eerie.

So all the more reason for me to be warning Doug not to make too much of a racket.

'All right...' he's saying, getting a bit agitated.

Schiebler's looking around nervously. He's shifting from one foot to the other, biting his lip. The others are behind us, waiting for Doug to break the door down so we can get in. It's all a bit tense.

Of course the door's been reinforced. Broken into too many times, and the windows have been boarded up as well. Half the street is now.

Doug is slamming it with his shoulder, grumbling about how we should've let him have some grease and then he'd have it off its hinges straight away, and me saying we don't want to make a fucking scene and that.

Finally, the wood splits, the door caves in taking the frame with it, and Doug almost falls flat on his face.

'Fuck it...' he says, and stumbles in.

It's dark, on account of the blocked out windows, and it stinks.

There's been no fresh air in here for a while.

I flick my lighter.

'Stay out here,' I say to the others, and Clara makes as if she's going to come anyway, so I throw her a look. *Please don't come in.*

The flame casts shadows and dancing light around the walls. It's a mess. There's graffiti everywhere, and fuck knows what else wiped all over the place. The sofa's burned out. The one that Ken used to lie on watching TV and wanking himself to sleep when he was too pissed to get it on with me or Debs.

There's needles. Lots of them, lying empty around the floor.

This was a nice little gaff for the crack-heads before the council came and shut it down.

'This is your place?' Doug's saying.

'I suppose so,' I say. 'I mean it was.'

I just wanted a look at it.

Here we are.

All at once it seems like a million years since I was last here, and like no time at all.

We're going to finish this right where we started it.

Back at the Links.

Surprised?

Not as surprised as me. The last thing I thought I'd be doing when I left was coming back. I was hoping I'd never see this shit-hole again. That my life before my black-dog and belt would be a distant memory. Nothing more than that. Something not to tell the kids (ha! ha!).

But here I am, standing in my living room, sucking in the smells of the junkies and their puke and shit, and the spunk where they've half-arsed tried to fuck on whatever they were pumping themselves up with. The ghosts of it all are playing out in those shadows on the walls.

Ken the monster.

Debs, who used to be a big sister, but's now just a memory of a scrawny, pock-faced kid. Dead and gone before she was fifteen.

Me not much more, and maybe heading in the same direction she went. If it wasn't for the belt. And the monster it made me.

'Well, I take it we're not going to be making our base here,' Doug says, casual like, as though he's seen plenty of this kind of shit before – which I guess he has.

'No,' I say.

What passes for fresh air is blowing through the door, sending the hum inside round in spirals. I can see it. All of it.

And amongst the stink the junkies have left, there's something else. Something familiar.

It's Ken.

I hold my lighter up and it gives out just enough for me to find my way up the stairs.

First, into my room.

Through these eyes now – my dog-eyes, the eyes that've seen everything I've seen over the last few months – it suddenly looks like a kid's room. There's posters with curling corners blu-tacked to the walls – David Bowie laid out with his dog legs stretched out behind him, all lean and hungry looking. He's got his red hair piled high on his head, and those funny eyes, one one colour, one another, staring out at me. And the two freak poodles behind him laughing.

The World's Strangest Curiosities, it says, and I'm thinking that could have been written for me. Half man, half dog. Born in this room really. At least, the version of me who knew how to get out. And I'm remembering me, dog for the first time, panicking and scrabbling around on my dog-legs, fit to go crazy with it all.

Then, into Ken's room.

Poor old Ken.

Left to rot on his bed all these months while the druggies were lying about downstairs getting fucked. There's hardly anything of him left. What I didn't chew off him has been eaten away by bugs, liquefied, sunk off his bones into the sheets in a black, sticky mess. To think that inside

Ken all this time had been that skeleton, man. He almost looks human (ha! ha!).

Maybe I won't introduce him to the rest of the gang. Something tells me they won't get the joke (ha! ha!).

You see it though, don't you?

You've been with me right from the start.

You're having a good laugh looking at what's left of Ken, not an ounce of flesh on him, laid out on his bed. It's not so much that the fucker deserved it, more that he didn't deserve anything else.

And you're seeing that this is what happens to people on the Links. They rot away, lying in a pool of their own shit, without no-one giving a toss about them. You see it. And that this is what was going to happen to me, until I decided something different, and, in finding my belt, managed to get the fuck out of here.

Fifty-three

First off, everything seems smaller.

Not enough room on the rec any more for everyone in the Crew and all our birds to be sitting getting stoned and drinking beer on hot summer days. The maisonettes not spacey enough for all the parents and kids that live in them. The towers not tall enough for all the people packed inside them. The trees stunted. The roads narrower.

The whole place in miniature.

I've grown and all this has shrunk.

Second off, it's changed.

This place looks like it's got cancer. I mean, when I was growing up here it was a shit-hole, right. All booze and cigarette smoke, the sweet smell of God's own ganja, rutting and fighting…

But it's dying now.

These really are the last days of the Links.

A broken window here and there is now a whole load of windows boarded up; in places the boarding's been ripped off, where someone's been eager to get in or get out. There's crap everywhere – rubbish stuck to the wet ground, black bags of it rotting on the streets – and where doors used to be open with people hanging out, and kids used to be sitting about in gangs on the streets puffing and drinking and laughing, now everything's quiet. There's something in the air: I can see the smell of it.

It's a mixture of fear and don't give a shit – people so fucked they're hardly even alive anymore.

Schiebler doesn't know what to do, poor fuck. He can barely bring himself to look around him. But he's too scared to say anything, what with me having given him the choice: you can fuck off on the run on your own (knowing now that you're just below Pete on Skeet's list of people most likely to end up ripped apart, chewed into tiny pieces and digested and shat out wolf-style), or you can come along for the ride. But you double cross me again like that and I'll tear your throat out. All nicey, nicey, of course. And he decided to come, but I'm not sure that this was because he really wanted to, or because he's more scared of Skeet than he is of me (which from my side is making a mistake (ha! ha!)).

The rest of us are alert.

We don't think that Cobb and his skin-rips or Skeet and his boys – we don't think that any of them will be here yet. But we're expecting them soon. Everybody wants Pete dead, that's a fact. Given time, they'll all be on their way here with one thing on their minds.

Fuck me, I've never had so much fun.

We've moved from the rec to outside what was Jack's house. It's not boarded up, but the windows have got those metal grills over them you've seen on shop doors, and every one of these is held fast by a dirty fucking great padlock.

I've got no idea whether the old sod is still alive, but I give the door a good banging anyway and shout 'Jack' a couple of times. We stand in silence looking round. Just waiting for some sign of Jack; that he's going to open up the door and welcome us in and say 'it's Pete, long lost Pete, where have you been, son? Why didn't you call and let us know you were OK?', and then a great bear hug and some tears.

I can feel eyes on us. I sense them. Someone's having a look but I'm not feeling we need to worry at this point. It's no dog.

Then we hear the sound of movement behind the door. Someone's dragging back a bolt or something or maybe clearing a load of shit out of the way... Then the door opens.

Jack comes blinking into the daylight. He looks pretty much the same, maybe a little more bent, maybe he's dragging the non-foot a bit more heavily, but he looks the same. Apart from his eyes, man, they're going milky white and you can tell by the way he squints and gurns that he can't see too well. He peers up at my face and I can almost smell the gin on his breath before he pulls back sharply.

'I thought it was you... Still a fucking skinny fucker, aren't you?'

'Nice to see you too, Jack.'

He arches his neck and looks at each of the gang, Clara last.

'Who the fuck are these?' he asks.

I don't answer him. This ain't the fucking Brady Bunch.

Jack fixes me with a white-eyed glare. *Come on, you old bastard, you could at least pretend you're pleased to see me.* I dunno. Poor Pete, brought up by no-one, never loved, never cared about.... (ha! ha!)

'So what the fuck you want?' he says.

He hawks and spits on the floor, right next to Schiebler's feet.

'I've got a list....'

I pull it out and he grabs it from my hand and stretches the paper between his fists to read. He mumbles as he goes through it, tutting and swearing under his breath.

'Don't want much, do you?' he grumbles. 'When?'

'As soon as you can. We don't have a lot of time.'

'I don't suppose you do... And how you going to pay for all this shit?'

Clara takes a bundle of cash out of her bag.

'You'll have to come back. Some of it I might be able to get today or tomorrow. The rest will take a few days more.'

OK, we can deal with a few days. I've got shit to do myself (ha! ha!)

He clunks back into his maisonette and slams the door.

Fifty-four

'What the fuck are you doing here?'

I mean, really nice.

Is there anyone who's pleased to see old Pete back round here? This is Tony – you remember – Lukas's brother. It all seems such a long time ago doesn't it? Remember him, right back at the start of the story – him and the rest of the Crew giving those nice Bruno boys a kicking after they popped my lung? Remember that?

My big surprise is that Tony is still king of the Crew. No-one ever used to last that long in the old days. I guess it was because there wasn't that much point to the job then... now there's more going on.

They've turned the garages at the west end of the Links into their HQ – there's even a couple of cars outside, man, unheard of in my time. I don't know what they are – nothing shiny and new, but it's a move in some direction, right or wrong.

Tony's got himself a fucking desk (I know, I can barely keep a straight face) and he's sitting behind it. There are other boys scattered round the garages, some sitting, some standing...

All very gangster stylie, so let's chew the scenery like we haven't eaten for a week.

'So how are things, Tony?' I say.

D'you know, I've no idea what I've done to upset him, but he really doesn't seem over the moon I'm back. I recognize a couple of the other boys, but they're avoiding my eyes.

'Where the fuck've you been?'

'Nice to see you too.'

'We heard rumours about you... I heard you took on the boys over at Marchwell...'

Well, well, well. This is what the dodgy looks are about.

It's true, I make an impression wherever I go.

Maybe some of the dealers and pimps I nicked from were putting two and two together and making something close to four or five. *Oh I see. Tony thinks I'm here to cause trouble for him.*

You don't stay top dog that long and take that many drugs without getting to be a paranoid fucker, do you? Well, if I wanted to be top dog round here I'd've stuck with Skeet and his plan. It doesn't interest me, Tony, you keep it.

'I've not come here for trouble...'

'Well maybe we'll give you some anyway.'

I'm thinking, looking around at all these pale streaks-of-piss skin'eads, with their gaunt, grey faces chapped with pocks and sores – I'm thinking, *no you ain't giving Pete no trouble. Not likely. Not any time soon. But I'm not here to play it that way.*

'I've got something you might be interested in.'

His beady little eyes light up, but he's suspicious. He leans forward across his desk and you can almost imagine him licking those dried and cracked lips of his.

'What you talking about?'

'Something that'll knock the shit out of whatever it is you lot are taking and dealing these days...'

He rubs the back of his hand across his nose, sniffing the snot back into his head.

'It's the rush of a life-time...'

I pull a small bottle out of my pocket.

Of course, you know what this is. You're way ahead of me. But you're also thinking, what the fuck is Pete doing? Why is Pete going to give the Crew grease?

Well, patience. I told you I was learning new tricks.

Just watch Tony's face.

He gestures to one of the boys slumped in a chair next to the desk. It's dimly lit in here, I can't tell who it is or if I know him, just the pasty face and dark eye sockets. He's a skeleton, man.

'Chalky.' They've all still got these stupid fucking nicknames. 'Take some – see what kind of hit you get…'

Chalky gets up, knocking over his chair. He comes towards me and goes to grab the bottle out of my hand. I pull it away.

'Let me do this,' I say.

I uncap the bottle.

Chalky is obviously thinking I'm going to feed him this, he half opens a slack jaw and I can see the dull glint of brown and yellow teeth, and believe me, I can smell the stink of his breath even though he's standing a clear three feet away from me.

'Come here…'

He looks to Tony, and his boss waves at him impatiently to get on with it.

I grab his T-shirt, pull him towards me, tip some grease in my hand and go to rub it on his head.

He backs off quickly.

'What the fuck you doing?' he growls.

I look back to Tony.

'Do you want this or not?'

Tony sits in the gloom, I can see his eyes, alive, reflecting the light in pin-points.

'Let him,' he says to Chalky.

I step back towards Chalky and smother his bristled head with the grease. He coughs, as the garages fill with the smell of it, and pulls back from me, rubbing his hands all over his greasy head.

'Well?' Tony says to Chalky.

Chalky looks blank and shakes his head slowly.

I turn to him and fix his eyes.

'Now.... You've got to make it happen...'

His face crinkles, then opens and he nods slowly. And I can see his neck and shoulder tense – tendons like string; he's pulling through the change, and he doesn't even know it.

Chalky bends double. He does a lot of writhing around, I don't know, maybe he falls to the floor and you can't really see what's happening to him due to the lack of light.

'What the fuck you done to him?' Tony, getting angry.

A couple of the boys stand up and reach for something – knives, could even be guns – not that any of that would worry me.

Then Chalky's back up on his feet. So fast, so out of control he knocks the desk over and sends Tony reeling. I've kept down the amount of grease that's gone on him, but he's such a wiry, aggressive fucker, he's making a decent Douglas style dog. He's looking round with these black eyes and baring these dog-teeth and getting all pumped up and ready to do someone some damage.

More chairs, and more bony skin'eads scatter and Chalky's bang in the middle of the room, growling and slavering. He's going to want to eat someone or something soon.

I can hear Tony shouting something. And there's a bang. A real crack that fills the garages and the smell of something like an explosion and I realize a gun's gone off and the bullet's hit Chalky straight in the chest. He's looking down at the blood spreading through a mix of ripped T-shirt and fur. Then he's taken a giant fucking leap across the room to the geezer with the weapon and taken his head off with a swipe.

Tony's shouting at me.

Okay, I've made my point.

All fucking super motion I'm across to Chalky and I've downed him with an arm round the neck from behind, until, even dog-form, he's not able to breathe and he sinks slowly to the floor, unconscious.

There's lots of breathing heard, mostly silence, a couple of 'fuck me's.

Then Tony:

'I want as much of that as you can fucking get...'

Fifty-five

'What did he say?' Clara asks, looking at me and not looking at me, the way she does.

'He went for it,' I say, sitting down on the sofa.

On account of my old maisonette being a den full of druggie blood and shit and dead-Ken, we got ourselves a different place to hole up in. A flat in the tower block, near the top. It's worked out better up here. We can look out the windows across the Links and have a decent idea about what's going on and what's not going on.

This is what Clara's doing now. Turning to stare out of the window.

'Who's watching Schiebler?' I say.

'Doug,' she says.

Good.

'So this is where you're from?'

It sounds funny coming from her.

'Yes,' I say, shrugging.

'It explains a lot,' she says, and leans against the wall next to the window. That almost curl of a smile across her lips. Her green eyes fixing mine, holding them so I can't look away. I can't tell if she's mocking me.

'You know what they say,' I'm saying. 'It's not where you're from, it's where you're going that counts…'

She laughs suddenly. Like what I've said makes her feel something unexpected, and it's leapt out of her mouth before she could control it.

'And where *are* you going?' she's saying.

My turn to laugh.

I have to pull out a cigarette and light it before I answer. I offer her one too and she cups my hand while I light it for her, and all the time she's staring at me, right in the eyes.

'Fuck knows,' I say.

We smoke for a bit, her lost in thought, me lost in thought about her.

'The most important thing was to get out of this shit-hole…' I say.

'Escape,' she half whispers this.

'I never thought of it like a prison until I got out.' I'm smiling. 'And by then I'd been thrown into another one.'

I'm saying these things, and realising this is the first time I've talked to anyone. Like this, I mean. I've got a whole life-time of banter behind me. Lads' banter about who's dealing what and who's taking what and who's been in what fight and where I can get something to drink or smoke or someone to crack into. And banter with girls about how I'm going to get into their knickers and what we're going to do together when I have. It's all been slang and swearwords, and big Pete being the boy, keeping up appearances and that.

And then this.

This being the first conversation I've ever had.

'What about you?' I ask.

Her eyes flicker, and there's a flash of red across her cheeks before she gets herself back together.

'Escape,' she says firmly. 'The same as you.'

'Not the same as me…' I start to say before she interrupts.

'Not as different as you think…'

'From Skeet?'

'Yes, from him. From my father. From all of it,' she says. 'Nicer than this place, but just as much a prison.'

I crush my cigarette out in the ashtray on the table, then I'm up and opening the window so we can get some air into the room. We stand either side of it.

'So why did you stay this long?'

I realise in saying it, that it sounds like I'm accusing her of something.

'I don't know. Why did you stay here so long?' she comes back at me.

I think about this for a bit.

'It took the belt... I suppose it took getting the belt to make me think I could get out... '

She nods.

'And for me, maybe it took meeting someone else who'd escaped,' she says. 'Knowing that escape is possible.'

Somehow we're closer to each other, we've moved closer together. And I'm wondering whether we're going to lean in and take our first kiss. My guess is that in the movie, that's what we'll do. And she'll reach out and cling onto me – the hero that I am – because she already knows it.

But this ain't a movie (yet, ha! ha!).

We're interrupted by Matti, Doug and Schiebler...

They stop-start for a second as if they're half thinking they've walked in on something.

'What?' I say.

'So did he go for it?' Doug asks.

I pull myself together. *Fuck me, I've got too much to get done to start softening up like a pussy.*

'Yes he went for it.'

'How many people's he got?'

'He reckons he'll have forty or so...'

Matti this time: 'Are you sure you can trust him?'

Me, making sure I stare right at Schiebler who's standing in the doorway, right behind Doug and Matti.

'Oh I'm absolutely sure I *can't* trust him. That's the whole fucking point my friend.'

Fifty-six

It takes a few days to really get going.

    First there's a girl dragged off the street, then somewhere else there's a bunch of gear goes missing, after that there's a fight where a couple of geezers with guns get knocked down by some boys with no weapons at all, and finally there's a hold-up where a few bags of cash get whipped away. Fuck me, if I'd given Tony the instructions myself he couldn't have done a better job.

    And to think that all I've done is get Doug to cook up enough grease to oil the wheels (ha! ha!), you know, as a gesture of good will to Tony, to seal the deal, like.

The Brunos (remember them?)

    The slick producer wants to do this in photos... he's saying think about it like holiday snaps, and I'm nodding although I've never had a holiday (except the whole of my life never being at work) or owned a camera.

    The pictures spin on the screen from one to the next:

    The first one's a couple of Crew-boys slapping on grease like there's no tomorrow, a snap taken half way through the change and one at the end when they're changed, both two-feet wolfmen like Doug, hardly really dog at all.

    Then you've got:

    The picture of them sneaking up to Brown-Town, early evening by the looks of things.

The one where they spy the good looking Bruno girl walking home by herself (there's always one isn't there?).

The one where they're grabbing her off the street, all leery looks.

And the one where the street is suddenly full of boys in turbans, waving hook-blades around, ready to pop some more lungs or worse.

The last one is of the Crew-boys being chased along the road and guess where they're headed. Right back to the Links.

The Greeks

The colours fade on the screen until we get black and white, silent movie.

This goofy music starts.

There's one of Tony's Crew-boys doing a Harold Lloyd down a street. He's off somewhere and up to something, all stripy top and swag bag to go with his drainpipes and Doc Martins.

After a while of him walking down the street he stops at a sign – Andover Estate – and turns smiling to the camera, giving it a wink and all that.

He scrambles over the wall they built to keep the scrags in, getting stuck at the top for comedy effect. There's lots of him trying to get his leg over (ha! ha!) then slipping back down, and he's getting more and more pissed off until eventually he makes it.

He jumps down the other side and now he's creeping along, down an alley and out onto a road with flats either side, and a couple of times he's looked at the camera with his eyes open wide, and flattened himself against a wall and waited – the music goes quiet – while one or two people walk past, somehow not noticing him.

He gets to the end of the road, there's a two-storey row of maisonettes, and the swag bag goes over his shoulder as he climbs up and falls through a window. Inside, he's tumbled amongst a whole load of sacks, and just in case you don't get it, we get a blank screen with the word 'coke' written on it. There's a lot of dust in the air and he's sneezing silently, then the door of the room swings open and in stumble a bunch of angry looking Bubbles, black hair and tashes.

One of them pulls a gun.

Plenty of dig-a-dig-a-din piano music

Our guy from the Crew looking scared.

His hand slowly reaches for his pocket. The Greeks are shouting silently at him, the music crashes on, the hand gets closer to the pocket and ... he pops out a bottle.

The Greeks make laughing faces, pointing at him.

Our man sloshes himself with what's in the bottle and pop, he's got a fake wolf head.

The Bubble with the gun shoots him.

Nothing.

He raises his arms and does one of those horror movie howls, and the Greeks all back away, then he grabs a bag of coke and leaps back out the window.

Black screen, with 'After him' written on it.

And it fades out.

You get the picture, right? Yeah, of course you do.

The Malis

This is psychedelic, man.

The cartoonist is on khat.

There's Mali boys twisting a real trip, and one of them's telling the others a story of something he's seen when he was reccying the Links.

Crew-boys blown off their skulls by some new stuff in town. Something that drives you crazy, gets you foaming at the mouth, and a foot taller than you were, and gives you arms strong enough to break heads.

And the other Mali boys are laughing, in and out of the mind-fuck they're having. They're all seeing cartoon Crew-boys dogged up like *Teenwolf*, man, running round tearing each other's heads off. They're taking it like it's a lot of fun, like it's got nothing to do with them in their little khat-den.

Until they get to the bit in their trip where the Crew-boys get tired of ripping Crew-boy heads off, and decide to pay a visit to Mali-town and put an end to the turf war that's been rattling along nicely for the last few years.

Trip turns to rip, and all of a sudden there's bucket loads of red Mali blood spinning round the kaleidoscope, and all the colours are whirling together and going from luminous to dark, and then darker and then it's black.

The Slavs

This is all *Goodfellas*, except with sub-titles.

We've got a bunch of tattoo-arm shaved-head Slavics, playing cards round a table in a room with no windows. There's a couple of lamps cutting through the dark, and the air's dense with cigarette smoke. They're staring at their cards, moving one now and then to another place in their hand, pulling on fags, and swigging from a bottle of vodka they're passing round between them.

Occasionally someone says something, but as it's all in their mish-mash of a language we haven't got a clue what it is.

Finally, one of them pulls a card from the pile in the centre, grunts, playing around with the other cards in his hand, then lays them down onto the table laughing.

A couple of the others throw their own cards down, pissed off they've lost, and the geezer that's won leans over the table so he can get hold of the greasy pile of coins and notes and pull it towards him. There's lots of what sounds like Slav cussing going on.

Then we've got banging at the door.

The geezer at the end of the table nods to one of the others who gets up and opens the door. Sunlight floods the room, the whole place is momentarily bleached out. Then our eyes settle, and we see another Slav coming in.

He stands at the end of the table, and waits to speak. We can tell he's shitting himself, he's sweating like a fuck – all white and shiny, man – and he keeps wiping away at his face, and we notice then that he's got smears of blood over his head… yeah, it's blood although in this light it looks brown like shit rather than red like proper claret.

The big bastard at the end of the table says something, probably, something like 'spit it out'.

So the geezer starts babbling man, eyes wide and his voice getting louder and louder until he's almost shouting and the big bastard has to stand up and threaten him before he shuts up. Geezer sits down, as if he's been told to, then sitting down, seemingly suddenly knackered, he slumps.

Big bastard starts throwing his hands around and shouting his Slav mouth off, and he's pulling the others out of their chairs and they're jumping up, and seems like they're getting organised, and this shouting and hands in the air stuff carries on as they wrench the door open and – all of them – are off out of it.

Wonder where they're going?

Well I'm not being funny, but we didn't need sub-titles to work out that naughty Tony's been up to something he shouldn't have (ha! ha!).

So it's taken a few days for Tony to kick things off properly, which is fine because it's going to've taken a few days for Skeet and Cobb to work out where we've got to. And once they've tracked us down, rather than it being Cobb and his boys, and Skeet and his boys, against me and my little gang, I've had enough time to stir the pot up a bit.

Oh yeah, you fancy-arsed cunts, you're going to be walking into the shit-storm of the century.

I know they're dogs. But they're posh dogs. And something tells me that Gideon and his lah-di-dahs and Cobb and his night-club bouncers might not be a match for the gangs of West London. Not when I've finished with matching up the odds a bit, anyway.

Fifty-seven

'So where is this place?' I ask.

The sun's thumping down from a clear sky, but I don't feel the heat: just a cool, damp something lifting off the long grass. The air feels liquid, my one-lung's supping up and feeling, for the first time in a long time, fresh and pink inside and not black and burnt and aching. I've got a different feeling from my belt. It's like a warm glow, no pain, no blistering heat.

'Where are we?' I ask again.

I notice that the others have drifted off, Schiebler and Sal are further ahead. They're just reaching the brow of a hill. Clara is next to me, but she isn't hearing what I'm saying, or else I'm not saying what I'm saying.

We're at the top of the hill too, now, and below us is a lake. Water flat, sheer like ice.

Around the lake, thickets of flowers. Red and yellow, with an occasional rush and swirl as wind gathers and spins them around. I can see (though I'm not in dog-form) the scents of these flowers buzzing like a cloud of insects all around and over and above the water.

In the middle of the lake there's an island, thick with trees.

On the other side of the lake, the ground's sloping upwards again, all grass until it reaches a craggy, gaping summit.

'Where is this?'

I see Doug now, at the edge of the water, stripping off his clothes. He throws himself at the lake, shattering the glass surface and scattering the smells from the flowers. He floats on his back, staring at *the sky and gradually the ripples die and he's lying on glass again.*

The other three – Matti, Schiebler and Sal – are sitting next to each other, in silence, amongst the red and yellow flowers. My head is thick with the smell of them.

I turn to Clara, and I feel my mouth make the words 'where are we?' but no sound comes, and I can see her mouth making an answer but I don't know what it is.

We sit down together, next to each other. I feel her hand wrap around mine. I've forgotten that I want to know where we are, and I'm thinking more about the smell. The thick, sweet smell.

Then:

I think I must have closed my eyes, because when I open them, I see a wolf standing in front of me. Just looking at me right in the face. His nose is about six inches from mine. He's got these red eyes, but the rest of him is pure white, man. I can see to my side that Clara is watching him as well.

I'm just sucking in that smell, and looking at the wolf's head in front of me.

This is like the mildest, purest buzz you've ever had from a joint. Better than that, you haven't even had to smoke the joint and get your lung(s) dirty. This is a perfect curve, baby.

The wolf's looking back at me.

We don't have to be afraid of him, I'm not saying to Clara and she's not telling me she knows.

I shut my eyes.

When I open them again (don't ask me how long it is, it could be the next second or the next day) the wolf's gone and in his place is a man, sitting there.

I'm so blown that it doesn't freak me out in the slightest that this is the man. The old guy. You know, from the house on Kensall.

He's looking better than he did back then. Alive, for a start.

And he's smiling at me through a fuzz of bristle around his mouth. His face is creased so hard I can barely see his eyes, just about make out a glint of pink and brown between the folds of skin. He's butt-naked, except for a pair of khaki shorts and I can see, round his waist, he's wearing a scar, like mine, a silver coil. But where on me you can see my dogstar buckle showing through the skin under my belly button, that space is empty on him.

Me, I want to ask questions. About him. About my – our – belt. Ask him whether he chose me, whether he was trying to kill me, why the fuck I ended up the way I am.

But I can't get the words out and he can't hear them anyway.

'Soon,' he says. 'Soon I'll come back for my belt.'

He smiles again, and then he isn't there in front of me anymore, and Clara isn't beside me and the smell evaporates, and before I open my eyes, I get a flash of a picture of myself – cut to pieces and hanging in wire with my stomach and chest wide open, so the insides are spilling out – and it looks like I'm dead.

I wake up.

With a real start. Like I'm choking. Like there's wire tightening round my neck.

Blinking my way to the real world from somewhere else I already can't remember. For a second I look around the room, that yellow half-light, and I'm fighting to get to where I am.

In the flat, overlooking the Links. The only place I ever called home, poor fucking me. Where Debs used to live, before she jumped off a roof, full up of pills. Where my mum, God eat her soul, sat rolling joints on her fat belly with me inside stoned before I could even breathe. Where Ken had humped away at us, first Debs, then me, until we were big enough to fight him off.

In that second, I can't remember anything between them days and now. I'm boy-Pete again. Fumbling for a packet of cigarettes so I can fill my lung with filth, before dragging myself out of bed.

That second where there's no belt, no dog for me, no dogs at all... no

Clara. Fuck me, with a lurch, this is what would have happened to me. I'd be sitting on my bed in my shit-heap of a maisonette. Sitting there staring into space, pulling a fag from the packet and biting it between dry lips.

Sitting there with no reason to move.

Going nowhere.

Rotting from the inside out.

I crack the lighter flint, and in that snap of light, I suddenly become aware of Clara sitting next to me. She's doing that thing she does, that thing that all dogs do: staring at me and not staring at me all at the same time. She's on the end of the bed, inches away from touching me.

There's a first suck on the cigarette before I'm going to speak, but she beats me to it.

'They're here,' she says. Softly.

And she just carries on looking at me and not looking at me.

After some time, I say:

'How long have we got?'

'Maybe an hour... I'm not sure...'

She's got that thing about her right now. What did for me the first time I saw her. Like she's queen of the world and a child rolled into one.

'Is Douglas ready to go?'

She nods.

This is the serious bit, you know. In the film, I'm half expecting Clara to break down and cry, and for me to gather her up in my arms and say, 'Trust me, babe, this is going to go our way... there ain't nothing for you to worry about.' Or maybe this would be the scene where we finally get it on, all sweaty bodies and last chance saloon. Yeah, I'm liking that.

Instead, she gets up and says:

'You better not have fucked this up. I'm just beginning to enjoy myself.'

Harsh but on target, baby.

Truth is, this is another one of Pete's plans. In a long line of plans that never go... how do I say this... like I planned them to (ha! ha!). I've got no fucking clue what's going to happen next. But one thing's for sure. Live or die, this has got to be better than rotting from the inside out on the Links for the rest of my life.

Fifty-eight

Look, I'm fucking sick to death of arguing, right?

How it really happens, well it's mainly in the dark, at least after the lights go out.

FAST FORWARD:

Pitch black screen.

Lots of shouting and sounds of fighting and dogs growling and barking, howling and shrieking.

You can't see a thing.

REWIND:

OK, fair enough. This isn't going to make much of a picture. I get it. The producer boy wants a full moon. Clara says it's a cliché, whatever the fuck that means, and I just say look bro, there's no full moon, no dog'd be caught dead having the kind of ding dong we had that night with a full moon out. But in the end producer-boy gets his way, because I can't be arsed to argue anymore. We're nearly there, babies, and Pete's getting a bit tired of this shit.

I get out of bed and pull on some clothes, follow Clara out of the flat, then it's down fuck knows how many flights of stairs on account of the lift being broken and full of piss. Once we get outside, we're seeing the whole of the Links lit by the moon.

What a fucking glow, man! What a glow.

The boys are on the heath behind my old maisonette. You remember, where I first ran wild and free on my dog legs.

That's where Clara's headed, and me I'm following, jogging to catch up and walk by her side.

As we get off the tarmac and onto the mud and the grass, I can hear Douglas and Schiebler arguing about something.

Schiebler's put in a special request to see this all out man-form and me agreeing to this because he's not much fucking use as his foxy kind of dog in any case.

Him and Doug have been cooking up grease in empty oil drums for the last couple of days, and the heath has got this low mist laid across it from the smoke of the fires they're using to do the cooking, and whatever it is that's drifting off the top of the drums and settling down on the ground. The whole place has got that grease stink and I can't decide whether I like it or not. Doug's Jock eyes are popping out of his skull.

He's never seen so much of his good stuff.

Sal and Matti have been backwards and forwards with buckets of grease to the tower block we've been holed up in. They're loaded up and making the last trip to the block and we've agreed they'll wait there while we see what happens. From up on top, they should be able to see everything that's going on across the Links. And they'll be able to see everyone who comes in. That's the beauty of the Links – just one way in, one way out.

REWIND AGAIN, BACK A BIT, THERE YOU GO:

Me in Tony's den, just after I've downed Chalky, after he's got dog-like and been shot and got up again. You know the score.

'You can have as much as you want,' I'm saying.

'How does it come?' Tony says.

'Raw ingredients, you have to cook it up.' (Me making it look like you brew it up from a shopping list you've taken to Costcutter (ha! ha!)).

'And how much do you want for it?' he says all sly-eyed and greedy.

'Nothing.'

He laughs.

'I've never met anyone who wants nothing,' he says.

'Not cash,' I say.

'What then?'

'I've got some... people... after me. I need help sorting them out.'

Those tiny beadies narrow even more.

'We're not getting messed up in your shit...' he spits.

I shrug my shoulders.

'As much as you want,' I say again.

'What kind of people?'

I lie a little here. Oh please forgive me, do (ha! ha!).

'No-one that's going to cause you boys any problems when you're all dogged-up, right?

Tony smiles, like he's going to lick his lips or something.

'Yeah. Well for that, my friend, I will take us much as you can make.'

'Be my guest,' I say and we spit and shake. 'We'll give you everything we've got.'

'And something for now,' he says, holding on to my hand, doing the big man and squeezing my bones, leaning forward and eye-balling.

I'm pulling another bottle out, and he lets my hand go.

'I've got another dozen of these. That'll be enough for you to have a bit of fun with in the meantime.'

FORWARD A BIT. THERE YOU GO:

We're at Jack's.

There's a flat-bed lorry reversing and I've got a couple of the Crew-boys piling stuff off the back. Oil drums, other shit. They're carrying all this, and stacking it up, and later they'll be bringing it round onto the heath.

'That's it,' Jack's saying. 'That's everything on your list.'

He's limping from his good leg to his wooden one, checking the gear as it comes off the lorry. Then I see him slip something into the hand of the geezer who's driving – danger money most like, who the fuck wants to bring a vehicle onto the Links these days?

Then me trying to say:

'It's going to kick off here pretty soon…'

And Jack peering at me from those glassy eyes. For a second looking like he might say something else, and then instead:

'You owe me another fifty… You were fifty short, you thieving little fuck-wit.'

Me pulling a thick wad of notes from my pocket and peeling him off a nifty. Him grabbing it out of my hand and stumping back to his front door, being through it and slamming it without turning round to look back at me.

THEN FORWARD ALL THE WAY TO HERE:

It's dead.

This place always knew when something big was in the off. And it knows that tonight. The lights are out, the place is silent.

Waiting.

Breathless.

Making me think of that first night I was a dog and how I noticed smells and sounds I never smelt or heard before. That even when it seemed like the Links was calm at night time, there was still so much going on. All the drinking and puffing, shagging, and back-chatting, TVs humming and microwaves pinging, the constant choke of the traffic. That I grew up in a place where there was always something happening.

But there's none of that now.

There's nothing happening but waiting for the bomb to drop.

The first thing that happens is the Crew make it onto the heath behind Ken's place.

Say there's about forty of them, maybe forty-five, who's counting, man?

I see Tony up front all swagger and zoot smoke, chest out and making the big entrance like he really is someone round here. *Well good for you, mate, I'm thinking. Let's see how you get on.*

The rest of them are a bunch of skinny, pale-faced fuckers, with teeth like grave stones and eyes bossed out from whatever it is they're tripping on. *Oh, that's gonna make some nice combination all mixed up with grease.*

Cobb and Skeet ain't gonna know what's hit them.

The Crew-boys are all here, standing around, or jigging on the spot depending on how much they've had of what they've been taking. Big Tone's puffing on an Afghan cheroot and looking just like he's in charge.

TONY: 'You got what's what?'

ME: 'Fucking bins-full. You ready for your end of the bargain?'

The big man nods to one of the boys next to him.

TONY: 'Gaw on.'

The same stick of shit, Chalky, that took the grease last time stumbles forward and I let Doug know he can splash him with some now. A proper dose this time. Really make him move.

Doug's got a bucket that he's dunked in one of the grease-filled oil drums, and you can tell that, rather than spraying this skinny prick with it, he'd give himself a face-full and play a nice game of chase and kill. But Doug's a good boy, so the skin'ead gets it and this time he's rubbing it into his own head and his arms and ripping off his T-shirt and giving it the crazy howl even before he's changed. This time, with more grease he makes a bit more of a dog although still a two-foot not a four like Pete. And then he's off, like a fucking mongrel, straight back onto the Links where the trouble's about to start.

TONY: 'So these people you got problems with, they're on their way?'

ME: 'Any minute.'

Then Doug's doing his own little production line and each Crew-boy's going through and getting his dose. And Tony just stands there puffing on his zoot-alors and making on about how nice it's going to be to see his boys having some real fun.

This is about when the next thing happens.

There's a crack.

Must be a gun shot.

Somewhere out on the streets.

Then there's voices, lots of screaming and shouting and another gun shot.

First to get here, judging by the fucked up language and the accents when some of the shouting gets into English, it's the Slavs. Things'll get tasty pretty quickly.

In the movie, you get a cut away to a bunch of the Slavics chasing Chalky-dog onto the rec and pumping him full of bullets from their tiny guns. I hear they've come by to pay Tony a visit on account of one of their dealers being done over by the Crew-dogs – who've been playing with my grease (ha! ha!) – and having his fat stash of cash stolen.

Oh, they're really unhappy about that.

Camera back to us, and Tony stands there for a second looking calm.

Then he's suddenly he's on at Doug.

'Well get a fucking move on then... we've got business to see to,' he says.

And as much as I know Doug wants to make a glove out of Tony's head, I'm telling him to carry on and douse the rest of them so they can go and kick it all off.

Slosh, growl.

Slosh, growl.

Slosh, growl.

Until all but a couple of the skin-types are done and racing away to the rec with more hair on them than they've ever had before. There's a right racket coming from that direction, with the Crew-dogs and the Slavs really getting stuck into each other and it being clear pretty quick that a dog will win out, even against a gun, every time.

Then Doug holds up a bucket for Tony.

'Oh no. Not me, mate,' Tony holds up his hands. 'Someone's got to keep an eye on the merchandise.'

Tone the man stands his ground with a couple of the boys behind him to make him feel tough enough to give Doug the eye. Doug looks at me, still holding up the bucket.

'Go on then,' I say.' Go on.'

I've hardly said it before Doug's smothering himself in grease, and cracking that great Jock dog of his. I promised him a fight, whatever, so what can I say? He wants to go and knock a few heads off and I'm not one to stand in his way. And just as he's made the best dog he can and is getting ready to make his way to the rec and join in the fun, it sounds like someone else has joined the party.

Until now, all the dog noise has been yapping and barking and growling like grease-boys do. And that in amongst gun fire and the odd scream where a dog jumps a Slav and gets to biting and using his claws.

Now there's something else.

Something deeper.

At first I can pick out the low chugging growls, and then there's some proper dog howling and roaring.

This has got to be Cobb and Skeet.

Clara looks at me and I can tell she's heard it too.

'Gideon's here,' she says quietly.

'Good,' I say, like my plan's working.

Time to have some fun (ha! ha!).

'You two stay here,' I say to her and to Schiebler (like he's going to offer to come!).

'Good luck,' Clara says.

No luck needed.

And as I'm racing off man-form, I probably see Tone giving Clara a bit of the eye and thinking this might just be his lucky day once he's dealt with the ginger prick, at which point she growls at him.

'Don't even think about it,' and he backs down like a baby.

She can look after herself.

Me, round the back way, to avoid the rec. And up into the tower so I can see what's going on.

Let's get this party started.

Fifty-nine

I'm still man-form cos I've got tactics to talk with Sal and Matti up the tower.

But I'm wishing I'd changed, because the stairs are killing my one-lung. I'm up about a hundred and ninety of them, spinning round. Neck aching looking up through the stairwell, like I'm stuck in some up and down tunnel cut off from the world. Something tells me I'm running out of time.

I can't hear anything from what's going on outside apart from the occasional firecracker of a pistol shot.

For this you'll have to rely on the camera that's hovering over the rec...

It's a full-on dog-fight.

You've got Crew-boys two-foot, tearing into the Slavs with their guns (and now we can see they've got bicycle chains too). The Brunos have made an appearance too, and they're laying in heavy with those curved knives they've got. Slash, cut and slice. There's blood spouting everywhere, man, and every now and then the film slows so you get a nice little close up of an eye popping or and arm being cut open, or some guts spilling out onto the streets.

If that's not enough, the Greeks come bombing in, and of course, as much as all of these gangs hate the Crew, they hate each other the same, and they're over the fucking moon (pardon the pun) to find themselves in the right place at the right time.

Last of the gangs has been the Malis. They've got something of everything. Bits of wood with six inch nails bashed through, axes, swords, the odd firepopper – at least one shotgun, a few pistols and a fucking machine gun for God's sake. And they're now shooting and cracking through, and it's a real every-which-way with everyone smashing up everyone else.

And somewhere in the middle of all of this is Doug, the six foot six man-dog, picking up two at a time, one in each hand and smashing heads together. And the more I watch him, and see how much fun he's having, the more I realise that he's somehow got himself in charge of the Crew-boys and he's shouting out orders, and gathering them together so they can fight as a team, and that way the Crew are taking less hits than all the other gang-boys who are just taking it on one-on-one and not so much caring what their mates are up to.

Well the Links has come alive now (ha! ha!). There's got to be a couple of hundred of them, smashing the shit out of each other.

And me I'm racing up the stairs.

Of course, Skeet's rolled up. Him and his boys in their smart cars, the like of which the Links has never seen before, and it's all skidding and spinning around with those, headlamps playing light across the battling gangs. And his boys are spilling out of the motors, and as they're doing it they're giving it the old skin-rip and you've got a whole bunch of four-foots ready to do some heavy wolf damage.

I'm almost at the top now. My lung is fit to burst. On fire, I'm sweating like a bastard.

Skeet himself just steps out of his car, sure to have a couple of his boys on either side. He pulls the cuffs on his shirt, and straightens his jacket. He's watching the carnage going on across the rec, and his dog-boys are all waiting for his signal before they get stuck in.

Him though, he's got something (someone) else on his mind.

'Where the fuck is the belt-boy?' he says, almost to himself, and so you can hardly hear his words over all the noise everyone else is making. Then he nods his head, and his dogs take that as a sign and there's howling and barking as they race towards the mayhem and start their good dog work.

Me, I'm finally at the top of the tower, out the door and onto the roof.

Sal, fag in his mouth or his hand, is laughing. I can hear him saying to Matti: 'Who next?'

And Matti seems to be enjoying himself more now than I've seen before.

'Hey, get the one with the gun,' he's saying, 'the shot gun.'

Then the pair of them are picking up armfuls of balloons they've filled with grease and launching them off the roof. Below they're hitting Malis and Brunos, Slavs and Greeks. The balloons are bursting and spraying grease all over the place, and whoever is hit is getting a little bit dog.

You've got boys and bits of dog and full-dogs, half changed and not changed and changed all the way. There's fur flying and teeth and claws slashing, and blood spraying in a mist, flesh splattering in great globs, there's knives and guns still popping off, there's shouting and howling and growling.

It's the fucking boom!

So far, so good.

What plan I had is working out all right. Get the gangs ripping it up, and drag Skeet and Cobb into the mess of it all, take out as many of theirs as possible, and leave me with what's left – even up the odds a little bit (ha! ha!).

'Glad to see you two enjoying yourselves...' I interrupt, just as Sal is launching another half a dozen balloons off the roof.

Down below, they're falling like flies.

Bodies and bits of bodies all over the place.

The grass and mud on the rec are soaked with blood.

What's left is mainly dog of one type or another.

Skeet's dogs are working in pairs, pulling people down and ripping them apart in a frenzy.

Doug's a one man army.

From a couple of hundred there's probably about forty of them still cracking heads. The guns are spent, so the two-foot dogs are using hands and claws, or still swinging chains and using knives.

Watching all this is Skeet.

Whatever he expected to find at the Links, he didn't expect this.

We're getting a close-up on his face. Then there's a close-up on mine. Then back to his...

Where the fuck is the belt-boy? he's probably thinking. And that he's walked into a trap, and that he's being played (which he is) and that he doesn't like to be played, and when he gets hold of me he's going to break my fucking neck, and that this is nothing compared to what he's going to do with that bitch of a wife of his, who he's more than half suspecting came along with Pete without that much persuasion...

Then the camera swings back to me:

I've got that bastard where I want him on the rec, I'm thinking, *it's just a matter of time before the numbers are thinned out enough for me to get dog-form and run down to finish all off nicely so me and Clara can ride into the sunset and that...*

And I'm standing back and enjoying watching it, Matti and Sal start bombing the whole place with grease again, and of course then Skeet's seen these bombs dropping and he's looking up and seeing Pete on the roof.

Back to him:

'There he is.' And his face is breaking into one of those smiles I've seen him make, where he's thinking okay, right, *of course* this is all going to go my way. Like it always does.

Then he's got that hand, with its finger nails all nicely clipped and scrubbed and polished, and he's lifting it up and he's pointing at us up on the roof. Even man-form he's got dog eyes that can see in the half-light. He's saying something, and the dogs that're fighting drop what they're doing – like he's called them back with a whistle – and the boys on either side of him are ripping some skin and getting themselves dog form. And altogether that makes about twenty of them, and they're all on their way up.

Back to me.

'Oh, shit,' I'm saying to myself.

Another one of Pete's top plans. I haven't thought we might get trapped up here. *Nice one.* I'm also thinking – *can me and Sal and Matti take on this many skin-rips at once?* I don't know. I was counting on there being less of them left, but they don't seem to have done too bad in the fight.

'We got some of Skeet's boys on their way up. It's change-time,' I'm shouting at the other two.

And there's Matti going off to drag his dog-pelt out of a sack, and Sal making ready to rip some skin, and me just hotting up to bring on the change, when something else jumps its way into my thick skull.

Pete... Pete...

And I realise what I'm thinking which is: *where the fuck is Cobb?* On account of I've been assuming that him and Skeet are going to come together and try to take me down as a team. But that I haven't seen him, and all the four-foot dogs I've seen have definitely been from Skeet's side... so where the fuck are his dogs too?

Just for a second I feel a tightening round my neck. Like I'm cut and I can't breathe.

Pete... Pete...

And then Matti's waving his hands at me and trying to get me to come over to where he is, and he's pointing down that way, and of course this is towards the heath.

'Pete, look! It's Cobb... look!'

And rushing over, I see it too. I'm looking down onto the heath and I can see Cobb there, with his team of dog-police or whatever they think they are, and they're all in a big circle around Clara and Schiebler and Tony, who've got absolutely nowhere to go.

Sixty

The camera swoops (yeah, swoops, man) down to the heath:

'So woss your story then?' Tony's saying to Clara.

He's walking around in between the grease barrels, trying to give it some, making sure she knows that he's the top dog around here. The sound of the battle's loud here, cracks of gunshots, snapping of bones and the screaming and tearing of flesh getting echoed about the place.

Schiebler looks horrified even that Tony's talking to them. You can tell he don't know what to think of the Crew... of the Links. This is about as far away from Schiebler's red-headed world you're ever likely to get. Right at this point he's wondering whether he took the right side in this argument, whether maybe he would have been better sticking with Skeet and trying to wangle his way out of prison and back into the dog good books.

Clara hasn't heard the question. She's listening intently to everything. She's got dog-ears and nose and she's sticking close to the fight and following what she can hear of me and the rest of our gang.

Oh baby... she's looking so fine. In real life, she's wearing whatever shit clothes we'd bought or ripped off. I mean, where have we had the time to go shopping, man? Of course in the film, they'll have her dressed up in something fancy, I'm sure. I don't care. She looks fine in a baggy sweat shirt and jeans... she looks fine whatever she's wearing. So long as the movie pricks don't put her in black leather. Every fucking twat and his elbow these days is dressed in black leather. Believe me, when you've got dog sense of smell the last thing you'd ever dress in is dead cow skin.

Tony grunts when he realises no-one's answering him. He stops at one of the drums, still simmering away over a fire.

'How d'you make this shit then? Eh?'

He dips in a finger and pulls it out sharply. *Yeah right you dick, it's hot.*

No answer again.

I can tell my baby's fretting.

There's something she's not liking.

She turns to Schiebler.

He's stressing still. So much sucked up inside his own head, thinking about whether he's made a big fucking mistake and how he's going to explain it away if Skeet and Cobb come out on top. So much that he doesn't feel anything.

But Clara's sensing something.

A feeling like they're being hunted, the fine hairs on the back of her neck standing up.

She's just about to say something to Schiebler.

To warn him.

To tell him they need to get out of here.

Then she visibly stiffens.

From behind Tony and the two Crew boys who're supposed to be watching out for him, a figure steps into the moonlight. It's hooded, in a dark raincoat There's a black shadow where its face should be.

Tony now sees Schiebler and Clara looking in his direction.

'Finally,' he starts to say, 'someone's going to answer my questions...'

Then even he – senses dulled by years of pumping himself full of booze and weed and coke and other chemicals – realizes they're staring through him, not at him.

He turns.

Good ol' Tone. He spits the wet end of the joint he's smoking onto the grass. He picks himself up, making sure his boys are close behind.

His hand goes to his pocket, where he's packing a gun. He pulls it out, like he's the coolest fuck in the world (making sure he gives Clara half a look and a bit of a wink while he's doing it). Then he pauses to make an impact...

'Who the *fuck* are-?'

All emphasis on the word fuck.

Unfortunately for Tony (and if I'm honest, and if it wasn't for the fact that he's a drug dealing scrag who deserves everything he gets, the beady eyed fuck), unfortunately for Tony, he doesn't quite get to the end of his question.

Before he knows it, there's been the flash of wood, and his head is spinning off his shoulders and his legs and body are kind of crumpling to the ground, and the open end of his neck is pumping and spraying thick blood all over the fucking place.

It's all too quick for the Crew-boys. They've got bashed-in heads and spurty neck-holes (ha! ha!) before they've had the time to wonder who it is that's wasted Tony.

The hooded shadow kneels down and wipes the blood off his cricket bat onto the grass, then as he stands up, the hood slips back off his head.

Me wondering where Cobb is?

Say hello.

In the movie this is the big reveal for his new burnt and fucked up face. Yeah, I know we've seen him before in a blur when me and the gang were making our escape from prison. But this time you're gonna get a long, lingering look.

Not so nice.

You can barely see the Bank's best dog-copper under all the red, scarred skin. There's something wrong with his face apart from that, too, looking like he didn't quite make it all the way back from wolf to man while I was giving him the flame treatment with my change. There's patches of matted hair growing out from the scars, and his mouth is twisted and stretched, looking like someone's given him a permanent grin, and you can see the glint of a mix of man- and dog-teeth in his mouth.

Wow, I fucked him up big time. He really ain't going to be happy with me.

'Good evening, Lady Skeet,' he says, sounding like someone's chain-sawed his neck. 'We've come to rescue you.'

Clara just gives him that look. She's scared but she's not showing it. This doesn't look like it's going to end well, and she knows it.

'You must know that's not necessary,' she says calmly back at him.

He pauses and it looks like he might be smiling through that twisted mouth, it being full of teeth all different shapes and sizes and surrounded by livid skin and hair in patches. Meanwhile Schiebler's standing there shitting himself, trying to shrink back into the shadows except there's no real shadows for him to shrink back into. Clara's standing tall, looking down at him.

'Well your father isn't very happy about this at all,' he says. And as he's talking he's seeming to stand a bit taller himself because he thinks he's got her and because of that he thinks he's got Pete.

'I can't say I'm all that surprised... you've had your head turned by the...' he looks like he's going to spit at the floor or something but manages to contain himself '... boy. Once we've dealt with him, you'll be back with your tail between your legs.'

At this point he laughs, and it sounds like someone's sawing wood.

'Once your father's back at the board table, he will, I'm sure, be looking to bring you and your husband back into line.'

She's barely seeing him now, even though she seems to be looking straight at him. But her eyes are red. She's fucking furious, man.

'You're looking very pleased with yourself...' she says.

Cobb kind of grunts and without saying yes you can tell he's absolutely fucking pleased with himself. He thinks he's got Pete. And maybe he has.

'... for someone that the "boy" made such a fool of.'

She shoots, she scores!

He strides towards her and gives her a good slap round the face with the flat of his hand. He's the villain, man, all villains give the leading lady a slapping. It's what makes you hate them so you cheer when they finally get what's coming to them, right? Blood trickles from the corner of her mouth, and those eyes are burning.

She reaches up to rip her skin.

'Stop her!' Cobb shouts and out of the shadows you've got a bunch of his men in uniforms, grabbing her, and it takes four of them to overpower her (even though she's not in dog-form).

Somehow Schiebler's been forgotten in this moment. He's backed off. Cobb is only interested in Clara right now. She's the prize, right? He can take her back home and his master will give him a nice pat on the head.

Back away Schiebler, you fucking coward.

That's right, you just let them take her and hopefully they'll forget about you... and just as you're thinking that's what he's going to do, and that Pete was all wrong to give him a second chance... something in Schiebler snaps.

It's that slap, man.

Clara being hit.

It's snapping back again and again in his head, and he's feeling something he hasn't felt for a long time. For the longest time.

It's anger.

And although he's only Schiebler the redhead freak, the thief of joy and the whinger, the least useful member of the gang, and although he's in man form and not even being able to use the fangs and claws of Skippy the dog-kangaroo.... Even though all of that is the case, he roars at the top of his voice and launches himself at Cobb.

Sixty-one

We've got to get to them.

I'm looking at three headless stiffs and Clara being slapped and then Schiebler launching himself at Cobb. *Fuck me, another one of my plans, eh?*

'Pete,' Sal says. 'They're coming up...'

And I'm realising not only have I let Cobb sneak up unannounced, like, I've also got us trapped at the top of this fucking tower, with half of Skeet's private army on their way to get us. *Well done, mate. Clever thinking.* There are twenty or more fucking Skeet-dogs humping up the stairs. You can already hear them baying, their claws clattering on the concrete, knowing when they get to us it'll be first one off with Pete's head gets top prize from the boss.

Down on the rec, I can still hear the fight going on. Douglas is doing some mopping up, I can't see this but you can, the Crew are winning out and Doug's doing his Jock-best to help.

'Pete?'

It's Matti this time.

'We've got no choice,' I say. 'We have to fight our way out of this one... time to change, boys.'

We've got less than a minute.

Matti does his...

He pulls his dog-pelt over himself and crouches down on the floor of the roof, and you've got Matti melting away into the skin and before you know it, he's starting to stand tall, and as he does, he's getting surrounded by this black smoke (*so that's why they call them smokers*) and growing from short-arse man-form into this fucking bear a good seven or eight feet high. He's filling out and getting pumped up and the hair from the pelt is covering him all over, until finally he's done. He picks up an axe he's brought up for the purpose, roars like he's going berserk and that roar echoes all over the Links. And just for the briefest of moments, Skeet's dogs stop on their way – for a kind of fuck me, there's something up there we should be worried about – before they carry on throwing themselves up the stairs, thinking they're more worried about Skeet than they are about what might be on the roof.

Sal does his...

He takes hold of himself at the mouth and starts to tug hard. He's pulling upwards, and at first you can hear the tearing sound as flesh rips apart from flesh, and then you get to see his skin turning itself inside out, and the dog-hair coming through and the dog teeth and his eyes turning yellow and before you know it he's four-foot.

And I do mine...

I bring on the heat of the change. It's white-hot man, searing, and I'm burning from man into dog. Then I'm cracking the ash, and breaking out.

And here we are. It's the three of us. Side by side. The bear, the wolf and the big, black and beautiful dog.

We stand on the roof ten feet from the door that leads down to the stairs. It's count-down.

Ten, nine, eight...

We can hear then coming.

Seven, six, five...

All three of us tensing up.

Four, three, two ...

Ready for what's going to hit us.

One.

Then blam!

The first of Skeet's dogs come crashing through the door.

Two of them.

Through the air straight at us.

Followed by another three or four.

And suddenly me and Sal and Matti are tipped upside down and making a bloody mess on the gravel rooftop, each one of us with a couple of dogs bearing down on us.

It takes me a second.

My mind ain't here, it's with Clara.

What are they doing with her?

Get back, Pete.

I can feel one of the dogs has got a mouthful of my neck.

Get back, or you won't be alive to help her.

I turn so I'm onto my back and get my hind legs under the dog that's got my neck. Back legs clawing at his belly. Then as he shifts in pain and tries to get a better hold on me, I've push as hard as I can with my legs and send him spinning into the gravel. The other dog crashes half-off at the same time. I knock his head with my front paw. A real bitch-slap. I've opened him up, a flap of flesh hanging off the side of his dog face. He's trying to get away from me now. I'm back on my feet.

Another half a dozen of Skeet's gang make it through the door. There are more behind.

These new-on-the-roof boys are standing back a bit.

Waiting.

Across from me, Matti's bear is doing a better job than Sal.

The bear's in some kind of roaring rage, what must be hidden under all of Matti's calm. The two dogs that took him on are wishing they hadn't right now. He's got one by the tail and he's swinging it round with one bear-hand. Then he lets go, and the dog flies off the roof. You get to hear what it sounds like when a dog screams, and what it sounds like when a dog hits concrete after flying downwards for a couple of hundred feet. The second one gets an axe through the head, and then Matti's off towards the door – where the others are standing back – looking for more fun.

CUT TO MATTI LATER:

'Okay, so I got a bit carried away,' he's saying, smiling and looking a bit embarrassed. 'It's the skin, it takes me over...'

BACK TO THE ROOF:

Sal's under a pile of dogs. Fucking cowards, half the pack are after him thinking he's the one they've got the best bet of nailing. There's got to be six or eight on him, and they're digging in and beginning to tear off bits and spit out the bloody muck of him.

CUT TO SAL LATER:

Sal, smoking a cigarette, looking straight at the camera:

'So, I'm better at fucking than fighting. What can I say?'

BACK TO THE ROOF:

So: it's me and Matti in a pincer.

Matti's dropped his axe to one side and he's trying to pick up a dog in each paw. Me, on the other side of the pile. I manage to break a neck. Then, I've got a big grey dog rushing me from behind and I've turned and sliced him open (nice and clean!) with my claws and as he hits the deck his guts are sliding out through the wrench I've made in his belly. But then there's more, streaming up onto the roof, another ten or so, more than I thought.

Matti's got four or five on his back now. He's turning, trying to rip them off. More than one's got teeth into him hard. He can't get at them. There's black blood and smoke drifting off him.

Sal's stopped struggling at the bottom of his pile. I don't know whether he's alive or dead. And there's me surrounded by too many. *Fuck me.*

All of a sudden, I'm thinking: *I hadn't realised it might end like this.*

Not like this (ha! ha!).

Just for a split second, though.

Of course it ain't going to end like this.

It's all growling. Gravel being sprayed. Blood and flesh splattered. All flickering and fast-cut in the moonlight so you can't see what's going on. Then:

'Stop!'

At first it sounds like a voice in my head more than a voice that's trying to shout above all the noise of the fighting.

'Stop!'

There's Skeet.

It's Skeet shouting.

'Stop!'

He's a silhouette against the sky. Standing right up on top of the hut where the door down to the stairs is.

And it stops.

Just like that, all his boys just stop.

There's a face-off.

Skeet's dogs back away, slowly, bared teeth and that, showing they're only letting us away because the boss has told them to. I look to Sal. He's a mess but still alive. He just about gets up onto all fours and limps across to me and Matti. I'm pretty much okay, the bear is full of holes and he's got that black blood sort of seeping out of him and drifting into the air like smoke.

'I want to talk,' Skeet says.

He waits.

To talk, I've got to change back.

Why should I trust him with that?

Man-form, if they're quick, they can definitely have me.

'I don't have all night,' he says.

It's a stand-off.

'And neither do you. Who knows what plans Cobb's got for your new girlfriend?' He really spits this, man.

I turn to Sal and Matti. They're giving me this look, like, what's the alternative? We're gonna get fucked up anyway so we might as well see what he's got to say.

I back up to the edge of the roof, and I can see and sense and hear enough from below to know that the fight's over and Doug and about half the Crew are left standing. And then I'm thinking of Clara. I have to get to her. I have to get to her before Cobb thinks about getting some revenge on me. In his burnt and fucked up state, who knows what he's capable of?

I breathe deep, and bring on the change.

This one, I make as fiery as I can.

The sky above me lights up.

We need you up here, Doug.

Then I'm Pete. Naked, bloody, scorched.

'I wish it was good to see you again,' Skeet says.

I'm out of breath still, from the change.

My one-lung is on fire.

Come on, you Jock bastard, don't let me down.

'Well, it's good to see you...' I say.

He laughs but not in a way that says he finds it all that funny.

Then just as quick, it's quiet.

Not a flicker from his pack. They're silent. Tensed. I can sense every muscle in every dog-body tight like steel, ready to move as soon as he gives the OK.

Keep concentrating on us.

Don't think about who's coming up the stairs.

'I didn't appreciate you running out on me,' he says.

'I'm sorry about that,' I say. 'But I thought about your offer and decided it wasn't for me...'

'It was a one-time only deal,' Skeet says. 'It was your chance to be something. To make something of yourself...'

I'm waiting.

'This is the deal now,' he goes on. 'I want the belt.'

'In return for what?' I say.

'In return for *nothing*,' he's almost shouting. 'In return for your life. You wanted to be back in this place, you get to come back to this place... To where you belong. That's the deal.'

Doug and the Crew-boys are coming slow up the stairs. Not making a sound. You can see this, I can't. But I know they will be. Doug's not going to miss a roof-top scrap like this one's gonna be.

'I'm not so keen on that deal either,' I say.

'I don't really care what you think,' Skeet says. 'Because it's either that way, or it's me letting my boys rip you apart and getting to the belt by pulling your guts out all over this roof.'

His dogs are all growling and showing their teeth now. Oh, how much they want to be let off the leash to finish what they've started.

'What about that?' Skeet's warmed up nicely. He's thinking he's got this one taped.

I'm not liking where this is headed.

I've still got half a mind on Clara.

Come on Doug.

'Look... we can sort this out without getting nasty...' I say.

'You already made it nasty...' he comes back at me, rigid with anger.

My mistake.

'So do we have to put you back in your place?' he says.

Come on Doug.

'Back in the gutter where people like you belong?'

Oh, he's liking the sound of his own voice a lot now.

Just keep him going.

A few more seconds.

Just keep getting more and more satisfied with yourself you posh-boy fuck.

Then all at the same time.

'Kill them,' he shouts.

Doug and half the still-standing Crew come crashing through the door, out onto the roof. As Skeet's dogs race forward towards us, they're bashed up with wood and nails, swung at with chains and bottled and leapt on from behind, and Doug's going crazy with a Bruno knife in each hand. Slicing and dicing. And before I know what's happened, Matti's picking me up in these great bear hands of his, and chucking me off the roof.

He lets out a strangled growl.

It's like he's saying something, trying to say something...

'Clara!'

And as I'm falling ten storeys to the concrete below, I've got just enough time to think that Debs did exactly the same thing, all those years before.

Sixty-two

I'm falling so fast I can't catch a breath.

Then the camera's switching to Schiebler and he's launching himself at Cobb. All Clara can do is watch as she's held back by four of Cobb's uniforms.

The camera's back on me.

I'm waiting.

I'm keeping it together until just before I hit the ground. Just before.

The camera cuts away again and Cobb's almost knocked off his feet. He's not seen it coming, any more than you did. He always had Schiebler for a coward.

Back on me.

Hold it, Pete.

The air's rushing at me as I cut through it. I don't have time to think, but I can feel it all. Below on the rec, I can see the bodies in pieces and piles. I can feel the ones who are still breathing, hear their hearts beating, see their faces clenched trying not to let go of being alive.

Back on Schiebler: he's gone at Cobb's face, thinking it's still going to be sore from all the burning, and he's right because when Schiebler takes a chunk out of Cobb's cheek and keeps at him scratching with his hands and nails, Cobb's screaming in pain and rage.

Back on me.

Hold it.

I can hear what's going on up on the roof. Ripping and slashing skin and hair and meat. Doug roaring, Sal ripping and re-wrapping and Matti's axe splitting skulls. Skeet and a couple of his boys running to the edge to peer over and watch Pete flatten himself on concrete, thinking they'll be able to come down and pull my belt out from the middle of the smashed and broken bones and bloody mess.

Back on Schiebler: Cobb's getting his balance back, and although he's hurting to fuck with everything Schiebler's doing to him, he's got hold of his red hair and is starting to pull him off, and by doing this helps Schiebler pull that mouthful of flesh out of his face.

Back on me:

Hold it.

All in this moonlight, man. This serious moonlight. The whole Links lit up like a Halloween lamp. And poor me, bundled up here after popping out the hole of a junkie and being buggered by my so called dad. Debs, taking the same leap off the tower block, pumped up with pills and slurring something before she fell head-first and cracked herself open on the hard ground below. All the years getting grown up here. Ziggy gutted by Lukas and Lukas being clinked up and ending up dead himself.

Back on Schiebler:

This happening in seconds:

Cobb's boys spring into action just now, and you've got Cobb pushing Schiebler off and two of Cobb's men dragging him off too. Schiebler's face is red with Cobb's blood, and his hands are a mess of burnt up skin and the flesh that he's gouged out with his nails. And Cobb himself is burning up with it, raw, man – completely raw. He's shouting something, screaming at his uniforms and they're pulling Schiebler away, and now it's his turn to scream.

Me:

Hold it, Pete.

And somewhere a flash of pale skin and white hair, or is it the ghost of an old man, who used to wear this belt, now mine, staring up at me in silence? The dead geezer on the sofa in the house in Kensall. The same geezer from my dream saying he was coming to get his belt back. Is that him, standing watching me, leaning on a walking stick with one hand capped over his eyes to block out the glare of the moon? Is it?

Now!

This change is my biggest. The best I ever do.

It'll never be like this again.

The force of it, the energy of it, right before I hit the ground, it bounces me back up into the air. I somersault in a ball of flames, and by the time and I come back down onto the rec, I'm four-foot again, and smashing out of my ash with a roar.

Ready to kill.

I'm still. Smoke and steam rising off me. My eyes are tight shut and I'm trying to find Clara. Trying to hear her, pick up her scent.

There's nothing.

Still.

I fill up my one-lung with air, then hold it. No breathing. I slow my heart until it's hardly beating at all and the blood stops rushing through my veins. A gentle flow. I'm centring inside myself, cutting out the crackle of static in my brain.

Everything cleaned down. Nothing in the way right now.

Listen again.

And I hear her. The faintest gasp… intake of air. As if something's being tightened around her neck.

In my dog-mind I see the Links spread out, and that tiny gasp, I can see where it is. In the garden. In the garden of Ken's house.

I'm coming to get you, baby.

Everything bursts back into flow. Breath, beating heart, blood thumping through my veins, brain fizzing with electricity. Muscles tensing into springs and I'm away, galloping across the Estate, back to Clara. *I'm coming to get you.* And Cobb, *I'm going to finish what I started with my little fire at the Bank, right?*

I'm pounding. As quick now across the Links as I was heading to the ground a few moments ago. I race back to my old street, and through the alley onto the heath. *You're not thinking, Pete. It's a trap for you.* Of course it's a fucking trap and I'm going to run straight into it and beat the living shit out of all them what's waiting for me.

Then I can see them, Clara and Schiebler.

They're strung up on the old chain link fence behind Ken's terrace. That twenty foot of mesh I clambered over when first a dog outside in the real world what seems like years before. They're hanging, star shaped, cut hard by the rope strung across their arms, chests and legs, heads down, hardly conscious.

Cobb's enjoyed some ultra-violence of his own, by the looks of things. I can smell and see the blood on them and I'm looking forward to crushing him even more.

I'm turning towards them, speeding up if anything.

I can see the shapes of Cobb and his security boys from the Bank.

I'm racing towards them and they're just watching me and all at once Clara raises her head and half-looks at me and shouts, 'No!' but it's too late because as I'm haring round, I can feel I've run into something which cracks me across my windpipe, it splits and chokes me with my own blood, and something else across my front legs, one I can feel break, splinters of bone cutting out through my skin and fur. I stumble and roll and roll, and then come to a halt, and my neck and legs are a tangle of wire. Before I can get up I'm surrounded and a dirty great fucking blade comes out of nowhere and stabs me straight through the chest, puncturing the one-lung and pinning me to the ground. I lay there, throat and lung filling with blood, and seeping more blood into the dirt.

Sixty-three

Schiebler's groaning. I can hear that. And maybe what else I can hear above the sound of the blood bubbling in the back of my throat, that's Clara sobbing.

Everything else is fading.

Over me now, a dark shadow.

I look up and I can make out a figure, black against the moon. A hood, dark but matted with blood. Its arms go up to pull back the hood and there's Cobb. All fucked up good, a real Pete barbecue (ha! ha! I'm choking on that last ha! believe me) with a side-order of Schiebler slice.

As he's standing over me, I realize I'm slowly making the change back. No burst of fire anymore. Just smoke drifting off me and then I'm Pete again, covered in ash as well as blood. A mess of wire.

'I told you we'd destroy the belt...' he says in a burnt up rasp of a whisper, then he leans in closer. 'I gave you the chance to give it up. But you thought you were better than that. Better than coming back to this. Now we're going to destroy it anyway, and you don't even get the chance to go back to where you came from...'

He spits on the ground as he says this.

Then he steps back, and Cobb's bitch comes into view.

'Remember me?' she says, and I'm thinking what a mess I've made of her face as well.

She pulls out the blade that's stuck me to the ground. It's hard and cold and shining in the light as she lifts it, then she reaches down and roughly pulls me over. I'm too cut up to stop her.

Calmly, she slices open my stomach, right where the dogstar buckle of the belt is. Then I can feel her hand inside me. Two hands digging into my flesh and undoing the belt by the clasp behind the dog's head. She takes the buckle in one hand and sets a boot on my stomach and pulls. I can't feel the pain. Just the sensation of the belt tugging itself out from inside me and at last her staggering backwards as it comes free and she's standing, holding it up, slippery and dripping globs of blood, staring at it.

I'm fading. I don't know what into, but I'm fading. Around the edges it's dark, I can hear Cobb and the bitch talking. And... I don't know what it is... tap... tap.

Clara hanging, in pain, full-on crying. And I'm lying here thinking that I can't believe I've let this happen to her. *To her.*

Schiebler's out of it now. They've given his face a good smacking. It's swollen, his eyes are closed up and his mouth is set at an angle where some of his teeth have been knocked out.

Then there's a new voice (and tap... tap), and I'm vaguely aware that it's Skeet, come down from the roof-top, following me, and he's saying something to Cobb.

'What the fuck do you think you're doing?'

Cobb is laughing, like he's lost it, man.

'Following orders,' he says.

'Whose orders?' Skeet's saying, and from the way he's saying it you can tell that he's wary, like he knows that Cobb's over the edge and that anything could happen.

'From you father-in-law,' Cobb goes on. 'Her,' pointing at Clara, '*father*. To get the belt *whatever the cost.*'

He stress that last bit.

'So you've got the belt,' Skeet says, not quite so fucking certain as I've heard him before. 'You can hand it over...'

Cobb's letting out a shriek of a laugh.

'You'll be interested to know that Daddy specified that I shouldn't let the belt get into your hands, not in any circumstances...' He turns to look at Skeet and Skeet himself steps back, shocked now that he can see the state of Cobb. 'I'm supposed to do whatever it takes.'

And this tap... tap. Getting louder. I'm hearing it and not hearing it, not knowing what it is.

'I'm not going to have to put up with you thinking you own me for much longer...' Cobb says.

He takes the belt from the bitch and she just tries to hang onto it for too long, like she's beginning to wonder whether she should really give it to him or to Skeet, and he raises a hand to her so she releases it.

Tap... tap... going on inside my head, everything greying over now. Clara not crying anymore, just hanging on the fence.

I'm aware of Doug, Sal and Matti, all dog-form, arriving round the back and onto the heath. Watching on. That kind of horror that roots you to the spot, watching on as Cobb takes the belt – my fucking belt – and circles his waist with it.

I'm just about seeing the belt tighten round him as it did when I first put it on. Cut into him. Dig inside him.

Tap... tap... tap.

He's bent double in pain.

Then the burning starts. And every inch of the flesh that I scarred with my fire is on fire again, and Cobb's writhing around, screaming, a ball of agony, man, so bad the whole Links is full of the noise of him. He's caking up with ash on the outside now, and through cracks in it he looks like molten lava beneath. This ain't my boom change. This is melting him and putting him back together in another shape. Everyone around him watching.

Tap... tap.

Then it stops.

For a moment everything's quiet.

The mound of ash that was Cobb is still for a couple of minutes, the outer shell starts to fall away, breaking off into pieces and dust. Then what's inside it, what the belt makes Cobb, stands up.

Be thankful for the half-light, that's all I'm saying.

Cobb's belt-dog...

He's a monster fucker. Bigger than my black beast. Eight foot tall at the head. Rippling muscles and all that shit, a face full of teeth and these red eyes, the whole of him covered in that burnt, fucked up skin.

He's still on fire, on the inside.

All that skin is burning him up on the outside.

It's all pain, man, every inch of it.

He can't stay quiet for the agony of it.

The tap... tap... getting louder, getting louder, but I can't see where it's coming from.

Skeet's standing there, just looking at him.

First off, Cobb finishes off the bitch. With the back of his paw, he takes her head off.

A couple of Skeet's boys – dog-form – charge him, and he just bats them away, splitting them into two. Half of one of them lands near me and I see its dead face, look into its eyes, as it slowly changes back from wolf into man.

Skeet's off. Away into the darkness before this fucking thing that was Cobb can get to him.

Oh, you're king of the world now, man.

Then Cobb turns round towards me.

Doug, Sal, Matti, they're looking as though they're going to make a run... to take him on.

Tap... tap... tap is so loud it's bursting my head.

Now I can see it.

Now I can see where it's coming from.

The tap... tap... turns into a duller thud as the old man walks out from the passageway and onto the heath.

I've seen the face before, of course, and I know it immediately.

There's something different about it. Like it's not real... or more real than everything else in some way.

Cobb's thing stops and turns towards him.

The face of the old boy, dead or not dead, on the sofa in the house on Kensall Road. Real but not real.

He stops, resting heavily on the stick he's been using to walk.

He says something.

I don't understand what it is, but I know he's talking to the belt.

I want to scream at Sal and Doug and Matti to get down. I want to be up on my feet and running to the fence and cutting Clara (OK, OK, and Schiebler) away from it. I know what's coming. I know he's calling the belt back to him. And what else he's asking the belt to do.

In that second, I think Cobb's understood too. In that second, my eyes connect with his. He's looking at me and I'm looking at him. Those eyes of his turning from burning hate to fear. And I'm guessing if you were talking to him, he might tell you that my eyes went from something like anger to something like pity.

Then... boom!

The belt explodes nuclear, taking out Cobb and all the uniforms standing round him, and, before it all goes black, I can hear the sound of the terraces and towers and maisonettes and the walls of the Links as they crumble.

THE NEXT DAY

Sixty-four

'I'll have gin and tonic...'

Why not?

This is me, laying back on the lounger by the pool. All sunglasses (even though we're inside) so I can get a good look at Clara's arse as she's drying herself after a swim, without her seeing me do it. Except of course she can.

'I'm celebrating!' I say because she's thrown me one of her looks. Then she smiles, pretending that she's pissed off when she and I both know she isn't.

Some oily twat from the film studio called today and said they've finished the final cut. We're going over to some big nob's house tonight – you know, one of these places in West London, it's got a cellar dug out underneath where they've put a full size cinema, all glass and gold and antiques, that type of shit – and we're supposed to be watching it there.

The boys won't want to come.

Schiebler just don't like people... and there's not so many other dogs around now (ha! ha!) for him to socialize with, so he's spending his time sulking. No real change there, then.

Sal's been fucking like a train ever since we've been hanging around on the set of the movie. Says he's got all that time in prison to make up for. Fuck knows what all these leggy wannabe actresses see in him, hairy arsed fucker that he is. I guess he's got a big dick and all that animal magnetism, right?

Doug's not been that much off the piss. We've already had to bail him out of jail once for splitting some geezer's face, he can't remember what for. Doug, you gotta love him.

And Matti. He's the only one that will come. Well, you can take him anywhere, although Clara will get the hump tonight because she'll see me and him whispering in the corner and assume we're casing the joint (which of course we will be).

Me, I'm not going to watch the film they've made. I'll leave it to you to tell me if it's any good or not. Do I give a shit? Not really. You've met me, right? And anyone who's met me will tell you I'm the boom. One of a kind. Don't get me wrong, I'm looking forward to the fame and fortune (ha! ha!) but I don't want that ruining my nights out running free. It works better for me if you don't take all of this too seriously, right?

No. I'll get tanked up (more tanked up) tonight and talk shit and look around for what might be worth nicking, and maybe who might be worth hunting down (ha! ha!) and Clara will rein me back in. We'll go back to the hotel and I'll tell my baby that I love her, and I'll sober up and we'll spend the night together like we always do these days. Awake, in the dark, holding on to each other. Her telling me about her. Me telling her she knows enough about me already.

Now that everything's all wrapped up, well I'm getting those itchy feet. It's going to be time to move on soon. We've spent long enough kicking back here in this fancy five star hotel with its spa and celebrity-chef restaurant. Sure, the money ain't going to run out any time soon. Especially when the tills start ringing at the cinemas and they're selling those little plastic dolls of me/ my dog and the gang and all of theirs, and all the other shit they'll do. And there's all Clara's cash on top of that, if we ever needed it. I've risen well and truly above my station (ha! ha!).

But money's no fun if you earn it. The best greens are the ones you've nicked and you can take that from me.

So the waitress brings over my G&T on a little silver tray, and I take the glass and replace it with a tip and try not to look too hard at those titties she swings right in front of my eyes as she leans over to clear the table next to me.

It's time for something new, for definite.

I'm fancying the country. Apparently, so Clara says, there's another family Estate up in Scotland, not so far away from where Doug came from (ha! ha!).

I take a sip of my drink. It burns a bit as it goes down. An acid burn. Different from all the heat burning I did back then. I'm shutting my eyes, and seeing myself under all that ash and rubble. Seeing Clara and Schiebler, and Halloween Jack all milky eyed, digging. Hearing Clara's gasp as they pull me out, almost in pieces, and she can see the cuts they made in me and the tangle of wire that's torn open my neck. I can't speak. My throat is full of dried-up blood.

Afterwards, they tell me, of course they do.

Afterwards, I get to know that Doug and Sal and Matti are still alive, fuck knows how. That somehow they saw it coming and started the race away through the alley and out onto the Links. That although the blast knocked buildings down, they were screened from the worst of the fire.

Then how Jack cut down Clara and Schiebler. How it seemed like everyone else had been burnt or blown to shit. And that from in amongst it all, the old boy had put on the belt and disappeared into nothing.

They all thought I was going to die. I didn't have the belt no more. I wasn't a dog. A man couldn't survive being ripped and rewrapped like I was. Me, even though I couldn't say it for weeks, even though it took me the best part of a year to (fucking literally) get myself back together... me, I always knew I didn't need the belt no more.

Even then, I could feel it running through my veins. What little blood I had wasn't man-blood. It was all dog. Now I was the real deal.

I'm remembering Jack leaving. His last words, 'Fuck you,' as he took the money out of my hand and got into the back of his cab. Who knows where he went? As far away as possible.

Then Clara reading to me out of the newspaper about the scandal at the Bank, what with them being involved in naughty things they shouldn't have done. Clara's daddy (out of hospital now although not so much on speaking terms with his dear daughter) and some of the other pin-stripes got done for it, although Clara reckons it is Gideon Skeet who should've got banged up for it all really. The rozz are still on the look-out for him but seems like he's disappeared. So there are new suits at the Bank (who knows if they're dogs?).

Then about the Links being laid over with concrete.

Two months after the belt blew, they were building Brent Heights – fancy flats for fancier people than ever lived at the Links. There's a whole load of bits and pieces of dog under those houses. Maybe one day all the right bits will makes themselves together again and the Heights will have its very own werewolf, just like the Links used to.

Time to get ready.

Clara nudges me. She looks so good.

Got to get myself ready for the screening tonight.

That'll be it, then. The finish. Tonight, they'll watch it all back.

Tomorrow? I don't know. It's time to get out of here. A change of scene. I'm thinking back to Scotland. Rich Lairds (whatever the fuck that means) with lots of money and fancy things to nick.

Yeah. That sounds about right.

I say let's go Jockways and make the sequel (ha! ha!).

Fade to black, and then the end credits begin to slide down the screen.
It's no game...

    There's another spontaneous round of applause.

    Then you're pulling your coat up off the floor, and dusting the popcorn off it. You're standing and stretching, and banging your way awkwardly along the row of seats – shuffling up the stairs – and you can hear people begin whispering, talking about the movie ...

    'Cool the way they make out like it's real ...saw an interview with Pete on TV ...getting myself a skin-rip T-shirt for definite.'

    ... until you're out of the screen and blinking into the daylight.

Enjoyed Dogstar?

Then please write a review online at Amazon.

Want more?

Then read on for the opening pages of Dog Gone, The Sequel:

Dog Gone

It's fifteen years after Dogstar. The streets are flooded with grease and the world's gone to the dogs. Amy's scratching out a living, scavenging by day and laying low by night. But when she picks a fight with the wrong pack, she realises she's not going to be able to hide anymore. The dogs've got her scent and they're on the hunt.

If she's going to survive, things are going to have to change. And maybe she's going to have to change too.

INTERVIEW WITH JAY FLETCHER, DIRECTOR, DOGSTAR: EMPIRE MAGAZINE (TRANSCRIPT EXCERPT)

INTERVIEWER: 'So, we've got to ask you about this. What about the rumours ...?'

FLETCHER: '... You know I'm not going to answer questions about that (laughing)...'

INTERVIEWER: 'Come on. Is it true that there is an original? That it was canned, and you were brought in to re-make it?'

FLETCHER: 'Okay, categorically, right (laughing again), just to make this absolutely fucking clear ...'

INTERVIEWER: (also laughing) '... and so no one else asks the same dumb question, right?'

FLETCHER: 'There is no 'original movie', okay? My movie is *Dogstar*. I don't know where these rumours came from, but they're not true.'

INTERVIEWER: 'Categorically?'

FLETCHER: 'Categorically.'

So, are you clear on that?

Really?

Good.

You'd better be.

Let's get going then. Make sure you keep up.

PARALLEL LINES

She must've been six when she first saw one.

Up close.

So close she could see every bent and jagged tooth as it snapped and snarled, she could feel the spit-spray on her face and taste the stink of its hot, grease-soaked breath...

... the memory dissolves into music as the lights've gone down, the screen stretches to letterbox and there's a crackle – like a needle jumping on vinyl – the soundtrack kicks in and the movie plays.

'Fuck,' she says, spilling out of the picture house with the movie still playing inside her head, and realising that it's dusk, and the streets are filling up with dogs.

REWIND

She must've been six when she first saw one.

Up close.

So close she could see every bent and jagged tooth as it snapped and snarled, she could feel the spit-spray on her face and taste the stink of its hot, grease-soaked breath. That same nightmare she'd had a thousand times since, it started real.

And somehow she'd been saved by the gate, it couldn't get its head between the bars of the gate, and if it hadn't been for some of the men on the Estate finding her and it down the alley, and if they hadn't managed to crack it over the head – first – and then drag it off her and pull the gate from off her too – the gate that'd collapsed as she'd closed it behind her and the dog'd leapt on it to get at her – if they hadn't managed to do that, even though it couldn't get to her through the bars, she'd've probably been crushed or suffocated to death anyway.

As it was they did.

Four or five of them, clubbing at it, and she saw its head split and the eyes pop with the pressure of that clubbing and she saw them leak out all watery blood. Mixed with the noises of the exertion of the men, and the dull slab slabbing sound of the clubs as they hit it, and the growling and then howling and then whimpering it was making, what stuck in her head was that... the pop its eyes made as the head caved in and the force of it pushed them out the front of its face.

It just went on fighting.

Even blinded and skull-cracked and twisted-limbed it carried on almost until they'd made a bloody pulp of it, and then the men were heaving, breathing deep, dark and painful breaths, backs bent, hands on knees and cricket and baseball bats dropping to the floor, until finally one of them remembered her laying there, and came over and reached out a hand and said:

'You okay?'

And she'd nodded quietly and got herself pulled up, trying not to cry, and as she stood the memory dissolves into music...

DOGSTAR THE MOVIE

... the lights've gone down, the screen stretches to letterbox and there's a crackle – like a needle jumping on vinyl – as the soundtrack kicks in.

A woman's voice... Amy hasn't heard it before, but it shoots through her like fire. It's cocky-angry, flirting and aggressive. Hey look at me and by the-way-who-the-fuck're-you-staring at? Blonde hair and steel-toed boots, rah-rah skirts and a leather jacket. It takes her breath away... partly because of the force of it and partly because – she realises – it's been so long since she listened to a proper song. Sometimes on the TV, part of one of the shows that Mum watches – there are snatches of notes that pass for music, but nothing like this. Not since she was a little kid; back in the days when windows were thrown open on the Estate and the thump-thump used to play out across the open spaces.

And then there's something else.

She can't place it right away.

Something in the background, a wheening, swooping sound behind the music, black and unreachable, and from nothing, the camera's lurching down into London from overhead and it's tunnelling through the streets, looking for something, hunting. All around is the life of the City – the shitty see-in-the-dark nastiness of it, and they're swiping by: a hold-up at a newsagents, a couple of guys shouting soundlessly, waving a gun at the old boy in the turban behind the counter and when he doesn't move fast enough there's a puff of dirt and smoke as they let off a shot; then there's a fight outside a pub, half-a dozen knuckle-faced yobs with the drainpipes, Martins and fuzz-hair crew cut, and one of them goes down and the others are kicking and wheeling and dancing his head to a pulp; a man in a suit being held up against a fence by snot-and-pale-faced kids in hoods, wiped out on something or other and jabbing at his throat with flick-knives, needing money to get some more; a girl being dragged off the street, silent screaming – and the music's crying for it, a whine of sadness, and then rage and frustration and then suddenly it's clear.

The sound behind it.

That's clear.

It's dogs howling.

Like a thin reed.

And the camera turns another corner, and there's a gun fight here, and people are being shot up – although the music's still so loud you can't hear any of it – shuddering between slow-mo and real-time and people are being blown away in arcing flight, spraying blood like dark confetti.

Then finally the music slips away and the screen fades to black. The voice is quiet, the howl of the dogs fades to nothing. Gone.

At first she can't make it out.

Metal – something mechanical, or blocks of it, a bolt-plate – rising to the surface in a pool of oil. Or the oil's draining away and exposing it.

Then, of course, she sees it.

Dogstar.

Find out where to buy your copy of *Dog Gone* at www.jezcampbell.com

ABOUT THE AUTHOR

Jez was born in London and brought up in the hills and woodlands of the rural Midlands in England. He studied languages and literature, specialising in medieval sagas and the German Romantics, before travelling & working throughout Africa and the Middle East, and then settling back in the UK.

By day he inhabits glass and steel tower blocks in the big smoke, helping people in big brands think more creatively and develop more exciting products and services, and by night he escapes to the country and transforms into an author of horror fiction. When not working and writing he runs wild and free with his mate and their pack of cubs in the Surrey Hills.

Twitter: @campbell_jez
Facebook: https://www.facebook.com/jez.campbell.666
Blog: www.jezcampbell.com

Printed in Great Britain
by Amazon